Praise for *Ghost Cities*

'*Ghost Cities* is a labyrinth of a novel that delights, terrifies, thrills and amuses in the very best of ways. An inventive and philosophical exploration of power, automation, art and love where nothing is as it seems; a decadent feast fashioned from tofu, a lush orchard carved from stone. Siang Lu's brain at play is a thing of wonder.' **Kate Mildenhall**

'What a pleasure to follow Siang Lu into his labyrinthine *Ghost Cities*. An instant Australian classic that stands both on the shoulders of giants and yet is somehow completely and delightfully new. Lashings of myth, absurdity, humour and pathos come together in this paean to art in all its forms. I want to crumple this novel into a ball and swallow it, whole.' **Hayley Scrivenor**

Praise for *The Whitewash*

'Audacious, original and a kick to the guts – in the best possible way.' **Benjamin Law**

'A literary star is born in Siang Lu.' **Chris Flynn**

'Searing, humorous and inventive.' **Mirandi Riwoe**

'[A] delicious satire of the film industry and its racism ... It's a blast.' ***The Sydney Morning Herald***

'Lu's tongue-in-cheek tone makes this novel a delightful read, a brilliant work of satire that hits close to home in the best and most unexpected ways.' ***The Saturday Paper***

T0340834

'A scathing satire of the big-budget film industry's ethnic and racial myopia. Original, critical and hilarious.' *The Conversation*

'A decidedly ambitious undertaking, synthesising real film history with invented detail ... the resulting novel is smart, playful and often very funny and explores its themes with nuance and insight.' *The West Australian*

'Totally bonkers, serious in scholarship and packed with pun-in-cheek playfulness ... a book about movies just waiting to be booked for a movie. A mischievous hoot.' *Sydney Arts Guide*

'With its accessible prose and film-history appeal, *The Whitewash* is an entertaining read from a bold new voice.' *Readings Monthly*

'A clever, layered work that animates a host of different voices.' *Sydney Review of Books*

Siang Lu is the author of *Ghost Cities* and *The Whitewash*, and the co-creator of The Beige Index. *The Whitewash* won the ABIA Audiobook of the Year in 2023 for its audio adaptation, which starred a large and diverse cast of fourteen actors. It also won the Glendower Award for an emerging writer in the Queensland Literary Awards and was shortlisted for a NSW Premier's Literary Award. In 2023 Siang was named one of the Top 40 Under 40 Asian-Australians at the Asian-Australian Leadership Awards. He holds a Master of Letters from the University of Sydney and has written for film and television for Singapore's Beach House Pictures and Malaysia's Astro network. He is based in Brisbane, Australia, and Kuala Lumpur, Malaysia.

www.siang-lu.com

GHOST CITIES

SIANG LU

First published 2024 by University of Queensland Press
PO Box 6042, St Lucia, Queensland 4067 Australia
Reprinted 2024

The University of Queensland Press (UQP) acknowledges the Traditional Owners and their custodianship of the lands on which UQP operates. We pay our respects to their Ancestors and their descendants, who continue cultural and spiritual connections to Country. We recognise their valuable contributions to Australian and global society.

uqp.com.au
reception@uqp.com.au

Cover design by Josh Durham, Design by Committee
Cover artwork: *Phantom Landscape No. 2*, Yang Yongliang
Author photograph by Andreas Weiss
Image on p. 20 by Du Zhiyu
Typeset in 11.5/15 pt Bembo Std by Post Pre-press Group, Brisbane
Printed in Australia by McPherson's Printing Group

Australian Government

Creative Australia

University of Queensland Press is assisted by the Australian Government through Creative Australia, its principal arts investment and advisory body.

A catalogue record for this book is available from the National Library of Australia.

ISBN 978 0 7022 6849 6 (pbk)
ISBN 978 0 7022 6973 8 (epdf)
ISBN 978 0 7022 6974 5 (epub)

University of Queensland Press uses papers that are natural, renewable and recyclable products made from wood grown in well-managed forests and other controlled sources. The logging and manufacturing processes conform to the environmental regulations of the country of origin.

PART I:

ASSIMILATED MAN

'And what if, after all this, it's a bad novel?'

—Mercedes Márquez, to her beloved Gabo

1

THE IMPERIAL TASTER

He wanted no story of simple ascension, wanted nothing of the truth of how He had won that slippery throne. For the youth knew Himself to be Exceptional, and Exceptional Men (such as He) had Exceptional Stories. They came to be Emperors through cunning, ruthless strategy and force of will. They certainly did not do it by gawping as their purple-faced fathers clawed and sputtered on what would later be determined to be an awkwardly lodged chicken bone. Exceptional Men did not watch, frozen, unable or unwilling to help. Exceptional Men did not wait, in lacklustre fealty, for that final breathless minute to expire.

Word travelled fast. By the time of His coronation, rumour was already circulating the courts that young Lu Huang Du had conspired to usurp His father's throne. Well, He certainly had not planned it this way, but He was nothing if not an opportunist. When whispers of patricide and regicide spread through the Imperial Court, He uttered no denials. Let them think Him ruthless. Why not?

His first act as Emperor was to order the executions of all who repeated the rumours. His second act was to order the deaths of the chickens – all of them, every last one throughout the land – for it was clear to Him that their traitorous bones were conspiring against His Imperial bloodline.

Even as the axes swung upon their necks, the rumour-mongers

and slanderers issued tearful defences, or else blamed political enemies or brothers and sisters and fathers, cursed the Emperor's tyranny and oppression, and cried out with their dying breaths.

The chickens – faced with their own impending slaughter, and inscrutable to the very end – made much less of a fuss.

An Imperial Edict was thus issued, forbidding the breeding, eating and harbouring of poultry.

Pork filled the culinary void. The effect of such sudden demand was disastrous for those who could not afford it. The breeding of pigs required double the land, triple the resources, and at the markets pork cost five times the flesh of the humble hen. Farmers lost their livelihoods, leaving their families hungry and destitute. The sons of a hundred fallen agrarians swore revenge against the Emperor.

All traitors born in the year of the Rooster were driven from their homes. But their younger brothers, born in the auspicious year of the Pig, were destined for good fortune and health.

The Imperial Taster, whose negligence was widely believed to have caused the death of the previous Emperor – the most heinous of offences under heaven – was mysteriously spared. Wracked with guilt, he grieved and prostrated himself to the brink of despair, but was awarded by the new Emperor larger quarters and a distasteful amount of gold, all against his will.

He had expected death, begged for it even, but instead received untold riches! His friends and neighbours grew to hate him for his lack of scruples. To all, it seemed that he had brazenly accepted payment for failing in his duties. And so, when he sobbed in great distress and confusion upon receiving the piles of gold, the others interpreted his tears as tears of joy. When he carted the gold back to the treasury to be rid of that sum once and for all, witnesses saw only that the Imperial Taster was a prideful man of the worst sort, parading his riches in public for all to see. And when he was beaten for daring to return the money, then sent away by the gleeful Emperor with an inexplicably *larger* amount of gold – how it shimmered in the moonlight along that quiet stretch of road – passers-by saw not his wounded body bent double, nor his limping form. They saw only the obscene stacks of gold in the opulent cart that the loathsome man seemed so eager now to tow.

Dear citizens of the Imperial City,

It is with mixed emotions that we proclaim that <u>Huang Zi Feng</u> has vacated the post of <u>Imperial Taster</u> on account of: ~~family reasons/exile/~~<u>death</u>.

Investigations have revealed the official cause of <u>death</u> to be: <u>a slow-acting poison, doubtlessly bound for the throat of our resplendent Emperor.</u>

We are hereby bound by law to note the dissent of the Shadow Historian, Sima Qing, whose pitifully worded records indicate that <u>the Imperial Taster was, rather, bludgeoned to death by an angry mob, the body showing no apparent trace of poison.</u> The Shadow Historian's fictional and disruptive accounts have, for too long, brought our scholarship into disrepute. Moreover, it must be asked: can a person be trusted if he, like Sima Qing, has shown himself to be physically incapable of growing a beard – even the most rudimentary one? No. So states the official record.

In any event, we are pleased to announce that the duties of the <u>Imperial Taster</u> are hereby passed to <u>the deceased's firstborn son, Huang Zi Yan, aged three months</u>.

<u>Huang Zi Yan</u> brings <u>00</u> years of experience to this role.

This parting of ways is a joint decision and comes after much heartfelt deliberation. May the heavens smile on <u>Huang Zi Yan</u>. Please join us in wishing him a prosperous life and death in service of our Immortal Emperor.

All the best to <u>Huang Zi Feng</u> in his future endeavours. He will be greatly missed. We recall fondly the time he _____

_____.

By Imperial decree,
The Order of the Eunuchs

The Imperial Advisers had cautioned their new Emperor against appointing an infant as an Imperial Taster, for the infant's mouth was yet even to produce teeth, and with such a limited vocabulary how could it sufficiently remark on the quality of the meal, or judge the food fit for the Emperor's palate, much less guard the Emperor from poisons, or anticipate the presence of serums, of rogue and suspect ingredients? But the naysayers had failed to grasp that under the Emperor's rule everything was permitted, that nothing was beyond Him, and that He would surely destroy those who had the temerity to defy His divine will. He, the definer of life, the defiler, the defier Himself.

So He threw these advisers into the Imperial Prison on the outskirts of the city – so named the Six Levels of Hell – and ordered the infant to be installed as the new Imperial Taster.

Mealtimes were complex fiascos. When the Emperor decided He wished to eat – His appetite was unpredictable, announcing itself at odd hours of the day – the infant would be rudely awakened and fed liquefied versions of the Emperor's meals, stray bits of fatty pork floating within the bottle that the baby was given to suckle.

But the richness of the pork and sweetmeats and abalone that the infant imbibed played havoc on his developing body, and he became sickly and so often prone to infection that nobody could tell whether the food was laced with terrible poisons or, in fact, safe for adult consumption. In this respect, the new Imperial Taster had failed utterly in his task.

It was noted that the baby seemed to thrive on breastmilk, but this was of limited interest to the Emperor, whose craving for such a thing was only slight and very occasional. With the baby's fussiness and incessant crying, and the intolerable delays that occurred while it was awoken and the bottle prepared, soon even the Emperor came to regret His decision.

But the infant could not be removed from its post, for the role of Imperial Taster was a lifelong appointment severed only by death, and the Emperor, though cruel, was reluctant to take the life of one so young (though such heartlessness would come later in His reign).

So there was a vacancy to be filled, for the role of Taster to the Taster.

There were those in the Imperial Court who came forth to express interest in the role. But one by one the Emperor found fault with each applicant. This one's palate was subpar, unable to differentiate even oolong from jasmine tea. This rotund one seemed interested only in filling his belly and was much too flippant about the life-or-death nature of the role. This one the Emperor could not take seriously for he had a drooping eye.

Day after day, the Emperor was presented with nothing but unimpressive specimens.

Then, heeding the words of His newest adviser, Tong Li Mo the Daoist, the Emperor invited all the beggars from the streets of the Imperial City to partake in a feast at the palace. Tong Li Mo had reckoned that the beggars, unlike the wealthy or spoiled inhabitants of the Imperial Court, might savour more greatly the richness of the food. That if called upon to comment on the flavour of a dish, their remarks might be plain-spoken and honest, a far cry from the florid and sycophantic words of the courtiers. Moreover, that among this great number of street urchins and bums who defiled the pristine palace halls with their muddied feet, there might be a handful with the inherent talent required of a taster.

At what came to be known as the Poisoned Banquet, the Emperor ordered a random portion of each dish to be laced with slow-acting toxins. By midnight, only one beggar remained unharmed. He had carved out only the safest portions of each delicious plate, while his neighbours had greedily taken the remainder of his untouched food and been among the first to die.

The next morning, the beggar was brought before the Emperor to explain how he had survived.

This beggar spoke of his ravenous and now-dead compatriots, how quick they had been to believe that the Emperor was kind of heart, when all tales told of the opposite. How, then, could the food prepared for the poor, that lowest and most hated caste, have been anything but poisoned? Only he had understood that this had been a test.

If the beggar truly held such suspicions, interrogated the Emperor, why had he risked his very life by eating at all? One wrong guess and he too would have joined the ranks of the dead. Would it not have been wiser to refuse the food entirely?

The beggar replied that he had been very, very hungry. Famished, essentially.

And so it was that this lone survivor, who through some miracle of intuition had managed to avoid every fatal spoonful, was bestowed the grand title of Taster to the Taster.

2

World Square Medical Centre – George Street, Sydney, Australia

My stomach is doing something weird, something loud – gurgling, frantically digesting that nasty chicken bun I had for breakfast – and I'm feeling uniquely betrayed because it's very quiet here and people are bound to notice this inner turbulence and, really, what does it say about you if your internal organs can't even present a united front?

The door opens and out comes Doctor Mok, who waves me into his office.

I shut the door behind me.

'哪里不舒服?' he says to his clipboard.

'Oh,' I say, because he has made an assumption about the language I speak – my culture, who I am or must be – entirely from my face. 'I don't speak Chinese.'

'Ah, you're Japanese? Korean?'

'I'm *Australian*.'

He tsks. 'No, no! I mean your *race*.'

'Is there another doctor available? I saw Doctor Collison last time. Maybe I'll just wait for her.'

'She's on leave.' He scrutinises me, eyes narrowed. '*Tell me where your ancestors are from.*'

I sigh. 'China.'

He slams his desk in joy.

'Ha! I knew it! You younger generation! Spoiled! What a shame.

Lack of language skills. Forgetting all about your culture. You are a bad Chinese! But anyway. What can I do for you today? Stomach trouble?'

'What? No. Why would you think that?'

'Your stomach is making a sound. Maybe you're hungry. Here. Have a cookie.'

'Thanks.'

'So,' he says. 'Why are you here?'

'My company sent me for an annual check-up last week. I'm just here for the results.'

'Ah, okay, yes, yes. Wait a minute. I will get them.'

Doctor Mok leaves in search of my file and so – I can't help it, all unattended rooms are seductive in this way – I look around at everything. The height chart. The blood pressure pump-thing. The medical qualifications hanging on the far wall. It's not snooping as long as you don't move around or touch anything.

Crayon drawings by the doctor's young son hang proudly on the wall, capturing his father in all his stick-figure portraiture: his stethoscope, his briefcase, the crucial essence of him. The boy's name scrawled in the corner like an artist's seal.

My dad used to have similar emblems of mine in his office. Toddler art, with its suspect lines and colours. He must have found me perfect, at that particular distance – and perhaps vice versa – in the brief era before one can truly disappoint the other.

I don't recall my dad proudly framing anything after I was five years old. My teen years were particularly fallow – I suppose, after a certain age, you outgrow those artistic impulses entirely, or you move on to other forms, other subjects, and, inevitably, you cease to sketch your father.

The desk is full of pharmaceutical swag: pens, calendars, a coffee mug. The mousepad is imprinted with a diseased, smog-ridden cityscape, bearing a clumsy slogan in English: *Port Man Tou, China: The City Where Anything Is Possible!*

Doctor Mok returns. He waves the test results cheerfully. He sits. He reads. The smile drains from his face.

My throat dries out. I set my cookie down on his desk.

'The results indicate that you have Taikophobia.'

'*What*-phobia?'

'Taikophobia,' he confirms. 'The fear of Chinese people.'

'You're kidding,' I say.

His face – a very Chinese face – indicates that he most certainly is not kidding.

'I know a good specialist who deals with strange disorders.' He taps his keyboard, avoiding eye contact. 'Oh. But his office is in the heart of Haymarket. *Chinatown*. Full of Chinese. Might be scary for you.'

But I am not listening. 'This is impossible. I can't be afraid of Chinese people. I *am* Chinese.'

'废话,' he mutters.

'What?'

Doctor Mok's expression softens and he extends his hand across the desk, either to double-check the test results and exonerate me, or to give my hand a sympathetic pat. But he does neither and with a slight grimace, as though he's afraid I might notice, Doctor Mok reaches for my half-eaten cookie and pulls it slowly from my reach.

En route to the Consulate-General of the People's Republic of China – Parramatta Road, Camperdown

On the bus back to work, my phone pings. I have mail. The bad thing about working at the Consulate-General of the PRC is that all email correspondence is in Chinese.

As always, I copy/paste the original text into my Google Translate app.

Subject: CAUGHT YOU!

HR Department <HR.chinaconsulsyd@mfa.gov.cn>
Friday 26/05/2017 3:04 PM

To: Lu, Xiang

Dear Xiang,

At first we thought you were just a fool. Dim-witted and slow. Later, we realised that this is much more than that.

Finally, we must congratulate you on making it to this point. Half a year, a real achievement! Did you know that a typical entry-level translator role such as yours, the average turnover rate of this sector is nine months? How close you are to celebrating this milestone!

Regrettably, we must fire you with immediate effect.

You may look like a Chinese person, but you cannot speak or read Mandarin. You are monolingual! The worst thing in this special context.

We regret the graduate program that secured your employment. We will destroy it. Really, the whole catastrophe is our fault. We made terrible assumptions.

Chinese name? Yes.

Chinese face? Yes.

Arts degree? Must be rich or stupid (we thought the former, but turns out the latter).

And the crucial mistake. Interviewed you in English. Forgot to test your Chinese!

We only have ourselves to blame.

But we caught you in the end. Do you really think we do not see through your silent behaviour? The time you had 'laryngitis'? Your terrible pronunciation, unintuitive syntax?

Do you really think we do not know you just copy and paste into Google Translate to do all your work?

Who do you think we are? We knew from the second day. The third day, at the latest.

At first we thought it was deference. The way you lowered your head passing us in the hall. Then we realised it was a fear of small talk. Fear of being exposed as a bad Chinese.

We bet that as soon as you receive this email message you will copy and paste into Google Translate (remember when the IT department blocked that website for one afternoon? Seeing your panicked face is too funny!). We had secret meetings in your absence (useless to invite monolinguist to bilingual meeting, agreed?). We estimate that you have a perhaps fifty-word Chinese vocabulary. A two-year-old knows more than your words! Are you not ashamed?

We all know you most dread our Monday roundtable meetings. Always quiet, always politely laughing. Remember the big joke Bo Wen Xia told in the meeting last month? It was a test. It was nonsense, a fake joke. You laugh at the absurd joke. The proof is indisputable.

Six months, we have let this farce continue, because we were worried maybe you are somebody's son or nephew. But the private investigator's comprehensive report reveals you are definitely not a spoiled child of diplomats. Just a middle-class idiot.

No such thing as 'half-yearly health check-up'! We sent you to the medical centre last week to hold our secret meeting and sent you again today so we can pack up your desk. Less chance of commotion from disgruntled employees (that's you). Please take your things from reception and go. Your replacement will commence on Monday morning.

By the way, we snooped your hard drive. Found some poetry you wrote. For a joke, we copy and paste it into the auto-translate website. It is bad. It is a bad poetry. And you are a bad Chinese person.

No use to swipe up. Your card is deactivated. If you try, security will embrace you.

Sincerely,
Dou Jin Bo
Human Resources Representative
Consulate-General of the People's Republic of China

3

THE IMPERIAL TRAITOR, LU DONG PU

Lu Huang Du was a jealous and paranoid ruler. Out of the corners of His eyes He saw only usurpers and assassins, and divined all manner of plots against Him. And so, in His madness, did He spill the blood of His brother-cousins and uncle-fathers so that none could lay claim to His throne. Those would-be betrayers, despite their ragged avowals of kinship, had been strangers to Him, with dark smiles and unknowable hearts.

But what of Lu Dong Pu, the Emperor's blood brother and successor to the throne? The Emperor Himself knew, with brotherly certainty, that Lu Dong Pu was meek of heart and harboured no designs on His crown, for the younger had long ago turned his back on the intrigues of the Imperial Court. He had chosen the scholarly pursuits and liked nothing better than to wander the scholarly gardens, to hone his skills in the chess game xiangqi and to muse upon philosophical quandaries.

It was often said – though only in whispers, far from the Emperor's ears – that Lu Dong Pu, who was mild in nature and possessed a keen intellect but not a single trace of ambition, was the inverse of his brother in these, and therefore all, respects.

The false empire of the Southern Song Dynasty had heard rumours that the new Emperor was made of weaker fabric than His father, and that His stomach unravelled at even the sight of poultry. Thus, they sent forth an army to test the Emperor's mettle.

The Tanguts of the North had heard similar stories, that the Emperor was built from brittle materials, and that His stomach unravelled at even the sight of poetry. Encouraged, but somewhat confused by these reports, the Tanguts redoubled their attacks against the Emperor's borders.

The new Emperor could not fight a war on two fronts. His forces were spread too thin, across too many outposts, their numbers halved to meet the threats above and below.

Sensing weakness, the South had set up embargoes, cut off trade routes and scuttled supply ships bound for Jing Hang Canal, hoping to starve the Emperor into submission. The cowards of the South had made their brutal calculations: if the Emperor mobilised His forces to defend against them, He would be weakened by the Tangut attack. But if He marched north to repel the Tanguts, then the South would advance, unimpeded, on the capital. If the Emperor chose neither action, then famine would strike and the Emperor's enemies would merely wait the winter out, and pick off the weakened border defences. One way or another, the Emperor would fall. Having arrived at this conclusion, the South – ever pragmatic – halted its army's advance, conserved its own resources and simply waited for a bloodless victory.

It was chaos within the palace walls. The Emperor's Imperial Advisers and Ministers were at a loss. Those who even hinted at surrender were executed for their cowardice. Those who bravely but stupidly beckoned for battle were exiled to the Six Levels of Hell.

The Emperor demanded a stratagem, but none was adequate.

Under siege, even the Imperial City's mighty stores of grain could not last forever. Unable to stand idly by as his own brother's Empire crumbled, shrewd Lu Dong Pu descended to the scholarly gardens where he had spent his youth learning xiangqi and chaturanga from the grand masters. Here, he partook in a game of xiangqi, having found a lowly palace aide with some measure of ambition.

Lu Dong Pu, easily the more masterful player, arranged to lose this game at the outset. He adopted a chatty persona, drawing the aide into idle gossip, talk of the Empire, how one might dispatch both North and South if one had the ear of the Emperor. This patient stratagem he teased out long into their endgame, so that it appeared to the aide that *he* had chanced upon the idea entirely by his own genius.

The aide rushed to request an audience with the Emperor, who, in His desperation, deigned to hear his words. The aide's stratagem was thus. By the Imperial City's spies and agents, let these whispers travel northward: that the Emperor had brokered a secret treaty with the South. But to the South, leak word that the Emperor had parleyed with the Tanguts of the North. Force each of their opponents to consider the enemy beyond their enemy, and second-guess their chances of success.

Neither opponent would have the strength to subdue two nations in alliance, and in a reluctant act of self-preservation, would they not each extend the hand of diplomacy, seeking to better the other's terms?

The Emperor had only to whisper into the winds and soon He would hold a treaty in each hand. The lie no longer a lie. The fiction indistinguishable from truth.

The mighty Sun Tzu had once written of a similar gambit – employed during the Spring and Autumn Period – in which the artful deception of the Yue had won them a similarly unwinnable campaign.

Upon hearing of the mighty Sun Tzu's praise for such a bold and unusual tactic, the Emperor's reluctance melted away, and He wasted no time in giving the necessary orders.

A new era was born, where diplomatic tension replaced the open wound of war.

This account of the Empire's famous stalemate over North and South was well documented in the histories. Only some centuries later in the Ming Dynasty did a certain Scholar Quan determine – through painstaking and methodical research – that no such gambit had ever existed, either in the writings of Sun Tzu or the official histories of the Spring and Autumn Period. It had been, in a word, a fabrication.

Thus did Lu Dong Pu construct three stratagems. The first to save the Empire, the second to save himself, and the third to establish false precedent, thereby creating the illusion – the slightest of sleights – that it had all been done before in another time by wiser and better men.

4

Apartment – King Street, Newtown

I'm sitting on my balcony, laptop balanced precariously on the railing as I apply for jobs, any and all, because Sydney living is not cheap, and this ratty studio apartment with a bathroom more spacious than the 'living room' isn't going to pay for itself.

'Oh god.'

Looking over my cover letter template, I realise that all of the applications have gone out with a critical error. I have misspelled *career*. My fingers – obeying some other impulse – typed it out as *careen*.

I read the offending line back to myself. 'I am a highly driven, *careen-minded* individual with great attention to detail. Fuck!'

My sent archive shows ninety-three near-identical cover letters, each announcing my heaving, vertiginous intent. What do I do? Revise and resend? Call each of them? Grovel? Joke? Pretend it never happened?

Through the paper-thin walls, I can hear my afro-haired thespian neighbour (badly) rehearsing lines from Arthur Miller's *The Crucible*.

I throw on my jacket and walk down the stairs, past the broken elevator with the cracked mirror and the bloodstain that still hasn't been cleaned up.

Need to go for a walk. Clear my head.

I check the mail. An envelope sticks out at me like a tongue. Odd. I never receive mail. My name and address are handwritten in messy script, along with the word '#BadChinese'. What the hell? I rip open the envelope, expecting a letter, but all that's in there is a ticket. A complimentary ticket to a screening this evening at the Sydney Film Festival for a movie titled *Death of a Pagoda*. Never heard of it, but that's my evening entertainment sorted. What a score.

The air out on the street is harsh, gusty. I quickly lose myself in the flow of human traffic.

Transcriptionist. Data entry coordinator. Office administrator. Media researcher. Junior administration assistant. Editorial assistant. Office all-rounder. Paralegal. Casual editor. Journalist assistant. Executive assistant. Policy framework facilitator. Temporary typist.

Careen. As in to rock, or lurch, or heel over.

I am a highly driven, careen-minded individual.

Fuck it. It's an improvement, if anything. A more honest accounting of the self. A glitch or slip that for once in my life might actually have said something real.

State Theatre – Market Street, Sydney

Drinks and canapés. The heady festival atmosphere. Closing night of the film festival. I had a vague intention to go last week – check out one or two films, three at most – and now, leafing through the program of movies I have missed, I feel pangs of regret, for they each seem to have promised the escape to worlds within worlds.

Under each film's title are a handful of curated words, accompanied by a lone image that someone, somewhere, has decided best represents the film.

An elephant, mid-street, mid-stride. A heavily bandaged woman peering through the blinds. Half-naked individuals. Inscrutable gazers in black and white. Foggy cities. Pristine mountains. Landscapes of the mind. It occurs to me, suddenly, that every work of art might be its creator's self-portrait.

I search the program for *Death of a Pagoda*.

DEATH OF A PAGODA

MON 5 JUNE 4:10 PM EV9   18+
FRI 9 JUNE 10:00 AM STATE
SUN 11 JUNE 7:30 PM STATE

China | 2017 | 106 mins | In Chinese with English subtitles | World Premiere
Director: Baby Bao | Producer: Farmstrong Tian | Production Company: Daedalic Productions
Filmed entirely within the mysterious ghost city known as Port Man Tou, this is the latest spectacle from China's self-proclaimed 'number one director, or at the very least number three, no wait, delete that, put number one'. Baby Bao's *Death of a Pagoda* – about the plight of gay

farmers – appears at first to be a blatant, note-for-note rip-off of *Brokeback Mountain*. But wait! Here comes a subplot set in ancient China. But wait again! These two competing storylines appear to have nothing in common other than their own poetic resonance, ah, but you, the avid filmgoer, the understander of tropes, have been primed to anticipate their neat intersection, as per some shitty *Babel* or *Crash* type deal. If that is you, then prepare for great disappointment. And neither will you like the middle section, not one bit, for that is when the work begins to fracture, to ruin itself and *careen* into some kind of dreamlike memoir, some labyrinth of the self ...

BABY BAO's film and television work has been reviled throughout the Chinese film industry. *Death of a Pagoda* is his eighth feature film.

The theatre doors open and the masses shuffle in. I find my seat. First row. Oh well. Can't complain with a free ticket. The place is packed. Not an empty seat in the house.

There is a longish wait. The audience starts to get jittery.

Finally, an anonymous middle-aged woman takes the podium. Her state appears to be one of thinly disguised panic. The microphone seems to swallow her words before the speaker system – or our hearing – adjusts.

'... but we seem to have lost the director. Hopefully we'll find him for the Q&A afterwards! Well, uh ... welcome to the world premiere of *Death of a Pagoda*. Our thanks to the director, Baby Bao, for giving us the chance to screen his film, and of course thanks go to the Sydney Consulate-General of the People's Republic of China Culture and Arts Department, without whom we wouldn't ...'

I shrink in my seat. To the side of the stage – each wearing film festival passes – are a handful of my ex-colleagues. Bo Wen Xia, department head. Fanny Something, HR executive. Have they spotted me? Did *they* send me the ticket? But … *why?* Bo Wen Xia nudges the guy next to him and points directly at me. Ugh. I un-shrink myself. If they've seen me, they've seen me. Can't fire me twice! I give Bo Wen Xia a sarcastic thumbs-up. He smiles serenely.

As the lights dim, two security guards approach. I am certain they are coming for me, courtesy of Bo Wen Xia, but it turns out their quarrel is with my neighbour, who appears confused and worried, before being escorted from the theatre. Soon after, a different man occupies the vacant seat. I can't concentrate on the film, because this new guy is an asshole, eating prawn crackers from a popcorn box, checking his phone, humming and laughing uproariously at parts that aren't even funny. Every so often, he nudges me and gives me significant looks, goading me, I think, into nodding with him to indicate that this movie is as much the bomb for me as it clearly is for him. I wouldn't know, dude, I want to say, you're kind of ruining it for me.

'不错吧,' he says.

Someone shushes him loudly. He sulks.

Two-thirds of the way through the film, he gets up and leaves and doesn't come back, and we in the front can finally enjoy the rest of the film in peace.

Polite, uncertain applause. The lights go up, and it's the same lady on the podium again. She offers profuse apologies that the Q&A can't proceed because the director still cannot be found. A murmur of disappointment. People begin to shuffle out. I stand and stretch. It seems that my annoying neighbour has left behind his wallet – fat with cash, credit cards, a hotel keycard – and a lanyard containing his festival pass. I pick up the pass.

It reads: *Baby Bao, Director.*

5

THE IMPERIAL SCHOLAR ZHAO

The Emperor's Feast was to be a grandiose affair, so it was proclaimed, to commemorate His triumphs against North and South. But it was all too soon. The Empire was yet to fully recover from its recent tribulations. The grain stores were near depleted, the farms and pantries empty, and only the first trickles of trade were beginning to arrive from reopened routes. Still, the Emperor – ignorant to the truth – demanded His feast, and so He would have it.

Tong Li Mo the Daoist, recently promoted to Chief Adviser to the Emperor, conceived of *two* banquets to be held in unison. An inner-palace banquet, and an outer-palace banquet.

The inner-palace banquet, held for the Emperor, his lords and generals and certain favoured ministers, was lush and overflowing. There, they dined on the eight famous delicacies: Desert Boat Sails on Clouds, Leaves of Wind and Sorrow, Deep-fried Ghost, Monkey's Sutra, Song of the Concubine, Butterflies Swarm the Lotus, Jade Pearl of the Dragon and Powdered Bear's Claw.

The outer-palace banquet was held for the lesser ministers, high-ranking eunuchs and scholars of note. Some had secretly anticipated an inferior menu, but – praise be the Immortal Emperor! – all the same delicacies were served. The pork skin crackled a perfect brown, the abalone tender, the monkey brain soft and pulpy. And yet, and yet … as each delicacy was unveiled, glazed and more visually stunning than the one before, the smiles of those at the outer-palace banquet began to fade, for their mouths tasted a different story.

Everything was made from tofu.

The wine was merely coloured water.

One insolent minister complained, and the feasters at the outer banquet watched in silence as he was promptly dragged away, no doubt bound for the Six Levels of Hell. All at once, their cheer and goodwill returned with force. For the duration of the celebrations – two arduous weeks – those in attendance at the outer banquet revelled and feasted as though their very lives depended on it.

In the second week of celebrations, the Emperor bid the minstrels to come sing His praises. So they presented themselves before Him with zither and flute and wooden clapper, and sang the song of Emperors.

But He had heard this song before. They had sung it for His father – the Sagacious Emperor – and his father before him.

The Emperor wanted an ode to Himself, unique. Were there not stories, after all, of *Great Emperors* who had emerged, newborn, from the skies, with pieces of luminous jade in their mouths? Men of prophecy, who communed with the heavens as though they were gods themselves? He wanted something like *that*. Something to make the man into the myth.

Thereupon He ordered Scholar Zhao – the most skilful of the Imperial Scholars – to be brought from the outer palace into the inner sanctum, to craft a tale that would precede Him, and strike fear and awe into the hearts of all.

Scholar Zhao listened to the Emperor's demand, closed his eyes, stroked his beard, and began to tell the tale.

In the beginning Mountain knew nothing. There was no knowing, in those days. Mountain did not know he was Mountain, nor did Mountain know that he knew nothing. Mountain knew not. Mountain merely was.

Lush vegetation grew upon him. One reclusive shrub at first, and later a small family of saplings, and then a wild and joyful proliferation of greenery that came to cover his entirety. This lent Mountain a certain air of grace and mystery, which in turn attracted the elk, the bird and the bear, and they too made their home on Mountain, nestling within his craggy folds.

And Man heard the commotion upon Mountain – the symphonies of growls and bleats and birdsong – and so came he to the foot of Mountain, for Man could not stand to be alone. And he built huts and farms with terraced fields and a school at the furthest ends of the village where the children sang folk songs. Mountain did not know the words, for he knew no words, but the melodies were pleasant with long and high notes that carried through the air, and Mountain learned to hum along in a low and faint echo that amused the children, prompting them to shout into his valleys at the top of their lungs.

And to the children's delight, Mountain would always shout back.

One day, a folk song came wafting along the breeze. Mountain had heard it many times before, but this time something about it was different. Mountain recognised his name! The song was about him! And he came to know the chorus, the refrain, and all the other songs in a lushness of words that equalled the lushness of his vegetation in the spring.

When the Mongols came, in a galloping rage, and burned the village to the ground, Mountain, who was nearby and had witnessed the commotion, was not terribly impressed, for he had seen fire before.

Eventually another village was built, though its inhabitants had forgotten the songs of their ancestors. Their minds were busier, filled with agrarian pursuits and petty politics, and so Mountain, who could not stand to be alone, began to sing his ancient song in the dark of the night.

The villagers awakened with this song in their heads, and henceforth they sang it day and night. Mountain was pleased to hear his song in the village once again.

At the base of Mountain, there was a deep and narrow crevice, which the villagers knew as Mountain's Ear, and it was here that they gathered for Mountain's counsel, whispering their innermost thoughts, seeking answers to their questions. *How shall we fortify our defences against those despicable Mongols? Why do Ugly Lao Zhong's crops sell better than mine? Why does Pan Pan ignore my advances?*

Mountain despaired, for he knew only the song and the echo, and it was only much later that Mountain began to truly *know*, to think with his own thoughts, to laugh with his own voice, and when Ugly Lao Zhong and Liu Wei's wife began to frolic within Mountain's hidden nooks for hours of hot passion, so too did guilt-ridden Mountain learn to yelp and moan and experience his own illicit joys.

Not content to merely provide an echo to man's words, Mountain began to give voice to thoughts entirely his own. Mountain composed poems. In vain he sought the attentions of some distant and slender hillock. To no one in particular he described that low rumble of delight he felt as Hummingbird would approach, that sublime instant before it alighted, wings aflutter, upon Mountain's peak. And always Mountain dreamed the dream that had burdened him of late, in which he found his entire self being plucked from the ground, like a tree, unmoored, and carried into the heavens by a tremendous wind.

When Ugly Lao Zhong was cast out of the village on account of his brazen midnight jaunts with Liu Wei's wife, he returned to Mountain's hidden nooks. As Ugly Lao Zhong approached Mountain's Ear, instead of uttering to Mountain some secret thought or confession, he ran his hands along that crevice, secured his grip and – with a strength unknown to him – began to climb.

Mountain said to Man, *Why do you climb me? Nothing awaits you at the summit. There is no settlement. There are no others.*

I know, Man replied.

Then why? asked Mountain.

I tire of this life and seek another.

Will you not miss the life you left behind?

No.

You will miss nothing?

A wistful smile broke out on Man's face. *Women, maybe.*

Tell me about them, said Mountain.

And Man spoke of women and the shape of their minds and bodies.

What will you do when you reach my summit? asked Mountain.

To this, Man did not reply.

The days were long with climbing, and not much was said between them during that arduous ascent. The nights, however, were filled with conversation, and they grew to know each other well. Man told Mountain of the dream that had burdened him of late, in which he found his entire self becoming fused into the inescapable earth ...

When Man was hungry, Mountain would cause the trees upon himself to shake loose their succulent fruit. When Man was thirsty, Mountain would split open a rock and water would flow. One pensive evening, Mountain asked again, *What will you do when you reach my summit?* But Man still did not reply.

In the final days, when Mountain's peak was in sight, Man's demeanour began to change. He was no longer quick to laugh and he grew sullen in the nights. To Mountain's dismay, Man spoke very little, and in the hours of light he climbed as though he were possessed.

Mountain did not have to ask a third time. It had come to him in a dream. He knew that when Man reached the summit he would throw himself from it, there was no persuading him otherwise, and so Mountain, who could not bear to be alone, altered his terrain in the night, creating impossible sheer cliffs that caused Man to backtrack and lose entire days of effort. No longer did Mountain shake the fruits from the trees. No longer did Mountain split open the rocks. And yet Man persisted ...

Then Mountain had a thought.

An offering.

A bargain for Man.

Not long after, it was said that the villagers never heard the mountain speak again.

Man descended from there, the same but changed, and ventured into the vast and open world. When Man spoke, it was with his own voice. When Man laughed, it was with his own laugh. And in the nights as Man slept – was it one dream or many? – he saw Hummingbird, its wings forever aflutter, in his brief but everlasting sleep.

The Emperor did not understand and demanded an explanation.

Don't you see, my Lord? implored Scholar Zhao. *YOU are Mountain!*

For this treason, Scholar Zhao was thrown into the Six Levels of Hell.

6

Lobby, The Langham Hotel – Kent Street, Millers Point

'Good afternoon, sir. Checking in?'

'Oh, no. I called this morning regarding a wallet I found?'

'Yes.' A warm smile from the receptionist. 'Mr Bao is expecting you.'

He gestures to a staff member, who escorts me up in the lift and directs me to room 301, the Observatory Suite.

I approach the room and knock.

A woman opens the door.

Behind her, slouched on the lounge, boots atop the coffee table, is Baby Bao in the flesh. The shoulder-length hair, the leather everything, the aviator sunglasses that he also wore inside the cinema last night.

I don't know whether to look at him (crass) or her (beautiful) or the suite itself (opulent) or the view of the harbour and the city's skyline (unfathomable) or the Sidney Nolan piece adorning the wall (mesmeric). It's all too much to process at once.

He speaks in a string of rapid Chinese.

My already lousy comprehension of Mandarin is worsened by his accent – Shanghainese, I think. I'm lost. Struggle as I might, I'm unable to detect even the slightest sliver of familiarity. Every sentence is dizzying.

'Baby Bao asks you to sit,' interprets the woman, but he interjects with an angry torrent and she pauses to take his instruction. She nods. Slips into her native tongue to clarify with him some point of articulation. They talk like this for a moment. Then, having reached consensus, Baby Bao addresses me once more, through her.

'*Sit! Make sure to use my words. Interpret one hundred per cent of what I say. Leave nothing out. Speak out every word so he can understand. Even my private instructions to you. So, for example, if, while speaking to him, I point at you and say "Her name is Yuan. She will interpret", then you must not say to him "My name is Yuan. I will interpret", but rather everything verbatim, in my words. "Her name is Yuan. She will interpret."*'

Each time she speaks, Baby Bao leans forward and watches her studiously, as though she might misrepresent him with a stray or careless word. He even nods at times. Does he understand some English?

'*And if I happen to whisper something potentially embarrassing, such as, "This guy looks like such a piece of shit", do not gloss over it, or pretend I didn't say it, but say it out loud to him, in English, so he can hear absolutely everything I have to say. Do you understand? Do not merely interpret me, but rather mimic me. Be an extension of me. So when I command him to sit, so must you command him. Sit!*'

They turn to me.

Confused and hesitant, I take a seat opposite the lounge. His grin is filled with mischief.

'*So, now that that business is out of the way, let us begin afresh. I am Baby Bao. If the film critics are to be believed, I make bad art. Let me pose to you a hypothetical question. Let us say that I am watching television, late at night, and I happen to catch an old movie made by some long-forgotten director, and let us say, for argument's sake, that everyone agrees it is a Bad Movie. If, for my next project, I decide that I will re-create this Bad Movie, shot for shot, and line for line, is the finished result a Bad Movie, as all the critics seem to agree, and therefore Bad Art?*'

'No?'

'*Hahaha!!! I like you. Just because something is indistinguishable from bad art does not mean it is bad art. Isn't that right?! Very few people can tell the difference. Let me tell you, I can't stand it when people say my films are filled with technical faults, as though I overlooked these things. Why shouldn't the boom mic be visible?! Why shouldn't I shift the camera's focus suddenly to a plane flying overhead?! Why shouldn't the ancient wuxia warrior carry an iPhone in his pocket?! People associate these anachronisms with bad filmmaking, but I embrace them as my own. These are my unique cinematic flourishes. Do you understand me?'*

'I do, actually. That maze-of-mirrors scene in the middle of *Death of a Pagoda*.' I laugh, recalling it – that climactic sequence when the lead characters Mao Wen Bo and Gu Ting Ting finally find each other and the image of these star-crossed lovers repeat infinitely across each mirror, the camera capturing the desire in their hearts, the music swelling for them and them alone, and then there it is in the mirror, in fact *all* the mirrors – a glitch? One mirror shifts away from the actors, and suddenly all the reflections in all the mirrors show an image of the set itself: the crew, the camera operator and Baby Bao himself, luxuriating in all his infinite reflected glory, so that as the lovers embrace we cannot help but be distracted by the repeated image of Baby Bao – grinning, shirtless, bearing aviators and skintight leather pants – who has stolen the moment and destroyed it completely. 'That scene was something else. Unreal.'

Baby Bao slaps his knee in self-satisfaction.

'Good! That was my intention! The whole movie, up until that moment, was classically shot. The acting, directing, cinematography, everything. Topnotch. I wanted to make my audience forget, momentarily, that they were watching a Baby Bao movie. Ah, but then. Having located the heart of my work, I set out to ruin it completely. Everything crumbles in time, but that which is conceived as a ruin is forever perfect in its ruination. Yes, you did not know it was me sitting next to you, did you? I had left you by then, but I was still in the theatre, watching from the back. When the scene played, you were all in shock, silent shock. And then, one person laughed, and this somehow relieved the tension, and soon, most of the theatre was laughing. But before the laughter, you simply could not comprehend what you were seeing. I created something indistinguishable from a good movie so that, at the crucial moment, I could ruin it in its entirety. Ultimately, it was good that they laughed; I intended the moment as a joke, of course, but on the other hand it was

serious too. My next project is ALL serious. Serious acting. Serious directing. Serious money. One hundred per cent serious. In fact, laughing is forbidden on set. Anyone caught laughing will be thrown into prison.'

I chuckle, but he glares at me.

'It will be my masterpiece. The film I was born to make. But I mustn't say any more. It's top secret.'

He shoots a conspiratorial look at Yuan and me. We remain silent.

'Okay, fine, I'll tell you since you want to know so badly! It is a historical biopic of the infamous Indomitable Emperor of the Jin Dynasty, Lu Huang Du. The film will make cinematic history, a twenty-seven-hour extravaganza – no intermission – in simultaneous worldwide release! No expense will be spared! We are going to reconstruct the Imperial Palace in all its splendour. My costume department will work around the clock to weave the finest brocade. I have already personally vetted each and every concubine, some even in pairs. But you mustn't tell a word of this to anyone. My investors think I am preparing to make a blockbuster spy film. You are wondering why Baby Bao would risk his illustrious career to make such a frivolous vanity project?'

'Actually, I wasn't—'

'I'll tell you why. I recently discovered that my lineage can be traced directly to the Indomitable Emperor! I always knew that I was destined for greatness but I didn't realise it was literally in my blood, coursing through my veins. After all, what other role in this modern world is more like that of Emperor than Director? Both are in full command of his world, his domain, his set. Fate has led me to tell the story of my famous ancestor! Everything was proceeding well until you threw my careful plans into disarray!'

'Me?' I ask, incredulously.

'Yes, you. Last week, when I arrived in Sydney with hotly anticipated film in hand, I fully expected all talk on Weibo to be focused on me. Instead, imagine my surprise when I see that the top trending topic is not about me but rather some idiot translator who knows no Chinese! Can you imagine how I felt? How rare it is to find someone more infamous than me? You are already a meme in China!'

I am stunned. I don't know what to say.

He pulls out his phone and shows me a Chinese social media app.

A scanned photo of my work ID – grainy, unflattering – along with what I gather are jokes at my expense. The hashtag, at least, is in English. #BadChinese.

I recall the hashtag written on the envelope of my free movie ticket.

'Wait. *You* sent the ticket?'

'*Naturally, I was curious about you. Why else would I arrange for you to attend my screening, sit next to you and bother you horribly through half the movie, then deliberately leave my wallet behind?*'

He cracks open the wallet and riffles through his cash.

'*Well, it's all here! You might be a bad Chinese, but I can see you are a good person.*'

Baby Bao peels off a wad of notes and hands them to me.

'*Here. Your reward.*'

'This is RMB.'

'*What are you? Lazy?! Go to a currency exchange! Or, better yet, you won't have to convert it at all if you come work for me in Port Man Tou!*'

'The infamous ghost city,' I say.

'*Ah, you know about it! Tell me what you've heard.*'

'It's been in the news, I guess. I don't really know much. Just that it's one of those huge, empty cities in China where no one actually lives. People were supposed to move there, but nobody ever did.'

'*Yes, the Chinese government has built dozens of these cities, yet has been unsuccessful in luring sufficient numbers of people to settle in them. I alone devised the solution! How? By turning Port Man Tou into the world's largest film set! As for your job, let's say part of it involves translation, which I know you have some experience in, however pitiful. Though its scope is far greater than that. What's more, if you take the job, you would be spending a lot of time in the company of Yuan*' – Baby Bao points at the interpreter – '*and to be honest, I think you might even have a shot with her!*'

Yuan stops to glare at Baby Bao, who laughs raucously and then says something to her to translate and, sensing her hesitation, goads her to go on, saying, '说呀, 说呀!' and pointing from me to her eagerly. Blushing, she continues, '*She thinks you are extremely handsome. Even more handsome than me, if you can believe it! My spies tell me she doesn't have a boyfriend. Go for it! You have a good chance! Tell him you said that. But then say to him, mysteriously, yes, say it, the whole thing, everything that is coming out of my mouth, "Did she really say that, or was it me instructing her to say it?" Tell him that.'*

I glimpse at her to try to gauge her reaction but, when she glances over at me, I grimace instead and look up at the ceiling.

Baby Bao laughs loudly.

'So Xiang Lu. What do you say?'

'Oh, I mean,' I begin, 'it's up to her. I'm pretty single …'

'No, you fool. I meant what do you say to my job offer?'

'Oh that! Right. It sounds interesting, and I *am* between jobs at the moment. But I've still got three months on my lease here. I can't afford to just up and leave the country and break the lease.'

'If you agree to come on board and return to Port Man Tou with me and my group on Thursday, I will take care of it. Your lease, your work visa, everything. Nothing is beyond me. Yes, yes, think it through. Think it through! But if you're at all interested, first I'll need you to complete a little translation exercise. Don't look so worried! You will be given a Chinese–English dictionary. Oh, we don't have one? Doesn't matter, there should be an app for that. Feel free to download it and make use of it. Take your time, but the whole test is just a formality. A final box to tick. If I deem it acceptable, I'll offer you a contract with Daedalic Productions, effective immediately.'

Baby Bao and Yuan chatter in low tones as they peruse my test results. Finally, they speak.

'Interesting,' says Baby Bao/Yuan. *'Very interesting! Especially this final paragraph.'*

He places the original Chinese text of the final paragraph above my English translation.

满透港正在逐步发展。包宝宝最近的两部电影都是完全在满透港拍摄的。附近的村民感受到了这个城市机会无限，甚至把家都搬到了满透港，成为了这座城市的第一批居民。摄制组雇佣他们提供餐饮服务、场景设计。这里有着公交车和货真价实的超市，还有着一所学校，让孩子们上学。但包宝宝觉得这还不够，他需要更多的龙套，他要把这座城市填的满满的。

Slowly but surely, Port Man Tou is growing. Baby Bao's last two films were shot here entirely. Villagers from nearby have even migrated to Port Man Tou, having sensed the city's boundless opportunity. They have become its first citizens. They are employed in catering and set design. They are paid a salary. There are bus routes and grocery stores with real food. There is a school for children. But Baby Bao needs more. He needs extras. He needs you to fill the city. Because if Man Tou is a bun, then the people are the filling.

'Why did you add that final line in your translation? It wasn't in the original Chinese text.'

I pause, and think back to my work at the Consulate, how secretly relying on Google Translate had often exposed me to bits of unintentional machine poetry.

'It seemed to fit the tone of the article.'

'And why did you shorten the name to just "Man Tou"?'

'Well, if my limited Chinese is correct, *man tou* is the word for, like, an empty bun?'

Baby Bao roars with laughter. *'Not correct at all! Different tones, different meanings. A perfect example of #BadChinese! But still, you seem to have added something valuable to the translation. The people are the filling! I like it!*

'Do you know that Yuan here was not at all impressed with your' – he turns to her – *'what did you call it? Embellishment? Yes, embellishment. But she is an adherent of that boring school of translation, where everything is strict and literal, where you must not deviate, even for the sake of beauty or poetics or truth. In fact, she advised me not to give you the job on this basis, but for me, it was this inspired and thoroughly unprofessional embellishment that breathed new life into the text. You have proven my instincts correct. Congratulations. You have the job. Now the two of you are colleagues! How awkward!'*

7

THE SCHOLARS YU, SHI AND DENG

After the banishment of Scholar Zhao to the Six Levels of Hell, Scholars Yu, Shi and Deng were summoned to compose an origin story befitting the Emperor.

SCHOLAR YU

... And in all that time lush vegetation grew upon the mountain, which in turn attracted Snake, Horse, Sheep, Monkey, Rooster, Dog, Pig, Rat, Ox, Tiger, Rabbit and Dragon, and they too made their home on the mountain, nestled within its craggy folds, filling the air with hisses and bleats, beating gongs and jingling bells. And lowly Man heard the commotion and so came he, to the foot of the mountain, for he could not stand to be alone ...

SCHOLAR SHI

... And when the Mongols came, in a galloping rage, and burned the village to the ground, only Liu Wei's wife survived. The woman, heavy with child, had feigned death and so had been the only one spared its touch. Amongst the aftermath of the ruins and the wreckage, Woman fled to the mountain in her melancholy ...

SCHOLAR DENG

… And at the base of the mountain there was a deep and narrow crevice, which the villagers knew as the mountain's ear, and unbeknownst to all, there hid a trickster spirit, and it was only Trickster who knew the truth, that the mountain was only ever a mountain. It did not speak, it did not sing – it knew not how – and so the mountain's voice and echo had, always and forever, belonged to Trickster. When the villagers came to the mountain's ear, Trickster amused himself by answering their many questions: *To protect yourselves from the Mongols you must bring me gold, lots of gold; Ugly Lao Zhong's crops outsell yours because he has good feng shui and because you are stupid, but I shall treble your income if you bring me virgins, lots of virgins; Pan Pan ignores your advances because you are her brother, but with enough gold, and enough virgins, perhaps …*

SCHOLAR YU

… and lowly Man was obsequious, and curried favour with the animals so that he might one day steal their secrets. Charmed by Man, Snake taught him how to lie. Horse gave Man his speed. Sheep, his wool to brave the winter nights. Monkey, his laughter. From Rooster, Man learned to separate the days from the nights. Dog gave Man friendship. Pig, his sustenance. Rat gave Man the gift of fear. From Ox, Man learned to till the soil. From Tiger, Man learned war. And Rabbit taught Man to multiply and soon he spread throughout the world, claiming dominion over the lands. Finally, Man asked Dragon for that which he most desired – flight – but to this, Dragon did not reply …

SCHOLAR SHI

… and within one of the mountain's hidden nooks was born a nameless child. Woman had survived the Mongols and the mountain had taken her in. That Child wanted for nothing, for he had been born of the mountain; when Child was thirsty, the mountain would split open the rock and water would flow; when Child hungered for meat, the mountain would shake the trees loose, causing the elk, the bird, the bear to become trapped beneath the falling debris …

SCHOLAR DENG

… and learning that the solutions to all their problems could be solved through offerings of gold, the villagers scrimped and schemed and saved to supply Trickster with all that he desired. But the villagers' wishes were never fulfilled and, in their bitter servitude, they worked themselves to the bone so that they might appease Trickster's insatiable appetite. They increased the scale of their farms tenfold, calling upon able-bodied men from nearby villages to work the land. Homes for the labourers were built, and soon enough came taverns, temples, schools. Beyond the distant and slender hillock came the new roads and the merchants, who marvelled at the village – its bustle and industry – the giant fields and the laughing mountain that glinted and glittered on the horizon …

SCHOLAR YU

… and, having been denied the gift of flight by Dragon, Man looked upon Rooster's wings and he pleaded with Rooster to teach him how to fly. But Rooster did not know the secrets of flight and in order to save face – for Rooster was a proud creature – he turned away from Man. For this, Man swore to destroy Dragon, for he saw that Dragon must have whispered poison into the ear of Rooster, to keep from Man that which was rightfully his.

Man descended the mountain. There he established a settlement and one by one, year by year, by force or deception, did he persuade the animals to make their own descent to join him and submit to his rule. But Dragon cared not for Man's deceitful pursuits, his petty politics, and so chose to remain upon the mountain in his perfect and unending solitude.

Years passed, but Man never forgot his vow of vengeance, and in his cunning he declared to all that Dragon had died. But the animals were not stupid and they required proof, so Man took them to the field in which the bones of Dragon lay. They knew not of Man's lies – that he had manufactured these bones from clay – and those remains sprawled in such an inelegant fashion that the animals, reconciling the fearsome creature from their memories and the pitiful corpse that lay before them, would forget the magnificence of Dragon.

And Dragon, high in the mountain, who knew all and saw all, was so angered by Man's insolence that he descended to the earth. To this day the animals recall that fearsome rumble as Dragon approached – the beating of his brutal wings and that deafening instant before he crushed those clay bones into the ground. There, before all, he took the world away from Man and punished him to suffer in eternal servitude under Dragon's rule.

SCHOLAR SHI

... and while Child was fed by the mountain, Woman nourished him with words and stories, to while away the days. At first they were stories of the village that once was, of things Woman had heard or remembered, but as Child grew older, and as those recollections from her life below began to fade, Woman made new stories to explain the world and the way of all things.

In this manner, Child learned why the pig's snout was flat, why rain fell down instead of up, knew the tale in which the mountain had learned to sing, memorised the names of the stars in the sky and was taught to speak in all the tongues of Man. In time, Woman grew old and feeble for whilst Child had been born of the mountain, she had been born of Man. Child grieved deeply his mother's passing.

One day, as Child ascended to the summit – the climb had seemed unbearably and infinitesimally shorter – he understood that even the mountain would erode, slowly but completely, and someday cease to be.

And, knowing this in heartbreaking clarity, Child descended from mountain-father's shoulders, for Woman had taught him the old story that there in the lands below was hidden the song of immortality. He had heard its melody in his dreams, and longed to know the words.

SCHOLAR DENG

... and Trickster reaped the fruits of Man's prosperity and left him with nothing in return. The years of bountiful harvests and good fortune gave way to drought and famine, and still Trickster demanded his tithe.

With no good soil to till, Man lay down his spade and shovel and climbed the mountain and opened it to the world, so that others would come from near and far to bask – for a fee, of course – in the mountain's splendour. Man sold trinkets and guidebooks, he built a temple as part of a deep and complex stratagem to part visitors from their money.

In this manner, Man appeased Trickster's demands, but in time the village no longer attracted the same numbers – it was said a village to the south had found a dragon's corpse and was charging a fair and reasonable price to view the bones – so the flow of money to the poor village began to dwindle. But still, Trickster demanded his tithe.

And in the hungry village, Man melted down his precious trinkets and his farm tools for meagre scraps of money. He sold his oxen, his children, his furniture, the very land on which he stood, and still Trickster demanded his tithe.

The village withered and scattered into the winds, but it mattered not, for the Trickster had finally had his fill.

The Emperor did not understand, and demanded an explanation.

SCHOLAR YU

... *Don't you see, my Lord? YOU are Dragon!*

SCHOLAR SHI

... *Don't you see, my Lord? YOU are Child!*

SCHOLAR DENG
... Don't you see, my Lord? YOU are Trickster!

For this treason, the Emperor threw Scholars Yu, Shi and Deng into the Six Levels of Hell and punished the scholarly ranks by ordering the destruction of the Imperial Library, and the burning of every book within it.

8

Lobby, Langham Hotel – Kent Street, Millers Point

We bump into each other in the lobby. Yuan is busy on the phone, so I give her a wave on my way out. She gestures for me to wait.

While she wraps up her conversation, I glance at her figure, her eyelashes, her slightly chapped lips. Away from Baby Bao, and in her native tongue, the tone of her speech is composed of gentler patterns that, strangely, make me think of siren song, her voice somehow lovelier when the words are foreign to me.

She finishes her call and smiles, as if to wipe the slate clean after all the bluster up above.

'Hi, thanks for waiting.'

'No problem,' I say, adding, 'sorry about up there.'

'Sorry for what?' she asks, surprised.

I have a tendency to apologise to beautiful women.

'Nothing.'

We walk towards the lobby's entrance.

'So, where are you headed?' I ask.

'Shelley Street. Wynyard,' she says. 'Back to my hotel.'

'You're not staying here?'

'Only Baby Bao is staying here. Farmstrong booked the rest of us in three-star accommodation. To save on costs,' she adds mournfully. 'At least the hotel is close to the shops.'

'So,' I say. 'What are your plans over the next couple of days?

I mean, besides all the shopping?'

'Well, Baby Bao is meeting with a potential investor on Wednesday. So I may be called on to interpret.'

'And how about today?' I ask.

She sizes me up, considers the implications of her answer.

'No plans today.'

Before I can chicken out, I say, 'There's an exhibition on at the art gallery that I've been meaning to catch. Want to go with me? Or maybe take a walk by the harbour?'

Yuan gives me a suspicious look. 'Aren't these dating activities?'

I shrug.

'How far is the gallery? Is it walkable?'

'Half an hour's walk, maybe?' I estimate. 'Want to take a bus? Taxi?'

'Walk.'

She smiles. We go.

Upper Fort Street, Sydney

'So, what's Port Man Tou like?' I ask.

'Well, there's the Canton of WF, which is modelled on 1930s Shanghai. The women wear cheongsams and carry parasols. Really! It is like stepping into a time warp! Recently Baby Bao opened that portion of the city to the Western media. There is much demand for interpreters.'

'Not what I expected,' I say. 'I guess I was picturing some apocalyptic scene. Deserted malls, empty streets, no cars or people. The modern ruins of man ...'

'En, that's always how the Western press paints these ghost cities. It's really a Western obsession, I think. In Zhejiang, where I'm from, no one really cares. Ghost cities aren't a big deal. There are over a billion people in China after all. It kind of makes sense for the government to build entire cities in advance. How else are you going to cater to the movements of such a massive population? Shanghai alone has more people than *all* of Australia. You would expect the town planning to be a little different.'

This way she has of walking with her hands in the pockets of her dress.

'What does WF stand for?'

'Western Facade. The canton is only a fraction of Port Man Tou. Large sections of the city remain under construction. Some of the crew members have seen other versions of the city. Rumours fly. By all accounts, the city is immense. Unfathomable. Baby Bao is always seeking more funding, more investment, so he can grow the city and the industry. One day he hopes it will become self-sustaining. But first he needs to consolidate his local mainland investments. And he seems to think that #BadChinese is the key.'

'I don't understand.'

'Baby Bao believes #BadChinese has captured the imagination of the mainland. He says all the major demographics are interested when it comes to cultural shame. Young, old, rich, poor. Just look at who is reposting that horrible photo of you. Movie stars, politicians, billionaires. He plans to announce that #BadChinese has become affiliated with the prestigious #BabyBao brand at the next investor meeting.'

'You look sceptical.'

She shrugs, then stops abruptly. 'Look. I don't want to start things off on the wrong foot.'

'Please. Whatever you feel you need to say.'

'... I'm not sure I can respect you as a colleague.'

My ears go red.

She bites her lip, but presses on. 'I've spent four years studying translation and interpretation at Zhejiang University, then another two years working with courts and governments and diplomats. Only to be told that I'm at the same pay grade and professional level as ...'

'As?' I ready myself, willing my ears back to their original hue.

'As someone who doesn't even *speak* Mandarin. And don't get me started on your translation. What you did to the final line of that text was … *unprofessional.* It's not the job of the translator to fabricate meaning. If you can't trust a translator to translate something with the utmost care and accuracy, then everything we do has a question mark over it. Your poetic licence diminishes my profession.'

It's been a long time since I've been taken to task by a girl, but I can already feel those dormant muscles limbering up, the mind racing to find the sharpest points of retaliation.

'It's true, I can't speak Mandarin very well. But I understand much more than I'm given credit for. For example, I understood perfectly well what you were saying about me on the phone in the lobby.'

'What?'

'You were complaining to someone about having orders to babysit me today. Why do you think I asked you on a date? It's not like you were going to turn me down.'

Now it's her turn to go red.

I continue. 'It's enlightening to hear what people have to say about you, in front of you, when they think you can't understand.'

'I shouldn't have said that. I'm sorry. Perhaps I misjudged you. In any case, one shouldn't judge.'

We resume walking.

'Didn't your parents ever teach you Chinese?' she asks.

'They tried. They sent my brother and me to Chinese school for a while, but it didn't stick. Well, not for me.'

'Your brother is fluent?'

'He's a better student. Straight A's. Honours in law school. Even now he enrols himself in language classes. He practises.'

'You should learn.'

'That's what everyone says.'

'You should.'

'I know.'

'I'll teach you.'

'What?'

'You don't want to be #BadChinese forever, do you?'

We pass by the entrance of a primary school. Some students, heavy-laden with backpacks, make their way to bus stops. Cars queue up, bored parents at the wheel, waiting for their children to emerge.

Our pace slows. We linger.

'It's interesting to see the subtle differences in cities and countries,' she says, watching. 'Back home, the streets and footpaths outside schools become *completely* clogged when school finishes for the day. Most of the children, in fact almost all of them, have someone waiting to pick them up and escort them home. Grandparents mostly. A lot of mothers, too. But here, it looks like many children get picked up in cars.'

'That, or public transport, yeah. When I was a kid, my mum would come by in the car to pick me up after school. I guess that wouldn't be possible in China.'

'No, that's rare. If every parent did that, it would be chaos.'

'Kiss and ride,' I say.

'What?'

'That's what it's called. Where you pick your kid up without parking or getting out of the car. Kiss and ride. Like picking up fast food at a drive-through.'

We set off again, passing a steady stream of children headed for the bus stop down the hill.

'I think that kids are more independent here,' I say, and then cautiously, in a conspiratorial whisper so as not to offend anyone nearby with my horrific blasphemies, 'but perhaps the parents and grandparents in China dote on their children more.'

'En. Ever since the one-child policy, the children have become more beloved and, dare I say, more spoiled. Up until recently, there were six adults in most families to heap affection on one child. Two parents and both sets of grandparents. That's the Chinese family unit. My nephew, he's so cute and adorable, and I love him so. But he is like a little emperor, changing favourites depending on whoever is nicest to him. If anyone displeases him or tries to discipline him, he rebukes them, ignores them. In the end, he gets away with everything because there will always be someone to give him what he wants.'

'Shit. Are you married?' I ask.

'What? No.'

'Then how do you have a nephew?'

'He's my brother's son.'

'How do you have a brother? Or do you predate the one-child policy?'

Too late, I realise my faux pas. I see from her expression that the damage is already done.

'Well ... first, the way you put it makes me sound old. Second, don't you dare attempt to calculate my age based on the date of the policy. And third, I don't "predate" anything of the sort. I was born after the implementation of the policy, but my mother fought to keep me.'

I hold up my hands in contrition.

'I didn't mean to presume. I'm hazy on the date of the policy, and frankly I'm scared to find out now. For what it's worth, you don't look a day older than, um ...'

'Than what?' She smirks, wanting to see this through.

'No, no, no. I refuse to continue. I opt out of that sentence.'

'You're not very good at this.'

'At what?'

'At complimenting a girl.'

Changing the subject, or rather returning to it, I ask, 'How did your mother fight to keep you?'

'She refused to give me up. We come from a small village. National policy sometimes doesn't take hold in the villages until years later. Plus, you can get away with a lot of things in China. You just have to be one of two things: very rich or very poor.'

'Which were you?'

'Both.'

9

THE IMPERIAL ARTISAN

Observe the works of the Imperial Artisan.

The nightingale automaton whose mechanisms delighted the members of the Court and whose chirps attracted even real members of its species into the halls, so lifelike was its birdsong.

The Moonlit Pagoda, by day so pale and unremarkable, but by night drawing admirers from all around, convinced they had glimpsed its true image in the water's reflection.

And the self-portrait entitled *A Simulated Man*, of which only rumours had been heard. It was like no other, said to have been conceived by the Artisan in a dream: he had seen a canvas in which a thousand layers hid, each beneath each other, so that day after day, year after year, the art would slowly corrode, the image of him as an infant disappearing into the ether to be replaced, in time, by the portrait of the child, the youth, the man. His ascendance and decline. He had worked with the Imperial Apothecary to craft a special sort of ink, comprising compounds that would decay with sufficient exposure to the light, so that he might paint the landmarks of his life, one over the other. Beginning with his death, that first and inescapable layer.

He had many admirers, this Artisan.

There were those, in fact, who even dared call him great, not realising how this might injure the Emperor in subtle and complex ways. Even the Emperor could not dispute that the Artisan, who had honed himself into an instrument of skill and expression, was remarkable. But was he *great*, the way the Emperor was *great*?

Of course not. The Emperor calculated the Artisan's worth. In His estimation, he did not occupy the same rarefied air.

The Emperor was uniquely talentless and took enormous pride in this fact. He had nothing to prove, after all. His greatness was immutable. Unsullied. Inherent and plain for all to see. The Artisan's 'greatness', on the other hand, was entirely dependent on talent, which, if it were to desert him – the Emperor smiled – would surely lose him favour with the Imperial Court.

Thus the Emperor commissioned the Artisan to create a wall sculpture of grand and heavenly scope, imposing cruel and arbitrary deadlines such that the Artisan could not but fail.

Nonetheless, the Artisan poured every aspect of himself into the work and, within the strict limits of time, fashioned striking pieces of unimaginable beauty.

After weeks of the Artisan's hard labour and inspiration, the Emperor conducted a private viewing on the eve of the sculpture's unveiling before the Imperial Court.

The Artisan unveiled the work. The Emperor observed.

He had underestimated the Artisan. This piece would only serve to heighten the Artisan's glory and He could not abide it.

The Emperor ordered the sculpture's destruction. The Artisan despaired as the Imperial Guards set upon it with their swords and feet.

After the guards had laid waste to the work, the Emperor – patron and patroniser – turned to the Artisan and commissioned him then and there to create *another* artwork of identical specifications. This He did to breed a sense of futility in his lesser, to remind him of the crucial and impossible gulf between a talented man such as he, and a *great* man such as He.

Disheartened, the Artisan began his second work. For long and agonising moments of the day he merely stared at the wall, struggling to recall the faint impressions on its surface so that he could re-create the original carving.

Working listlessly, the Artisan realised he could not match the previous work, for this was merely a replica and therefore meaningless. But in a momentary lapse or madness – perhaps he was merely anticipating the sculpture's fate – he gouged at its centre, rending the work in two. Better that it be from his own hand, better that *he* be the one to strip it of its beauty. But before he could destroy the work entirely, the Artisan wavered. For he thought he saw, suddenly, in the deep and intricate riven, something in the cracks and fault lines, their repetitions, a meaningful echo or conflation. And, inspired by this ruined and ruinous centre, he returned to the unsullied edges of the carving, seeing it anew.

Upon the sculpture, he rearranged the features of some commoner into the unmistakable likeness of the Emperor. And, guided by his hatred, he repeated the image of the Emperor on each and every face in the wall thereafter.

The Artisan unveiled the re-created work.

Its sight displeased the Emperor greatly, for it was not what He had ordered. Even from afar He could see that some mischief had been wrought. Nonetheless He casually ordered its destruction.

But the Imperial Guards, approaching with swords drawn, hesitated at its form. They studied the ruined centre, unsure of how to destroy it further. Instead they moved to the sides of the carving, which were intact and therefore more recognisable as something worthy of their attention and attenuations. Their eyes came to rest on shapes and compositions that seemed particularly lovely to each man and, beginning their labours, they swung their weapons at these sites of resplendence.

Only at the proper distance, where the Artisan and the Emperor stood, was it possible to see that His destroyers had been subtly guided by that ruined centre, and with each successive strike the Emperor – in some Delphic confusion – saw before His eyes a certain symmetry restored, the art acquiring an unstoppable grace, as though it had been completed by its very ruination.

In later days, when He would come to banish His deceased father's most favoured concubine to the Six Levels of Hell, He would recall some measure of the sculpture, how every blemish and loss had made it perversely more impossible in its beauty.

Troubled at the ease of His triumph, the Emperor locked eyes with the Artisan. But something in the man's expression – pride? defiance? joy? – assured Him that He was somehow being made a fool of, and in a daze He approached the sculpture, ordering His men to cease their destruction. Here the Emperor saw His likenesses repeated across the wall and in shattered pieces on the floor and He smiled, for He had been bested.

For having destroyed His sacred image, the Emperor ordered the execution of each of His guards.

But what to do with this treasonous Artisan? It was plain to see in the work that he had acquired some glimmer of greatness. From where? From whom? From the utmost source of greatness, of course: the Emperor Himself, who had infected the Artisan's art, corrupting it completely. What strange pride He felt.

He decided that He would commission one final work – a piece of unprecedented scope and ambition – which He would extract from the Artisan before executing the man for his mischief.

As for this sculpture, which could no longer be seen or destroyed, the Emperor gave orders for the room to be sealed, leaving the art to forever languish in the darkness.

10

George Street, The Rocks

We wander through the old tourist haunts. The cobbled brick streets lined with terraced houses, cafes with handpainted signs. Yuan lingers happily at store windows, contemplating opals, wood-crafted kookaburras and other Australiana. Down the street, a taxi driver gestures at us to hop in. We shake our heads and continue along our way.

'So, do you have family back in China?' she asks.

'Only distant. In a village called Min Qiang, in the Fuzhou province. There's an old joke that goes Min Qiang is the armpit of the armpit of China.'

'Have you gone to visit?'

I hesitate. 'Once, as a kid. My grandmother's cousin gave us a tour of the family hall, the farms. Later, he took us back to a tiny hut and showed us the most outrageously extravagant hi-fi system I've ever seen. The speakers were taller than me. It seemed crazy to me, that a poor farmer would have a hi-fi as big as his living room.'

Yuan laughs. 'Did he play any music on it?'

'No! I wish he had. That village really was the armpit of the armpit. Kids playing on dirt roads. Babies with holes cut out of their pants so they could pee wherever and whenever they wanted. The "hotel" my family stayed at had pillows filled with sand! My brother and I still joke about it to this day. But it's that thing where

I look back *now* and think, okay, maybe I'm remembering it wrong. What if the stories have replaced the memories? It would be such a disappointment to go to the village and see, maybe, that it wasn't at all how I remembered it.'

'You should go back.'

'Maybe I will ... someday. Or maybe it's better left alone, untouched, just beyond my grasp or understanding. Does that make sense?'

'In a way. When I was sixteen, I met my friend Xiao Ling in the city and it started to rain, but we only had one bike and one raincoat between us, so I climbed onto her back while she rode the bike. We covered the raincoat over both of us. We must have looked like a weird hunchback girl riding through the streets! She went through a red light and a policeman pulled her over. After the bike stopped, I tried to balance but I couldn't stay on, so I jumped off her back and gave the policeman a fright! Luckily, he saw the funny side and let us go with a warning. Xiao Ling and I, we were inseparable. Like one person. But years later we had a falling out and lost touch. I still think about her a lot. Sometimes, I want to call her, but I never end up doing it, because ... I don't know.'

'Because the friendship wouldn't be the same?'

'En.'

'That's very self-defeating.'

'I guess so. But we can never get it back. The magic of how it once was. And if we try too hard to reclaim that thing we might lose it even more. Even if, in your case, it is a memory of a dirty village with a huge hi-fi and pillows filled with sand.'

'I remember distinctly thinking of the villagers as my *ancestors*. It felt like I was looking at ancient people. Even the kids were ancient, somehow. I could never have articulated this at that age, but that's how I felt then, in the village. Like an *anachronism*. Like I was peering at some vision of the past. I'll never forget.'

'You know, in Chinese, the word "forget" is *wang ji*. And how we say the word "remember" is *ji de*. So the two are linked by a common root, *ji*. But in English it doesn't make sense. *Forget. Remember.* There's nothing telling you that these two words are related. Doesn't that seem wrong to you?'

'English is a messy language.'

'I *know*, it's so frustrating, isn't it? The messiness.'

'Well, no. I think the messiness is quite beautiful, actually!' I blurt out, feeling surprisingly defensive. 'I've been reading Nabokov's *Invitation to a Beheading* and there was a phrase that stuck with me, I think, because of its messiness. *The road wound around its rocky base.* And just the other day I read it as wound, as in "hurt". The wounded road. Rather than wound, as in "coiled". And it was a wonderful and confusing image. A wounded road. Like a wounded animal, somehow. I wondered if he had intended it.'

'I like that. You must have a head – heart? – for poetry,' she says. 'Did you know the French government has a department, the Académie Française, that acts as the official authority on the French language? I think the Israelis have something similar, to preserve Hebrew. If only there was an authority on the English language! I would write to them and request that they fix "remember" and "forget". Because to me, the natural opposite of "remember" is "dismember".'

'But that's already a word.'

Yuan sighs. 'En, I know. That's what I mean. It's too messy, the English language! But when a memory eludes me, like the edges of a dream, where no matter what I try I can't remember the details – only it was important and now I have lost it maybe forever – then I *am* dismembered. I have lost a part of myself. Violently so. That is actually how I feel. A dismemberment. Is that strange?'

She looks at me, expectantly. But I'm somewhere else, suddenly seeing the outline of the memory of my grandmother's death, my father's mother. Remembering it, or perhaps the opposite, for I have always been bothered by its ... incompleteness. The gaps in my recollection, which begins only on the day of her funeral, only coming into focus when I'm lifted out of bed by someone, Mum or Dad, and then dressed in white robes of mourning. She lived with us and was sick for months and I never knew it. I had to ask to find out that my own grandmother had died. How old was I? Three? Four? But that is no excuse.

The loss of my memory protected me from her dying, her death. But my brother, three years older than me, *he* remembered everything and was not protected in the same fashion. He watched the entire funeral in complete silence, and afterwards stood before her grave. For a long time, like that. The moment Dad led him away, he burst into inconsolable tears, and to this day he cannot bear the sight of a grave.

I never thought too much about this in my teens. At that age, I suppose, there isn't enough time; you have better things to do. But I have been thinking of her lately. Her death, her dying, some damaged pathway of my memory which I can never recall.

A wounded road.

Customs House Library – Alfred Street, Sydney

If I am the navigator, she is the explorer. Other than confirming the right direction, I let myself be led by her. She seems so enraptured by the city – its streets, its sights – that it would be a shame for me to insist on faster routes.

We take a quick detour through Customs House Library, where we spend some minutes marvelling at the miniature of inner Sydney encased in glass beneath our feet, before heading up the spiral staircase, in search of the company of books.

'When I was a teenager,' says Yuan, perusing the stacks of fiction, 'I would always borrow the same book from our village library. *Xibao* by Yi Shu. If I love a book – really love it – I could spend my whole life reading and re-reading it. Just that one book. I read *Xibao* so often and returned it so often that eventually the librarian offered to sell the book to me. He said it was practically mine. No one else ever borrowed it.'

'Librarians can do that?'

'It was a small village. The rules are different. So I bought it for two RMB.'

'Why didn't you just buy it from a bookstore?' I ask.

'I *like* library books. They have more personality. They never quite belong to you and must leave you eventually. So you race through them to make sure you don't have to return them unfinished, and savour every minute you have together. And besides,' she says, 'I grew up poor, or did you forget that already?'

'How did your family lose everything?'

'It was long before I was born. We owned a lot of property in Xian Ju, my village, but my grand-uncle gambled it all away on mah jong and cards.'

'That's awful.'

'In the beginning he was very successful, actually, and everybody in the village knew him as something of a genius.'

'Well, it's only called a gambling problem if you lose.'

'En, that's why nobody minded at first. But one day, the talent left him mysteriously and he sort of went mad trying to recover it. He would scribble in his notebooks day and night. Trying to find the winning strategy. He had so many notebooks all over the place, and nobody could decipher them. According to my boh boh's stories, he would visit fortune tellers, sleep sideways on the bed, visit the prostitutes only on alternating months ... He was always devising new theories, convinced that some missing element would perfect the puzzle, and turn all those losses into victories.'

'I've read,' I say, 'that the same pleasure centres of the brain light up whether you win or lose. Either way, you feel the same.'

I wonder if it's the same with love, I want to add, but don't.

'It's a kind of demon, isn't it?' Yuan says. 'But *his* demon saved us. He borrowed my family's money and never gave it back. In the end, he outright stole until there was nothing left. But my boh boh says he did the family a favour by getting rid of all our bad money. You see, not long after, the class struggle of the Cultural Revolution came. During the struggle sessions, many landlords were tortured or executed. But by then, *our* family was too poor to be accused of being class enemies. We had no land or money. We were spared because of my grand-uncle! So we all think of him kindly these days because, in a very strange way, he was able to reverse our fortunes by reversing our fortunes.'

An announcement goes out over the library PA system.

'Ah, damn,' I say. 'It's almost closing time. We won't be able to make it to the gallery at this rate.'

'Tomorrow, then.'

'Right, tomorrow.'

We head outside and walk back towards her hotel.

11

THE EMPEROR

In melancholic moods the Emperor would summon His brother, and they would take midnight walks throughout the palace grounds.

The Emperor was comforted by this sibling dynamic – the younger at His beck and call – and during these aimless jaunts He spoke of many things: His philosophies on life and war. The constant burden of His greatness. His deep annoyance at the volume at which one of His concubines snored. A poem He had forgotten but for a fragment (and in its shaky recitation therein a hope that His brother, Lu Dong Pu, might recall its remainder). Once, staring into the Moonlit Pagoda, He had come very close to asking for help, though for what exactly He was not quite sure.

At times, He found He had nothing whatsoever to say, and in these moments – fearing silence – He bid His brother to speak, though in truth He hardly listened.

This particular night they found themselves traversing the servants' hallways, passing dumbstruck maids, errand runners ...

That first assassin, in pageboy's garb, armed with hidden blade and calm demeanour.

As they passed, in this cramped and darkened cloister, the way he pivoted and sank his blade into the Emperor's rib.

No. Not His rib. His *brother's*. For Lu Dong Pu had anticipated the movement and, with no intent or conscious thought, slid between the two, his body now a shield.

The Emperor did not sleep for days.

In His terror, He saw how easy it would be to murder Him, in His city, in His Court, in His sleep. And who might do such a thing? Not just the enemies of His state but His very own subjects, whose loyalty – He realised – had always been in question. Look at them! How they fawned and grovelled but detested Him deep down! He saw it when they smiled or bowed. He saw it when He closed His eyes.

The Emperor ordered the execution of one of His concubines who, in the blissful aftermath of lovemaking, had lain beside Him, and with the tips of her fingers sensuously traced the length of His arm, the path of His vein, and He saw now – how could He not? – the very causeways of His vulnerable, precious blood, and He knew that there was no other explanation for her wandering fingers except that she was a spy, sent to construct an intricate catalogue of His weaknesses, a map of His vessels and all His meridians, all the more information for the endless assassins that awaited Him in every nook, in every shadow and in every darkened corner of His sprawling palace.

He heard the sharpening of blades whenever He nodded off, and would awake in the coldest of sweats. He divined the presence of poisons in every meal and refused all food and drink, and when He grew weak and gaunt as a result, this only seemed to confirm His most bitter suspicions.

The Emperor could not keep these thoughts away and they visited Him in His dark and suffocating chambers, night after night, terror after terror. He relived the assassination attempt relentlessly, the events shifting, revising themselves constantly – the stance and the trajectory, the angle of the attack – each version papering over the last, until He had constructed the perfect simulacrum that He replayed over and over in His mind's eye.

He had always suspected that the world favoured His younger brother in subtle and indefinable ways and, in the clarity of His madness and delirium, He finally found the piece that had eluded Him all along: the assassin had aimed straight and true. His brother had been the intended target all along. Not He.

It could not be forgiven.

The Emperor examined His memory and traced the length of His brother's betrayal – the path of their approach, the turning page, the blade and bloodstained cloister, that slow and fatal dance.

And in the darkened corners of His sleep, He saw it – how could He not? A map of all His brother's meridians.

Dear citizens of the Imperial City,

We are pleased to inform you that Lu Dong Pu, brother of the Emperor, has been banished to the Sixth Level of Hell.

Furthermore, the Emperor has also taken Wuer – Lu Dong Pu's beloved wife – as His own concubine.

No doubt there has been a great deal of conjecture and well-meaning gossip as to the reason behind such drastic actions! To quell any confusion, we offer the following rumours, officially sanctioned by the Emperor Himself:

- Some say Lu Dong Pu plotted a coup against the Emperor. You know how the Emperor feels about coups.
- Also possible, is that the Emperor secretly desired the beautiful Wuer for Himself and had merely been waiting for an opportunity, a pretext, to make her His own.

Please draw your own conclusions.

We are hereby bound by law to note the dissent of Sima Qing, the Shadow Historian, who begins with a lengthy and boring preamble about how the Tanguts and the false empire of the South have found the current 'chaotic' state of our Empire most favourable to their own affairs. He goes on to question what feats the Empire might have achieved had the throne been ceded to Lu Dong Pu. Would Lu Dong Pu have allowed our border defences to crumble and lapse by diverting important resources towards a vast and mysterious construction project beneath the palace? Would he not have instructed the Imperial Apothecary to craft medicines for the poor and needy, instead of hounding them day and night to produce an impossible elixir for everlasting life?

Sima Qing claims that the enemies of our State employed an assassin to dispatch not the *Emperor*, but Lu Dong Pu himself! That the Emperor was never in any semblance of danger, and that consequently, He was wounded only by the knowledge that His brother was considered the more important target.

We, however, would hesitate to believe the crackpot theories of Sima Qing. So what if he matriculated from the prestigious Confucian Academy? One does not require a flimsy diploma to be inducted into the scholarly ranks. Just look at us! We, the Official Historians, are living proof.

In any event, citizens, please note that Lu Dong Pu has been stripped of all rank and standing in society. It is now a crime to invoke his name. If you absolutely must refer to him, please do so only in hushed tones and by the ignominious title of the *Imperial Traitor*.

By Imperial decree,
The Order of the Eunuchs

12

Royal Botanic Gardens – Art Gallery Road, Sydney

The next morning, we cross the grassy expanse of The Domain, leaving the chatter of the city behind us. A bride and groom pose for wedding pictures. On instruction from the photographer, the couple gather bunches of leaves and throw them towards the camera with arms outstretched. The photographer requests another take. The bridesmaids and groomsmen stand to the side, shooting the breeze. We give them a friendly smile as we pass.

Yuan says, 'Have you heard of the marriage markets in Shanghai? Retirees gather in People's Park to find spouses for their unmarried adult children. They post photos, vital statistics, career prospects.'

'Sounds nightmarish,' I say, thinking of my own career prospects.

'En, but it's even worse for girls. In China, if a girl is over twenty-five and still unmarried, she's considered "over the hill". They call us *shengnü*. "Leftover girls". Often, the children aren't even aware their parents are advertising them.'

'It's like a dating app,' I say, 'except the algorithm is our parents.'

Yuan shivers. 'Thank god there isn't a marriage market in my village. If there was, my mother would probably live there.'

'Mine too. When I was a teenager, my mum had only one golden rule when it came to dating.'

'What was it?'

'*Don't marry a white girl.*'

Yuan bursts into laughter.

'What's so funny?' I demand.

'You *are* white,' she says. 'If not in skin tone then in demeanour. You might as well have blond hair and blue eyes to go with that Australian accent.'

I am about to protest when my mind flashes to Doctor Mok's diagnosis and I lose my train of thought.

'When we depart for Port Man Tou, are you going to miss your friends and family in Sydney?' she asks.

'My friends and family live in Brisbane. I don't really know anyone here.'

'Have you told them about the job?'

'Sort of. But if I told them the whole story they'd probably prefer I come home, let them set me up with a nice Chinese girl. Settle down. Have kids. Like a line graph, everything neatly plotted out.'

'So, you moved to Sydney to draw your own graph?'

I shrug. 'I think there comes a point when you must abandon all that's familiar, your friends and family, and strike out on your own. Exile yourself.'

She eyes me with gleeful suspicion. 'Your exile wouldn't have anything to do with a girl?'

'What girl?'

'I have a sixth sense about these things.'

'I don't want to talk about it.'

She persists. 'Were you running *to* her or *away* from her? A or B?'

'I resent that binary classification. Isn't there an option C?'

'You tell me.'

'The weather in Sydney is better,' I offer. 'And the economy.'

She considers my response. 'So, it's ... A?'

I sigh. 'B.'

Yuan pauses her inquisition as a jogger passes by.

Finally, she says, 'You look like the type of guy whose relationship status is always "It's complicated". You have that look.'

'What look?'

'The look of someone who invites girl problems.'

'Is that so?' I ask, incredulously.

'En. Take today, for example. You're less scruffy than yesterday, when perhaps you weren't expecting to talk to a girl. You dressed up,' she teases, 'for me?'

'You're full of theories, aren't you?'

'*And* you shaved.'

I am taken by the urge to kiss her. But I lose my nerve, and the moment is gone.

13

THE IMPERIAL CONSORT, WUER

The Imperial Concubines wept upon hearing of the exile of Scholars Zhao, Yu, Shi and Deng, for they had been promised a trove of new stories to while away their summer. Now a chorus of melancholic sighs could be heard emanating from their quarters in the palace. It was bad enough to know they would never again receive new volumes of Scholar Shi's austere poetry, which struck the hearts of the Emperor's fair and lovely maidens. But to be deprived of the classics and past writings of Scholar Yu and his fictional alter ego the Warrior Bard? To be denied all those forbidden tales of adventure, earth-shattering sex and rollicking hijinks along the Silk Road? It was almost too much to bear!

In their desperation, the concubines arranged – through back channels and clandestine agreements with rogue academics – the delivery of Scholar Deng's *Death of a Pagoda*. His exile had come midway through his writings, resulting in an incomplete manuscript, which the concubines took turns passing around. Those who had had their turn kept watch for approaching guards or, God forbid, the Emperor Himself. But one by one, the readers' ecstasies turned to disappointment, for the manuscript was so smudged, so unfinished and so unsatisfying – rife with dull notes and private digressions and plots-in-progress – that they regretted ever having set eyes on it.

But it was for Scholar Zhao that the concubines grieved the most, for he was the finest of the four laureates (and, it was rumoured, the most handsome) with his dozen wuxia epics and sweeping romances. The latter captured so accurately the innermost thoughts and secret sensualities of his heroines that each concubine secretly fancied herself the protagoness of his haunting, ethereal tomes.

The newest concubine and recently appointed Imperial Consort – Wuer – had in fact been the subject of one of Scholar Zhao's earliest works. Zhao had long ago been a suitor of Wuer's, and was left heartbroken when she chose to marry Lu Dong Pu. The scholar forever blamed himself, convinced that, in failing to capture his subject's breathtaking beauty adequately on the page, he had somehow lost her affection.

In time, the concubines realised her true identity. They recognised her from Zhao's stories, and their jealousy towards Wuer fell away. It occurred to them that they loved her – the way that Zhao had loved her, as though his feelings had jumped from the pages of his books into their hearts.

The concubines took Wuer under their collective wing. They instructed her on how she must behave so as not to incur the Emperor's wrath; they walked hand in hand with her throughout the gardens and plied her with questions. For Scholar Zhao had written Wuer into each of his successive works – though never so directly as that first time – and it became something of a game for the girls to spot that stray but recognisable detail in a priestess or a wench, a lady of the Court, or even perhaps a man, a hero, that belonged only and indelibly to Wuer: her poise, her intellect, the upturned nose, the gentle voice, that impossible memory of hers (for Wuer remembered everything …).

Time and skill had enabled Zhao's work to reach new and sublime heights, but then so too had his living muse grown more radiant with every passing year, her beauty forever exceeding his words and grasp.

Befitting her new and elevated status, Wuer was assigned a number of servants. They were led by the eunuch known as the Grand Prolonger of Autumn, the title bestowed upon the chief of the Imperial Consort's retinue. She was beloved by them, and by him above all.

Wuer's charms were, however, lost on the alchemists of the Imperial Apothecary.

She was always requesting special medicines and poultices, for when her servants and their children fell ill with fevers they could not afford to treat, Wuer would descend upon the Apothecary. But the alchemists, who were already occupied with the Emperor's odd demands, soon became wise to Wuer's tricks. They denied her requests unless she could demonstrate that she *herself* suffered from such ailments.

When the Grand Prolonger of Autumn was made bedridden by some mysterious infirmity, so too did Wuer take on her servant's illness, feigning his symptoms, perfectly simulating the pox that had struck him down. Inspecting her pallid skin and dried lips, the alchemists had no choice but to deliver her the rare ox bezoar which Wuer then administered to save the Grand Prolonger's life.

Thereafter, she feigned illness frequently, and with great authenticity.

In spring, Wuer simulated her chamberlain's rheumatism. She confounded the alchemists by presenting hands that had grown wizened and gnarled overnight. When the soothing salves arrived, both she and the old chamberlain were instantly cured of the affliction.

She cured her guard of consumption by conjuring a blood-choked cough and mimicked the embarrassing infection that her youngest maidservant had caught in the Emperor's bed.

The grateful families of her subjects honoured the Imperial Consort. Expectant mothers secretly prayed not for sons but instead for daughters who might embody Wuer's grace and selflessness.

Wuer acquired a false reputation throughout the Imperial City as the most delicate of flowers, whose frailty seemed a cruel symptom of her extraordinary beauty. This romantic image of her echoed throughout the commons, in shop corners and watering holes.

The number of guards assigned to the concubines' quarters tripled, for the gardens had received an unprecedented number of attempted break-ins from thieves and rogues and adventuresome men who had become mad for Wuer, risking life and limb to glimpse her beauty just once, and perhaps hoping to win her by saving her from the clutches of the wicked Emperor.

It had never occurred to Wuer that she needed saving, much less from anyone other than herself.

In summer, sensing a telltale bump, the Emperor ordered a thorough examination of the Imperial Consort. Indeed, His suspicions were confirmed. Wuer was pregnant, and the child belonged to the Imperial Traitor, Lu Dong Pu. Wuer put a stop to her catalogue of simulated sicknesses, for fear that her child might be born sickly, inheriting not only the symptoms but also the disease.

A midwife was assigned to Wuer, replacing her youngest maidservant, who had recently become a favoured concubine of the Emperor.

In autumn, however, Wuer fell ill once more.

Her midwife, Fan Mei, received a letter from Min Qiang, her ancestral village in the Fuzhou province. But she could not read, and so requested that Wuer recite the letter for her. It seemed that Fan Mei's sister, the town gossip Yang Ying, had lost her voice. As she read, Wuer herself began to lose all faculties of her own voice. The last sound that came out of Wuer's mouth was her gentle laughter at the midwife's colourful ode to Fuzhou: a province so dirty and backwards that it was known as the armpit of all the provinces; and Min Qiang, a village so tiny and forgettable that it could only be the armpit of the armpit.

The alchemists devised a complex mixture of roots and herbs to cure her muteness. During this time, the other concubines watched over her. They chattered to fill her silence, kept her up to date on Court intrigue and rumours.

Unable now to distract herself with the ailments of others, Wuer began, with increasing regularity, to shed the weight of her burdens in deep and heavy tears. No longer was she able to hide the heartache of losing her husband, Lu Dong Pu, or the ache of knowing that he would never look upon the face of their child.

In the gardens, where Wuer would convalesce, the leaves fell interminably, seeming to hold in midair, forever spinning in languorous arcs designed to delay the inevitable … But all autumns must pass.

They came for her in winter.

14

Art Gallery of New South Wales – Art Gallery Road, Sydney

We reach the looming columns of the art gallery, with immortal names adorned upon its sandstone facade: Canova, Jean Goujon, Giotto, Raphael. After purchasing our tickets for the exhibition called *A Simulated Man*, we cross the whitewashed marble floors of the entrance court and go down the stairs to the lower level, where lines of people have already begun to form. There is a visitor limit for the exhibition. We wait. An octogenarian security guard ushers us in.

And here, in this hushed and reverent space, we gather before the master work of the unnamed artisan. A protective cordon surrounds the canvas. The flow of patrons in a collective daze, arms crossed, whispering to each other, appraising the artwork.

We read the plaque. The self-portrait depicts the course of the artist's entire life, from birth to death. A thousand and one paintings, layered atop one another, the inks designed to corrode with sufficient exposure to the elements so that each layer will disintegrate and reveal the next. A living art that breathes, ages and decays. A dying art, ever in flight, from the Musée d'Orsay to the Guggenheim, to here and beyond.

We try to commit it to memory, before it is lost forever and there is nothing but the empty frame. And even then, perhaps, we would still come, arms crossed and whispering, to see such a thing. To see the place where there once was art.

We pass the old security guard on our way out, exchanging friendly nods.

Once we're out of earshot, Yuan says, 'That old man reminds me somehow of the Terracotta Warriors in Xi'an. Have you been?'

'No, I haven't.'

'It's amazing. I'll take you there, one day.'

I scan her expression for romantic intent. She holds my gaze playfully.

She continues, 'There's an old man who sits outside the gallery – or sat – I don't know if he's still alive. The story goes that *he's* the farmer who unearthed the Terracotta Warriors decades ago. He's been sitting there since the seventies. That's his job now. People take photos of him in his dusty Mao suit. I found it really funny at the time, but the more I think about it these days, the old man just sitting there like he is part of the art, the more it makes me sad, somehow. We should go to see him before it's too late.'

'I've heard only a tiny fraction has been excavated so far.'

'En, the archaeologists know exactly where they are, deep inside the ground. But if they were to excavate them now, the paint would fade immediately. This is why the Terracotta Warriors appear the way they do, like unfinished clay, because they were discovered before we had the technology to preserve them. Perhaps they were better off in the ground, unspoiled, instead of in ruins.'

'So by that logic you'd rather that *A Simulated Man* had never been discovered?'

'I'm conflicted. The galleries have special low-UV lights to minimise damage, but even the most well-cared-for pieces are slowly being ruined by their exposure. I don't know. Maybe the only way to truly preserve art is to keep it locked up, in the dark, forever, where no one can ever see it.'

15

THE LABYRINTH

The Emperor ordered the Artisan to spare no expense in constructing a labyrinth beneath the palace. He had only two requirements: that no map of the labyrinth could ever exist, and that the Emperor alone be taught a foolproof method to access its very heart. He did not care for other details, and left the design to the Artisan's discretion.

The Artisan embarked on his most ambitious work. Already, he dreamed of passageways angled with mirrors, endless rows of luminous jade, a sonnet made from stone.

He would pattern the interminable maze in his very own image – his bones and memories – and pour every part of himself into the labyrinth. One intersecting series of paths he designed to match the worry lines upon his palms, another the spiralling whorls of his fingertips. Lines and layers. Stutter stops and dead ends. Here, the shape of that month-long fever, where his body ached but the colour of his dreams had seemed so vivid. There, the abstract recollection of a lover's scent. Every turn and passage was imbued with a meaning known only to himself, so that wandering the memory halls he would recall entire conversations – every bitter argument, every sweet nothing – with perfect clarity.

Each room led to other rooms, with scant regard to time or logic, so that the room whose contours formed the pattern of his mother's gentle laughter might give way and plunge, inexplicably, into hidden spaces and dark territories marked by petty jealousies and secret sorrows.

Overseeing these grand designs, he sent out a hundred men into the depths with tools and materials and detailed instructions. They did not know what they were building, and could not conceive the scope of their labours. The monstrous scale of such a thing. The unthinkable cost.

In the absence of maps the men were guided, instead, by lengths of rope that threaded through the labyrinth.

With the labyrinth nearing its completion, the Artisan left the men to toil the safer outskirts while he alone struck out into the dark in order to craft the final chamber: the ambage to the heart.

And deep within, past suffocating crawl spaces and deceitful traps, the Artisan alone concluded his labours in some gilded fever dream. In perfect darkness he worked, his hands guided only by some primal notion that, in retrospect, he recognised as terror.

On the eve of winter the Artisan glimpsed a secret procession. The foreman led a woman, heavy with child, and half a dozen behind her, each bound and hooded, into the chamber at the heart of the labyrinth.

The Artisan watched his men as they worked. Did they know that none would survive the labyrinth's construction, for the Emperor would not abide it? Their faces betrayed no such knowledge.

He tried to explain to them the subtle inspirations behind each room or pathway – the memories, the heartbreaks, the secrets they held – so that, when the time came, each man would have the knowledge to escape. But the men, not realising his confession was their salvation, only pretended to listen to his breathless ramblings, and knew him no more in the end than they had in the beginning.

It was too late, in any case. With the labyrinth nigh complete and every man accounted for within it, the Emperor ordered the burning of the ropes. The men tripped over each other in their haste to escape the fire and the smoke. Some died quickly. Others survived for agonising moments longer. They ran, they crawled, they scratched at the walls with their fingers. They cursed the Artisan with their dying breath. None could find the exit. None survived.

The Artisan, who had spirited himself to cowardly safety, could only watch and listen, haunted by their desperate cries.

He knew he had not done enough.

In all his works thereafter he hid some secret sorrow – his vivid brushstrokes coding and concealing his grief within the landscape – in the hope that this might absolve him of his pain.

It did no such thing.

Dear citizens of the Imperial City,

A terrible accident has occurred. A fire has broken out within the bowels of the labyrinth. One hundred labourers have been confirmed dead, including the Imperial Artisan. What a mishap! His works were much beloved.

The Emperor ordered the obliteration of all of the Artisan's known creations: the Moonlit Pagoda, the nightingale automaton. His paintings, his portraits. We searched high and low but could not find *A Simulated Man*.

We are bound to note the dissent of the Shadow Historian, Sima Qing, who claims that the Artisan survived the fire by crossing the airless gulf between the outer labyrinth into its inner portion, and its secret heart within.

We have attached a petition, for the perusal of the Imperial Court, to have the troublemaker Sima Qing exiled to the Six Levels of Hell. His frequent disruptions have taken their toll on us. Our hair is falling out in clumps. We don't sleep well at night. All of this has undermined the effectiveness of our administration of the Court. Please sign it. Help us help you.

By Imperial decree,
The Order of the Eunuchs

16

Darling Harbour – King Street Wharf, Sydney

On Wednesday we take the scenic route along the harbour, towards the Chinese Garden of Friendship, where Baby Bao is charming an investor for last-minute funding.

'You seem distracted,' I say.

Each day we part, and the next day it is as though we have become strangers all over again and must find some way to know each other once more, to dust off the rusty rhythms, fall back into step.

'Do I?' she asks. 'I guess I'm just worried about the investor meeting, how it's going. Whether I should be there.'

'Didn't you say the investor was Chinese?'

'En, but still. Maybe he's not so fluent, like you. What if something gets mixed up that I might have been able to clarify, and the deal falls through because I decided to go for a walk with you?'

Last night I dreamed of you, I want to say. In the dream we continued our conversation, walking side by side, as if we had never parted. But I don't dare reveal such a thing.

We walk along the harbour in silence for a while.

I watch a father and son board a private water taxi. The water taxi lurches, unexpectedly, and the boy instinctively wraps his arm around his father's leg while the father grabs the railing to keep from pitching forward.

This is the state we long for. Surely. A tender position that one cannot help but outgrow, in time.

I'm certain I did the same, once, in some different configuration, on a bus or train perhaps, reaching out to steady myself against my father's leg – a faulty ballast – in the time before I could understand that should he fall then so would I.

'How old was I?' I say aloud. 'Four? Five, maybe. I had my first wobbly tooth. My father asked me to open my mouth so he could look at it. I refused because I had seen him do this to my brother, time and again. He would just yank the tooth out. No dentist, no anaesthetic. No tooth fairy. I made him promise not to pull it out. He promised. I just want to look, he said. Then, as soon as I opened my mouth, he yanked it. I was shocked. It had never occurred to me that my father would lie. He pulled a few teeth over the years, in exactly the same way, and I kept falling for it. I vowed to repay his betrayal.'

'How did you get him back?'

'I haven't yet. Maybe one day I'll write him into a story. Like, I don't know. Like *he's* a kid, and he bites into what he thinks is an apple, but it's actually a stone or something. I haven't worked out all the details.'

'Literary revenge.'

'The best kind.'

'Speaking of betrayal, *my* father also betrayed me. Do you know the card game Hong Wu?'

'Red Five?' I translate from my meagre repertoire of Mandarin, eighty per cent sure.

'Oh! You know it?'

'Actually, no. I was just trying to prove that I know *some* Chinese.'

She looks disappointed.

'Anyway, yes. Red Five. Or Red Heart Five. Six people play, with five decks. The rules are very complicated and they sort of change with each game. I guess it's similar to Bridge. People team up and form alliances. Everyone watches the dealer closely to see if he has a good hand. If he does, then you want to join his team. If he doesn't, you want to hold on to your good cards so that other people will be forced to join him. Then you won't be on the loser's team. It's very strategic. Sometimes if you have a bad hand, you must pretend you have a good hand so you can join the dealer and improve your own chances of winning. One time, the dealer didn't have a good hand and my dad said to me, "Oh, we will totally kill the dealer, we will slaughter him", and he kept nudging me, saying, "Only we two need to team up and we can definitely win."'

I laugh. 'I think I know where this is going.'

'En, based on the information and the way he played his cards, my dad was the least possible person to be the dealer's ally. I thought my dad was *my* ally, so I gave all my points to him. I thought we were teaming up to win. Do you know what I mean?'

'Not really, but go on,' I say.

'Well, when I ran out of spades, my dad didn't throw any spades.'

'That's bad?'

'Usually it just means that your partner has run out of spades too. But by the end of the game, my dad revealed that he had all the aces of spades in his hand! He just tricked me into joining him and giving him all the points, and at the last moment he teamed up with the dealer and betrayed me! I was so mad at my dad. I said, "Baba, I am going to disown you!"'

'Wow. Your family takes cards seriously!'

She smiles.

We watch the water taxi depart.

I say to her, 'When I left home, my father said two things to me. The first, which was deeply embarrassing for both of us, was that I should "use protection".'

Yuan cringes. 'Do you mean sexual protection?'

'Indeed.'

She laughs, and then chokes, which I accept as instant karmic retribution.

I continue, 'I wanted to tell him that I am not quite the ladies' man he must have mistaken me for, but I said nothing and prayed that the moment would be over as soon as humanly possible.'

'And the second thing he told you?' she asks.

'He enveloped me in a long hug and whispered, "I wish you didn't have to go, but I know you have to." Something like that.'

'Was he right?'

'I'm sure, deep down, he didn't quite agree with my way, probably didn't think it was necessary for me to leave the city. Seems so dramatic now that I put it into words. There were other reasons, of course. Not just "a girl". But I needed a fresh start, and in that moment he said what I needed to hear.'

'Tell me about him. He must mean a lot to you.'

'Yes. I remember when I was nineteen, we were on the way to the airport to pick up my brother, who was coming home from Melbourne to visit. I drove, and Dad was in the passenger seat, which, to him, is the height of luxury, to be driven around by his sons. He becomes very philosophical in the passenger seat and was doing most of the talking, and I can't remember the context of why or how, but I blurted out – naively, I now realise – that it seemed to me that a father's love was inherent, you know? Some immutable, guaranteed thing. And whenever I'm back in Brisbane visiting my folks, I can't travel that particular stretch of road without thinking of those words, which must have caught him by surprise.'

'But that's very naive of you to say or think such a thing, when so many people are from unhappy or broken homes.'

'Yes, exactly. It was a selfish moment, maybe, where I had mistaken *my* experience for the whole. That everybody's fathers must be like him. He looked out the passenger window for a while, and then mumbled, "I guess so." And I felt instantly stupid, because I had forgotten my own family history. My grandfather – *his* father – had abandoned the family when my father was a kid.'

'But to think this way must mean you had a good childhood. Good parents. To have been so protected. And what about your grandparents? Are they still alive?'

'My mother's parents, yes. But on my father's side, both are gone. My grandmother when I was three or four, from dengue fever. My grandfather a few years later, from … I can't remember. Sometimes – not often – my dad talks about her. Things she used to do or say. A certain method to cure heartburn by moving your arm up and down.' I simulate the movement, like doing scissors paper rock.

'Does that really work?' she asks sceptically.

'My father swears by it and he's not normally a superstitious man. He's a man of science.'

'Your father is a scientist?' Yuan asks.

'A veterinarian, actually. He'd get heartburn at the dinner table but would wave away the water we brought him and keep doing the hand movement instead. We used to roll our eyes when he did it but he'd spout off words like "physiology" or "peristalsis" to make his case.'

I do the movement again. More freely this time, and with less embarrassment.

'A few years ago, I started dreaming of my grandmother all the time, though I never had as a child. Did she like living with us, that first year or two in Australia? Sometimes I wonder about her life back in China, and I find myself missing her so deeply it aches, even though I hardly knew her and can barely remember what she was like.'

That jolt. That deep and instant regret at having said too much, too clearly. Because I don't speak like this, have never spoken like this. And it is not only the words ('so deeply it aches') that I can't stand but also their pitch and timbre – the soap operatic – and I want, all of a sudden, to take those words back, as though in their desperate intonation I had recognised a key I wished I'd never spoken but had thrown away instead.

I should have stopped at peristalsis.

17

BROTHER'S PROTECTOR

Wuer, who did not often give herself over to superstition, nonetheless believed that deep in her womb a creature might be growing – some beast befitting a labyrinth – for at times she felt and witnessed its many pressing limbs against her belly, and knew it could be no ordinary child.

Her midwife offered a simpler explanation. Twins.

During their long gestation, Wuer formulated plans to keep them from the Emperor's grasp. It would not be difficult for her to raise them in the labyrinth. Though the heart was most hospitable, she knew well the darkest corners of the outer labyrinth where the Emperor dared not venture. With care and vigilance, her children would survive the labyrinth. As they grew she would teach them to navigate its pitch-black wings and orient themselves by the faintest flow of westerly breezes that whispered through its halls. She would remain alert at all times, ready to hide them at the first sound of His leaden footsteps.

She fretted over their future and happiness, wondered if this would ever be enough. Each day she conjured new scenarios, new ways to keep them safe.

Nothing could surmount the pain. No act or thought or reason.

She had not been prepared. There had been no way to know that only one would survive her womb.

She held them both, for as long as she could. One, whose cries echoed about the labyrinth. The other, whose silence tore irreparable holes in her heart.

Just a moment longer. Until the Grand Prolonger of Autumn approached, eyes lowered. The Emperor might come at any time. Indeed, they could hear footsteps in the labyrinth.

But she knew, even in her state, that these were not the footsteps of the Emperor. Their pace was softer, slower. She had heard these footsteps before. They belonged to a man in hallowed space. The labyrinth's creator.

It must be done now.

The Artisan, in some kind of bitter tranquil, ventured into the heart of the labyrinth. He knew his life was forfeit, and wished only to make something of his final hours, to make his peace with the world, to walk the passageways of his designs one last time. Selfishly, he thought he might like to see the Imperial Consort, that rarest of beauties, with his own eyes.

He found, instead, her loyal servant the Grand Prolonger of Autumn, and a crying infant in the old man's arms.

The Grand Prolonger of Autumn explained that this was the Consort's child, whose life the Emperor sought to snuff out. He held the infant forth, and pleaded for the Artisan's help.

But the Artisan had not come to save any child. He took a step back.

The Grand Prolonger fell silent. He appeared to be receiving instruction from another, behind him. The Artisan thought he glimpsed the form of a woman, he thought it might be the Imperial Consort herself, and he wanted, suddenly, to paint her, to better chart her enigma. But it could have been a shadow. It could have been nothing. The Grand Prolonger spoke once more.

'This corridor, so dimly lit, is as far as we, the servants of the Imperial Consort, dare to go. But our lady master does not fear this labyrinth, and often ventures from the heart. She knew you would come, someday. She read it on these very walls. Once, returning from her travels, she described to us a room, deep within some ruined wing, with such strange latitudes. Do you know it? It was the room in which you once strove for greatness. In time, it became the room where you attained it. Only to become the room in which you came to know that it would never be enough to solve you.'

'I built no such room,' said the Artisan.

'And yet it exists …' Her words coming from his mouth.

And that moment of surprise when the confession tumbled from the Artisan's mouth: how he wished that he, too, had perished in the flames. He regretted such words almost immediately, for now that he had placed his aches, he could no longer misplace them.

The Grand Prolonger pressed the child into his arms. This time the Artisan did not resist.

The Emperor came some days later.

Of course it was no pleasant thing to take a life – much less a newborn's – but who in their right mind could argue with the potential threat to *His* throne, *His* life, the lives of *His* people. Priorities. Silly to think that anyone might disagree. Though He empathised. He certainly empathised.

Was that the word?

The Emperor had come to take the child and was pleased, in fact, to see its lifeless form. His work already done. A decree would be issued, the body displayed as proof. Especially pleased was He that the Imperial Consort seemed to offer no resistance.

He left the labyrinth in good spirits none the wiser.

Wuer wept at her own callousness, for how easily the plan had come to her. As though her clarity of mind were some evidence of lesser love or, even worse, self-preservation.

Thereafter, Wuer ventured out into the lightless corridors, ignoring the entreaties of her servants and wet nurses, who feared that she would be lost forever, not understanding that this was, in fact, her very wish. For days at a time she would disappear into empty spaces, the darkness in which she knew herself more completely. There she would contemplate her sons, the ache of their parting never dulling in her infinite, perfect memory.

Even in the unrelenting dark, it was easy for Wuer, whose hands trailed endlessly against these mysterious walls, to create a mental map of the labyrinth over time. Each path, each blemish unique and unforgettable, for they seemed to her like tokens of memory and heartbreak.

In time, she knew the labyrinth. Where ordinary men might despair at its inscrutability, its repeating rooms and echoes, she persisted, pursuing pathways that seemed truncated or, at their outset, impassable. It was nothing to her. The more she ventured out into the margins, the more she felt she understood the labyrinth's creator. She did not seek an exit and, consequently, found all of them. A false panel that led to the concubines' private quarters, a hidden door into one of the pantries of the Imperial Kitchen, an alcove near the Emperor's private wing, a concealed trapdoor behind an empty shelf of the Imperial Library.

But every winding labyrinth is filled with secrets, the most trivial of which are surely its solutions and egressions, and in her wanderings she came unto a hidden room, filled with the creator's tools: stone cutters, hammers, mallets, saws, picks and chisels.

Ink. Parchment.

18

Chinese Garden of Friendship – Darling Harbour, Sydney

A hidden oasis in the heart of the city, filled with water lilies and weeping willows. Tiny stone bridges inscribe arcs over inlets, the circles completed by the water's reflection. Golden carp dance beneath the surface. A painterly scene. Even the people in the distance seem composed of inscrutable lines.

The atmosphere in the Teahouse Pavilion is hushed. Production types, leggy models, worried moneymen in suits hunched over steaming bowls of oolong and chrysanthemum. Eyes flit expectantly across the lotus pond, scanning the walkways, the pagoda atop the hill, all the visible nooks and alcoves for Baby Bao and his billionaire investor.

Yuan introduces me to Farmstrong Tian, Baby Bao's producer. He looks like a normal-sized Yao Ming. She translates as he speaks.

'*Ah, Xiang Lu, the bad Chinese! Are you ready to see Port Man Tou with your own eyes? I am jealous of you! The first time is the best. Unforgettable!*'

'What's up with the mood in here?' I ask. 'Everyone looks worried.'

'*Nonsense! Production always costs a lot of money, yes, more investment money is always good, yes, the deal will go through one hundred per cent, yes, but even if not, we have many more investors, new and old. Port Man Tou is a glorious city, far from bankrupt. Once you get there, you never want to leave. The worried faces you see are of people who cannot bear to be away from Port Man Tou. A lesser city like Sydney has no meaning for them anymore. They are anxious to return home.'*

A murmur goes around. Someone has spotted Baby Bao emerging from the direction of the Rinsing Jade Pavilion. He and the entourage of investors walk side by side along the far path, engaged in conversation. Everyone on our end averts their eyes, feigns nonchalance, while casting sidelong glances, attempting to glean whether the news is good or bad. We look for clues in their posture, their gait. The body's prose.

Across the pond, Baby Bao slips a mobile phone from his pocket.

Farmstrong's phone rings. He answers enthusiastically. They speak back and forth for a while.

'好. 好. 好.'

Farmstrong hangs up the phone and beckons me over.

'The investor wants a photo of you.'

'Why?'

'I don't know. Baby Bao says the funnier the better. Do you have any funny faces? Ah, yes, that one is good. Use that face.'

'That's my normal face.'

Farmstrong directs me to one of the tables bearing yum cha dishes, laid out with napkins and utensils. He sits me down, then switches his phone to camera mode.

'Eat the food. But with that face. And use the fork.'

'I *know* how to use chopsticks.'

'Fork is better for the #BadChinese!'

Fork in hand, I swallow the shao mai, along with my pride.

Farmstrong giggles and snaps a few photos. He sends it off. A moment later, we hear loud gales of laughter from across the pond.

Soon, I am told, #BabyBao and #BadChinese are trending once more.

Baby Bao confers with Farmstrong at the Teahouse Pavilion while the rest of us wait expectantly. After a few breathless seconds,

Farmstrong gives the thumbs-up to rapturous applause. Out comes the alcohol, champagne and hard liquor. A DJ materialises, and what was once a tranquil and traditional tea house has been transformed into a boisterous party zone.

Farmstrong leads the festivities, pouring shots for everyone.

I watch Baby Bao slink off, strangely muted. Yuan and I follow.

We find him outside, contemplating the Rock Forest. He notices our presence, and deigns to let us approach.

'来,' he says.

'*Come,*' Yuan interprets.

A moment passes in silence. I wait for him to speak, but he seems to be preoccupied with other thoughts.

'Congratulations,' I say.

He waves me off dismissively, like securing tens of millions in funding from an individual private investor is nothing special.

'*Maybe, maybe not.*'

'Is something wrong?'

'*It's the same old story. Once again, the artist has to compromise his vision. It is a lot of money and, of course, it comes with certain … strings attached.*'

'What strings?'

Baby Bao sighs theatrically. '*I'm required to cast that idiot financier's girlfriend as my lead actress.*'

'Oh. Can she act?'

'*Who the hell knows? Probably not. But it doesn't matter. We are shooting many movies at once. I'll move her into one of the more low-key productions, shoot a few glamour scenes, try to sleep with her, and then phase her out of the production. It's the other requirement that unsettles me. He insists that I appoint Farmstrong as my backup director. It is a key stipulation in the contract.*'

'That doesn't sound so bad,' I say.

Baby Bao leans forward, grabs me by the shoulders.

'*Don't you see? They want to replace me! Farmstrong is in bed with them. I thought he was my friend, but now I see he's only ever been jealous of my talents. That artless fool. A director? Ha!*'

87

'Maybe you're reading too much into all of this?'

'*Help me get rid of him.*'

'What do you mean "get rid of him"?'

'*You know what I mean. You're an outsider. The only one I can trust.*'

It's impossible to tell if he's joking. He seems incredibly paranoid, different from his previous self. But maybe the paranoia is mine; maybe Doctor Mok's diagnosis has some truth to it.

'What about Yuan? She's trustworthy,' I say, desperate to lighten the mood. She doesn't seem pleased at my having included her in the discussion, but nonetheless doesn't miss a beat with her translation.

He doesn't even glance at her.

'*No, you mustn't trust beautiful women. But I see the way you look at each other. You have a real connection, I can tell.*' Yuan takes on a distinct shade of red as she continues translating. '*As long as you don't tell her anything important, I have no problem with you pursuing a relationship with her. Do what you will with her. You have my blessing.*'

'Um … thanks.'

'*Go. I want to be alone.*'

With that, he dismisses us with a flick of his hand.

'Did Baby Bao just ask me to help him *kill* a guy?'

Yuan and I are walking back to the Teahouse Pavilion. I ask her this as much to break the icy silence as to confirm my understanding.

She casts me a furious glare and picks up her pace.

'What?'

'All you could say was *thanks*?!'

'I didn't know what else to say,' I offer.

'Then you shouldn't have said anything.'

I lose her in a sea of people and words I don't understand.

Baby Bao makes his belated entrance, sauntering into the Teahouse Pavilion wearing sunglasses, hair tied into a samurai's ponytail. He pushes his way through the mob and puts his arm around me in a friendly embrace as though I hadn't just seen him minutes ago. Together, we make our way to one of the lounges. We drink. It is the hard stuff now, some stratospherically high-proof Chinese liquor that makes us choke back tears and then beckon for seconds.

The rest of the entourage joins us. Farmstrong toasts Baby Bao, who smirks and wags a knowing finger back at him.

All night long, Baby Bao says things into my ear, then leans back and laughs outrageously. I don't know what he's saying, but I can guess at his intent. *Look at him. Farmstrong. He doesn't know a thing.*

We drink.

A lot.

People in my periphery move like missing frames in a film. Everything lurches forward in strobe-light succession.

At some point I demand to inspect the bottle – fuck, man, you know, the *shit*, lemme look at the label – because there's got to be something else in there, some, I don't know, Chinese hallucinogenic. Because I'm feeling *fucked-up*, dude, but in a good way.

Yuan is nowhere in sight, so I'm left to overcome the language gulf through gestures and bits of broken Mandarin. But it's working, almost. Baby Bao knows what I'm babbling about. Farmstrong dances with the models to the pumping music. Baby Bao nudges me and mutters derisively.

Farmstrong doesn't know we know. Only *we* know the truth, the truth about his traitorous ways.

Baby Bao speaks Chinese whispers in my ear. Only he and I know. In our darkened moods, we *know*. We know everything. We understand each other *completely*. You see? We manly men have broken through the membranous walls and acquired fluency in the universal language of alcohol. To hell with glasses, we pass the goddamn bottle back and forth – *brewed and packaged exclusively in Port Man Tou*, Baby Bao tells me – and we spend the next few minutes with arms around each other's shoulders, squinting at the bottle, scrutinising it, its secrets ever more clear to us with every subsequent swig. We take turns telling each other extremely funny jokes. We feel our brains enlarging by the second, approaching a perfect understanding of everything. Somehow, in the babbling stream, we have rediscovered our vestigial tongues.

Now, nothing is beyond us.

19

THE GRAND PROLONGER OF AUTUMN

Dear citizens of the Imperial City,

Behind our beloved Emperor there are certain men – powerful men – who, at crucial moments, might bend the Emperor's immortal ear or proffer sage advice, and in so doing make their own indelible mark on history.

We are not these men.

But if a keen observer were to stand at *just* the right angle of the Imperial Court, he might see, behind those men, certain *other* men.

Those men are not us either. But we were once mistaken for them.

Doubtless, this preamble has indicated to you the proper extent of the scope of our power, the *considerable* sway we, the Order of the Eunuchs, have over important matters of the State.

So it is in this context that we proudly announce a bold and exciting change! The Emperor has seen fit to reward our ambition by promoting us to wardens and administrators of the Imperial Prison, known as the Six Levels of Hell.

We have established an outpost on the First Level of Hell, where we will be better placed to oversee the administration of the underworld. In fact, to better aid such a process, we have been ordered to close our offices here in the Imperial City effective immediately.

Please note that during this period of transition you will no longer receive any further missives from our Order. Rest assured, we will continue to serve our purpose as the true mouthpiece of the Emperor, if only for the denizens of the Six Levels of Hell.

Citizens, do not despair! Remember the koan: if a tree falls in the forest and no one is there to hear it, it does not cease to serve our beloved Emperor.

We are hereby bound by law to note the dissent of Sima Qing, the Shadow Historian, who claims that our mass relocation is, in fact, an order for incarceration, and that we are to be stripped of all entitlements. Ludicrous. Do not make us laugh, Sima Qing! Your veracity as a eunuch has been called into question. Though we did not see it ourselves, we have no reason to disbelieve Brother Gu's report that once, while you were seated in the breezy gardens, a gust of wind caught your robe as you casually adjusted your position, and there apparently – intact, and dangling between your legs – was a penis and two perfectly uncastrated testes. Of course, Eunuch Gu has been blind for quite some time, as we all have been, for the removal of our eyes was necessary, we were told, for our rule over the Six Levels of Hell. Now we write forever in the dark.

All praise our benevolent Emperor!

By unofficial decree,
The Order of the Eunuchs

The Imperial Consort returned from her latest sojourn to find her subjects grief-stricken and inconsolable. The Grand Prolonger of Autumn was dying.

In the time she had been away, the Emperor had ventured into the labyrinth to seek her company, only to find her missing from the heart. The Grand Prolonger refused to explain her absence. Enraged, the Emperor beat the Grand Prolonger senseless.

On her return, Wuer took the Grand Prolonger into her arms, and was nurse to her beloved subject, developing sympathetic bruises and welts upon her own body as she presided, for weeks and months, over his slow recovery.

During this time, the Imperial Consort began ferrying her vassals to safety, leading them by hand – midwife, chamberlain, wet nurses – through the interminable maze, each to a different exit, so that none could ever find their way back to the heart. They could escape the Imperial Capital and, over the course of their lives, do what she could never do.

Forget.

So it was that the Imperial Consort's retinue disappeared into the ether. All but the Grand Prolonger of Autumn, who long ago had pledged to serve her till his death. When he recovered the strength to walk, Wuer led him to the room filled with the Artisan's tools. She taught him to memorise the labyrinth's many openings and, more importantly, the Emperor's preferred route so that the men might never cross paths.

She taught him how to navigate the labyrinth, to the extent that was possible for him. To never rely solely on one single route or method. To never backtrack, for the labyrinth played tricks, presenting avenues that only seemed identical, and seduced you into committing to false and ruinous paths. She taught the Grand Prolonger the secret method to reach the exit from any point within the labyrinth should he become lost. And she instructed him that he must never attempt to make a map, lest it fall into the wrong hands.

Then she led him out of the labyrinth.

After his escape, the Grand Prolonger of Autumn slept in the homes of fellow eunuchs and scholars, and was never far from the labyrinth. He became her secret emissary within the Imperial City.

Save for the Imperial Consort, the Grand Prolonger knew more about the labyrinth than any other, and yet, in his comings and goings, in narrow and nameless corridors, he would feel that godless fear rushing upon him, sure he had made a wrong turn somewhere. Then he would strain to remember the method of escape she had taught him, but such a task required his full and undivided concentration, and he was not always able to return to safety.

Stumbling in these cold and pitch-dark spaces, hopelessly lost, he would call out for Wuer to save him, sensing that she was just beyond him, in adjacent rooms or pathways.

Once, she met him at the limits of the labyrinth, and placed a book in his hands.

In the era after the Emperor's grand burning, such objects were rare and more precious than jade.

The Grand Prolonger of Autumn dared not inspect it until he reached the home of his host and benefactor, Scholar Ping. The Grand Prolonger studied the book. There was a clumsy beauty to it, as though it had been put together only recently, with imperfect materials, by one unskilled in the art of binding.

He read the words within, which began: *Every now and then a landmark is revealed to be a fallacy after all* ... The Grand Prolonger of Autumn was befuddled, for the 'I' of these writings was a man, yet the graceful brushstrokes that gave them voice were written, unmistakably, by the hand of the Imperial Consort, Wuer.

In the home of the eminent Scholar Ping, the Grand Prolonger and his host pored over the words, the taps and strokes of ink.

They recognised these words as the opening lines to the exile Scholar Deng's unfinished masterpiece, *Death of a Pagoda*. After having read it once, so long ago, Wuer had transcribed the work from perfect memory, capturing its heights and all its perfidious imperfections.

From then on, whenever the Grand Prolonger of Autumn returned to the labyrinth, under the cover of night, and traversed the pathways to that hidden room, he would find new books awaiting him in greater abundance, bound and sealed with ever-improving skill. Classic texts, once thought lost forever to the flame. The forgotten tales of the Warrior Bard. An expert's guide to chess.

When the Imperial Consort was low on ink and parchment, he would replenish the raw materials she required to feed her obsession. Though paper was banned within the Empire, his brother eunuchs had a source in the Six Levels of Hell, and were more than willing to supply it to him.

She wrote from the heart of the labyrinth, single-handedly reconstructing the glory of the Imperial Library by transcribing the language of her soul. By what strange methods did she imbue her own element into these works, which would have appeared word-for-word and line-for-line identical had their originals been spared the fire? How was it that the prime works, which the Grand Prolonger remembered to be filled at times with ordinary and unimpressive turns of phrase, had been elevated by their repetition into objects of unimaginable beauty, passages that – in perfect replication – now moved him so deeply?

Clandestine meetings were held at Scholar Ping's home. His colleagues studied each of the tomes, and declared these volumes of poetry, fiction and philosophy to be perfect simulations. Only once in the entire canon did the scholars suspect an error on Wuer's part. In Scholar Shi's seminal work – *River Merchant's Wife* – each learned man could have sworn that the penultimate line had once read 'This, *the cage for my grief*'. However, in the Imperial Consort's version, the line read 'This, *the vessel for my grief*'. That change seemed, to them, to have produced an object of vastly different proportions. But in the end they could not know, their memories were faulty, and it had been too long since they had read the original.

In time, Wuer restored every single book that had once been destroyed. But she did not stop. Instead, she continued in the same method, simulating new and unfathomable works: her brush forever dancing across the page, her lips moving silently as she intoned the words – perfect and incorruptible – from the works of authors who had never been, and were yet to be.

Soon, there were too many books to fit in Scholar Ping's den. Sympathetic colleagues offered their own homes to house the ever-growing library. But despite the scholars' best intentions, each book somehow escaped from its hiding place and entered the slipstream of the Imperial City.

Somehow, the concubines came to possess a number of volumes and a chorus of sprightly, buoyant sighs once more emanated from their chambers.

The guards, the ministers, the farmers – each committing tiny acts of rebellion – began to read in secret.

But no one dared hold on to the books for long, for they still feared the Emperor's reprisal. Instead they sent the books to friends and relatives in far-off provinces, flung them over the borders of the Imperial City, sold them to travelling merchants, smuggled them onto ships at port.

The books were swept along invisible currents like autumn leaves caught in a southerly wind, always south, as though each and every book had a mind, a heart of its own, knew its home, and longed to return there at last.

There was a time she felt as though she might have been sustained by words and words alone – their urgency and meaning, the way they arranged themselves upon a page – and she gave herself completely to this new obsession. If her words emerged lifeless, she could yet resuscitate them, revivify them, rewrite them into something whole.

Every other act thereafter was in service to the word: she ate only to have the strength to write. She had no use for sleep except to dream, and in her reveries she conjured stories that mingled and migrated from one book to another, forming new and illicit narratives.

On occasion, she would hear the Grand Prolonger of Autumn stumbling in the outer labyrinth, and she would go to him. Even then she was elsewhere in her mind. As she walked the passages, her every step and footfall recalled a rhythm, a beat, a recitation she might someday commit to ink and paper.

The Grand Prolonger would bring news of the Empire, supplies, materials she might require. And though she was buoyed by his friendship and loyalty, some part of her was most anxious to bid farewell, to return to her secluded spaces, to write once more and capture the words flowing from her thoughts and fingertips in a ceaseless stream.

It was the only way to expel the longings of her heart.

How could she have known that each of these words, these books in flight, would find her son and one day bring him back to the Imperial City?

20

Sydney International Airport – Airport Drive, Mascot

I stumble through the check-in ritual. It is a blur of ticket counters, bags and trolleys. The immigration officer inspecting my passport looks at me like I'm an inconvenience.

Shouldn't have drunk so much last night.

I consider buying a coffee, then decide to wait till I'm at the lounge so I can get it for free.

The guardian of the lounge scans my boarding pass. She flashes a bright smile and says, 'Welcome!'

I intend to say 'Good morning' but all I can manage is 'Good'. I am not yet properly calibrated to the day, and wasn't expecting to have to make small talk this early. An unreasonable amount of time elapses between my first word – 'Good' – and the second, which remains unuttered, and we stand here in the foyer, puzzled at each other, wondering why I have said 'Good' to her greeting, as though I were marking her on her presentation, her delivery, her diction, perhaps. I should have bought that coffee.

'Uh ... please, sit wherever you like.'

'Thanks.'

We are both relieved to be away from one another.

Where is the coffee?

I float around the mini-buffet, eyeing each hotplate – bacon, scrambled eggs, roast something – allowing my testy stomach to figure out what it can handle after such a night. Only fruit, it seems. And, of course, coffee.

Here's Yuan, fresh-faced and lovely.

She ignores me and sits at another table. She orders a coffee.

I go over to her table.

'Good morning,' I say to her, the words in perfectly reasonable proximity to each other. 'Is this seat taken?'

Yuan sets down her bag and heads for the buffet.

I nurse my coffee and wait.

She returns, plate full, and begins eating. The calm before the scorn.

I focus on my fruit.

This dragon fruit is amazing. I cannot stop at one mouthful. I must have more.

Yuan reaches over and wordlessly takes a piece of dragon fruit from my plate.

And in this moment of casual familiarity, I sense a thawing, of sorts. You grow accustomed to this sort of behaviour, these hidden olive branches, if you have grown up with a sibling. When I was young, my brother and I would fall into deep and bitter arguments – I forget the specifics of these fights now, who started them, who was at fault, so let's lay the blame at fifty-fifty – which would always be followed by minutes, hours or, in the worst cases, days of silence. As I was the younger one, all my attempts at repair were futile, met with hostility. I was always extreme, always wanted things to be over immediately or else never. And it was up to him, the forgiver or forgivee – never me, I never had such rights – to arrive at our armistice through side doors and strange paths, as though he could skip over the need for apologies by asking if there was anything good on TV tonight, or if I might be interested in a game of Scrabble or chess, or like now, with Yuan, announcing the end of our separation by picking a piece of fruit off my plate.

I test the water.

'How was your night?' I begin.

But she shoots me a cold look and maybe a piece of fruit is sometimes just a piece of fruit, and not a peace offering, after all.

The boarding call sounds and we make our way onto the plane.

21

THE SIX LEVELS OF HELL

Of those first days he remembered nothing,
only pain without respite; Imperial
Torturers, those men of wicked substance,
with strange instruments and blades for skinning
had meted out their cruellest art, for here,
upon his spine, from shoulder to pelvis,
did they unstitch the bindings of his skin,
leaving behind a pulpy mess from which
he bled profusely, and only then our
Emperor deigned to cast His brother out
into the darkness, shackled, left to rot
in this, the Sixth and deepest tract of Hell.

Alone but for one other, the guard that
they had sent to watch him, feed him, keep him
breathing, in order to prolong his pain.
There was no rest, for rest caused him to sink
his back against the jagged wall, to cleave
his skin, to open up old wounds, and so
in agony he spent his waking hours
outstretched, but no, his chains were cruel and far

too short and, succumbing to exhaustion,
he relented and fell into deep sleep,
unable to protect his open wounds.

In his darkest imaginings he saw
himself consumed, osmosed into the wall
like in some grotesque assimilation,
as though he had become it (or it him).
Would his veins extend into the surface,
seep into the deep substratum, and in
their unnatural manner trace some network
of his being into this rock and fuse him,
skin and bone, into this monstrous structure?

He knew the pattern of his pain. Each day
awakened by his own tormented screams.
His weeping flesh congealed against the wall.
Through gritted teeth he tore his half-healed skin
away, his wounds made raw, time and again.
Sleep followed sleep, pain followed bitter pain.
Inspired by his mortal terror he found
some way to contort his broken body,
so that even in rest his limbs would form
strange angles, impossible positions,
these lesser pains he forced himself to bear,
to give his festering wounds relief, to clot,
to harden, and, in slowest time, to heal.

Awakened from his stupor by a noise
that shook him from his darkest apathy.
A knock of something not quite wood, of bone
or ivory, perhaps. He knew that sound.
That weighted thump so pleasant to his ear.

In it, he heard some whisper of escape,
however faint. The guard owned a chessboard ...

How many days or months or years were lost
forever, time he might have spent in thought
to methods of escape but instead had
squandered in lapses of delirium?
His beloved wife forgotten amidst
his base survival, selfish miseries.
How he tortured himself for his weakness.

Now, with clarity of mind returning,
he took to observing the guard, whose lamp
lit his every movement in the distance.
His post was at the cavern's furthest end,
where a large steel door barred the passage up.
The briny walls shimmered in the lamplight
above the trough where the guard pumped water.
He could not help but lick his own parched lips.

On rare days, the guard would open the door
for eunuchs who brought down food and sundry,
and the Prisoner knew he would receive
a precious few drops of water, and a
piece of mouldy bread whose taste he savoured.
But on most days, the guard stayed near his post,
in contemplation of a game of chess
upon a board that measured eight by eight,
some ancient variant born from foreign lands,
whose rules were nonetheless familiar.

He recalled, in the time before his fall,
the Court's fascination for this game, called
Chaturanga in Agra and Lahor,

Chatur on the Golden Chersonese, and
Shatranj by the Persians in Ecbatan.

The board was fine, some worthy spoil of war.
How had it come, then, from the Emperor's
collections into this lowly guard's hands?
The guard played his games through correspondence,
passing coordinates to the eunuchs
to ferry to his opponent above.

Patiently did the Prisoner observe
the passage of their play, waiting for some
impasse of the board to present itself,
where one move might spell victory or loss,
and now sensing the guard's indecision,
the Prisoner murmured a suggestion.
An emboldened and unorthodox play.
The guard pretended to have heard nothing,
but, hours later, could see no better way.
He took the suggestion, played the move, found
the balance returning to his favour.
Before, defeat had seemed all but assured,
but this gambit had spelled his victory.

It was not long before the guard began
to seek the Prisoner's analysis
of each and every move, to plan and plot,
anticipate their unseen foe's designs
and orchestrate a tactical defence.

He urged the guard to proceed with patience.
Adopt a languid stance to lull their foe
and in some brutal lateral shift then seize
the board's command and, without mercy, force
their opponent's shah into a checkmate.

The guard grew to dislike the pace of play,
the long days between each correspondence,
awaiting lax and fickle messengers
who often passed on wrong coordinates
and caused each of their boards to misalign.
Those arduous weeks lost to unfinished games.

So as not to raise any suspicion
he kept silent, bided his time, allowed
his frustrated captor to come to that
spontaneous thought as if it was his own ...

In his impatience the guard suggested
that they might forgo the correspondence
entirely, and play, instead, each other.

Where once each occupied a corner of
the room — he seated at his post, he chained —
they sought to play each other, man to man
(or close to that ideal as was allowed
by circumstance). Still, he was required to
dictate his movements, for his hands remained
in chains. On this, the guard refused to bend.

Of late it seemed their talents were equal
(indeed his captor won many a game),
but in truth he cultivated struggle
where there was none, to make them closer than
they were, and in careful modulation
of his skill he crafted narrow losses

and orchestrated clumsy victories
that seemed somehow illicit to his foe.

How had that piece gone missing? In panic
they searched for it in vain upon the floor.
A shah, no less! That all-important piece!
But it was truly nowhere to be found.

They conceived a stopgap in its absence,
agreeing to play the piece in abstract
by recalling its imaginary
placement – the lacuna, reconstructed –
and, in time, they did not lament its loss.

Rumour made its way around each Level
of the Prisoner on the Sixth who had
invented some potent variation
in which there was but one shah to defeat.

The matriarch on the Fifth Level of
Hell, leader of the fallen concubines,
came to hear of this intriguing version.
She studied the game, discerned its secrets.
Was it not plain for all to see that in
the seemingly innocent omission
of the shah there was a hidden meaning?
Such veiled critique against the Emperor!
One side a shah; the other, a faceless
wall of bitter subjects aligned in hate
against Him. To play the game was treason!
So play it she did, with greatest fervour.
And soon the fallen concubines began
to play the game to while away their hours,

106

until obsession took hold, surpassing
now all of their other fickle follies.
To keep themselves engaged they resolved to
play each other only for the pleasure.
If a piece so bored them they would change it,
mould it into something else entire,
allowing new expressions of the game.

On the Fourth Level, the old ministers
— former advisers to the Emperor —
studied the intricacies of this game.
They could not separate the board from the
Imperial Court, where once they held such sway.
Blackmail and coercion had been their tools.
Each word and whisper hid some evil ploy.
Inspired by their former expertise,
they devised a rule that every piece could
be corrupted, turned against its master.
But without a shah there was no checkmate.
How, then, to quantify a win or loss?
They sought to broker a stalemate, which was,
to them, equivalent to victory.

The players on the Third Level of Hell
refused to accept this inglorious rule.
They were the proud and fallen cavalry,
men who knew true victory and defeat.
To better suit the nature of their souls,
they abandoned this rule for another.
If even a single piece remained in
opposition, there could be no defeat
until it, too, were slain. This was their code.

On the Second Level resided the
battle engineers, who once built chariots

and weapons and siege engines for combat.
In time they would build an automaton,
capable of speech and reason. And chess.

Up each Level like a game of whispers
until the First, where lowly eunuchs dwelled.
They maintained the systems of the prison,
kept each Level stocked with food, and ferried
rumour of the game. It was they who were
the true propagators of this pastime,
who viewed each Level's ever-shifting rules,
and revelled in their new-found influence.
They, too, had their own interpretation:
a style of game that favoured pawns, sought to
promote them above their modest station.
They lived in service of the Emperor
but beneath their obsequious facades
hid fantasies of murderous intent.

In due course, the Prisoner on the Sixth
became weakened in both breath and reason,
ravaged as his body was with illness.
His mutterings fell, barely audible,
and his friend, the guard, strained to make out his
incoherent instructions for the board.
But all he could manage were muddled plays,
a sneak attack too easily read, or
some defensive pattern left incomplete
– crucial errors in his calculation –
until, on the cusp of defeat, did he
whisper some illegal coordinate,
an impossible move that caused his friend
to approach now, ear inclined towards him.

And by the length permitted by his chains
— the feigned illness disguising his true strength —
did he seize the guard in a rough embrace
— his last stratagem so slow, so measured,
those secret nights in which he did not sleep,
but toiled in silence on the missing piece,
for it had taken time to grind the shah
into a makeshift blade of ivory —
and in a brutal lateral shift he sliced
a jagged wound across his captor's throat.

He took keys from the guard's lifeless body,
and in addition stripped it of its clothes.
Ill-fitting though they were, and sure to fail
any close inspection, he thought, at least,
that they might provide a way to better
navigate the Levels of Hell to come.

∿

He thought he would find joy in freedom (or
freedom of a kind, from chains and shackles),
but as he climbed the steps up to the Fifth
he knew he yearned no longer for his life.
Instead he longed for vengeance absolute
and thought himself a weapon, of a kind,
sent forth to break his brother's precious throne.

He trailed his hands along the walls where lay
depleted veins of salt. He recognised
this place now. In generations past this
was no prison but, instead, a salt mine
whose riches birthed a mighty dynasty.
But in their excavations at the depths
the miners fell sick to noxious spirits,

and many died until they sank bamboo
shafts that routed the pernicious vapours
to the surface where they were set aflame.
Thus was born the furnace everlasting
with roaring fires that pierced into the sky.
Visible even from the Imperial
City, it struck the hearts of men with fear
and they dubbed it the Six Levels of Hell.
Years hence, exhausted of its resources,
the place was fashioned into a prison
and there its moniker remained unchanged.

He thought his senses deceived him, for on
the Fifth he encountered children playing
in the dirt. How could this be! What madness
had caused the Emperor to cast out youths?
He noticed there were no boys, only girls.
Despite their tattered rags, some among them
wore the brightly coloured flower brooches
that were worn by the Imperial Harem.

He knew then that they had been born within
the prison, mothered by the concubines,
but fathered by whom? He had an inkling,
for when they saw him, and his uniform,
their sallow eyes refused to meet his own,
and quickly they scattered into the dark.

He followed piercing cries in the distance
and came to a filthy hovel filled with
screaming infants, jaundiced and malnourished.
Their gaunt mothers attempted to nurse them
but had not the milk to ease their hunger.

At first they paid the Prisoner no mind,
but then began to notice as he lurched
forward, clutched at his head in agony,
and finally collapsed onto the ground,
unable to stave off his exhaustion.

Approaching now, they saw he was no guard,
for his beard was unkempt, his body hunched
and scarred, his nails so outgrown and gruesome.

Unable to agree as to his fate,
they sent a girl to summon their leader.
So came the matriarch – who once had been
known as the most favoured concubine of
the Emperor's late father – to decide.

After the late Emperor's death and the
coronation of his son Lu Huang Du,
the matriarch was showered with trinkets
and promises, for the new Emperor
was sick with lust for her and desired to
possess her as His father had before.
But she refused Him, choosing death instead.
Indeed death came, and swift, but not for her.
In the Imperial Court it was said that
whosoever scorned a man three times his
better would be repaid in triplicate.
The Emperor, in His infinite worth,
therefore, repaid His scorn infinitely.

Though she had hidden her two children well
(for they were the Emperor's half-brothers
and would not have survived His jealous reign),

111

His spies had plucked them from their hiding place
and brought them there, before her, to the Court.
Now she *became the one to shower* Him
with vows and promises and desperate
capitulations. Anything He wished.
But the Emperor had lost all reason.
He gave orders for the execution
of her sons before her eyes, and cast her
to the depths to live out her days in grief.

The matriarch bade her Prisoner speak.
Who was he? The guards upon this Level
misliked venturing into this hovel
– indeed, they knew not of his presence yet –
but she had only to raise her voice and
they would enter, and run their swords through him.
What purpose had he to breach their sanctum?
The Prisoner spoke the truth, explaining
that he had escaped from the Sixth Level
and sought to continue to the surface.

His voice seemed strangely familiar to her.
She studied his features – somehow regal,
even in his wretched state – finally
she recognised the father in the son.
Moreover, her captive's resemblance to
his brother, the Emperor, drove her mad
with thoughts of vengeance. She ordered him scrubbed
clean and fed what little they had to spare.
Then she spoke her plan to conceive an heir
with which she might usurp their jailor's throne.
But she could see that he misliked her scheme
and, pre-empting his resistance, ordered

her concubines restrain him, the way the
guards had once restrained them for their pleasure.

The matriarch disrobed and straddled him
on an encrusted sheet upon the ground.
She must have thought herself a beauty still,
and could not reconcile his impotence,
confused to find him unwilling, for she
had not known rejection by any man.
She ordered her concubines unhand him
and dismissed them so that she might complete
the act with him in privacy, though the
screaming babes and their mothers still remained ...

She thought him nervous and sought to calm him
as his father had calmed her once before
when she had been but a child. She spoke of
his own father: a man with doubts and fears
far removed from the one he thought he knew.

He repaid her tale with one of his own,
recounting his father's subjugation
and conquest of the scattered northern tribes.

Until dawn, he remained unmolested.
She left him in the hovel to repose
and returned to him the following night.

When on the next night she asked him what lay
below them, on the Sixth Level of Hell,
he described his prison not as it was,
but as a place of dead spirits, instead.
A lie: he did not know from where it came,
but he committed himself to the tale.
He gave account of imposing structures,

vague at first, in adumbrate, that provoked
her fascination, and sensing some thread
to pull he continued in this fashion.
If, perchance, his descriptions displeased her
he would alter them to reflect her whims.
Cleverly he incorporated her
responses, at times her own suggestions.
Until, finally, he knew the rhythms,
the secret landscapes they had made, of her
childhood memories, her grand obsessions.
And in nights thereafter with greater skill
and eloquence did he reconstruct the
ancestral village of her memory.
He caused her, by design, to recollect
loved ones she had lost and was yet to lose.
He described an impossible village
in which dead men and women lived and breathed.
This anachronistic place that held all
times, all places, all people, all at once.
In one tale, with no apparent error,
he described her father as a child; at
the same time, her mother as a woman.
The village grew, and in some grief-filled prism
she saw her lifeless children grown before
her eyes, the lives they would have had. Their loves.

(Were you there as well, my neverborn child,
your face almost familiar from afar?
Always, I have ached that you were nameless
in this life and once, as though in a dream,
I recognised you: brother's protector.
There are times I catch the pain receding
– and how I mourn its loss – but only now
I understand the truth: that the pain has

never left me but has sought, instead, some
darker corner of me in which to hide.)

Each night she returned to the hovel, so
that she might consummate her carnal schemes,
but night after night he spun such stories
into dawn. She knew that these were fictions
– to delay her bold advances – but bade
him to continue. Entertained, at first,
to see his mind at work, then curious
to see how long he could withstand her charms.

In time she did not bother to disrobe.
Having distracted her with fantasies
of her loved ones, he turned his strategy
now to muting her desire for vengeance
that she might relent and grant him passage
to the Fourth. Was it truly within her
to create a child born out of hatred?
He thought not. Would this son be lesser than
her others? What wretched life would he live,
so singularly of poisoned purpose?
And if perchance she failed in her designs
was she prepared for harm to befall this
child – to lose once more the blood of her blood?

He did not tell her of his own desire
for vengeance against that very same foe,
and yet she saw the barely disguised rage
in his eyes when their conversations turned
to the Emperor. She understood now
his persistence, his skilful manoeuvrings,
the ways in which he sought to sway her from

her plan, and instead free him and assist
his passage to the Fourth. Halt not his own
ascension, for this much was clear to her:
the Prisoner from the Sixth sought greatest
harm against his brother. Let him have it
and allow his vengeance to be her own.

She arranged his safe passage to the Fourth
by ordering her most nubile consorts
to clear a pathway of seduction through
the Level and, amidst all the drunken
bacchanalia, allow the Prisoner
time to slip through the door, with key lifted
from the pockets of the slumbering guards.

On the Fourth Level he came upon crowds
of men gathered among the dirt and rocks.
They were seated on the ground but maintained
the haughty visage of noble statesmen.
Casting his eyes about he recognised
familiar faces: fallen diplomats,
advisers, ministers of old, who stirred
his memories, long lost or forgotten.
He understood what game they played at now.
What a pale mimicry this was, of the
structure of the Imperial Court above!

In the belly of this infernal court
a grand assembly was called to order.

The Minister of Rites stepped forth and, with
much conceited airs, addressed his brothers:–
'Celebrate the depths of our grand cunning
with which we corrupted our own captors,
by promising power we had no right
to give! Willingly did the guards accept
the poison that we poured into their ears,
and ceded their sovereignty unto us.'

On hearing this, the guards shared looks of mirth
but permitted the farce to continue.

'Now we rule this unhappy inferno,
a poor reflection of the Court above.
Time and again do we pose the question:
Shall we accept this as our final place?
The highest peak to which we might ascend?
Shall we be happy with our current lot
within this foul dominion we have won,
to rule it with what small pleasures remain?
Or might we attempt to recapture our
former glory in the world above, and
in so doing risk annihilation?'

With practised eloquence did the highest
of them – the Grand Minister – take the floor,
answering these questions with another:–
'Does a sapling accept the sunlight and
one day say, "Enough! I have had my fill"?
No! That is against the way of nature.

'The eunuchs on the First Level of Hell
protect the gateway to the world above.
There, the cowardly hide beyond our grasp

and it will take the might of Hell combined
to breach their walls and find our sweet release!'

Then spoke the Minister of Public Works:—
'We lack the strength to overrun our foes
and must enlist my battle engineers
to build us battlements and siege engines.
But who will man such instruments of war?
Surely not our kind! Though we are somewhat
willing, our courage unquestionable,
we must protect our precious intellect
and cede this task to men of lesser wit.
Let us beseech our brothers on the Third,
the cavalry, to aid us in this task.'
All present bellowed in strong agreement.

The Minister of Rites then rose again:—
'We turn to you, O Minister of War,
for your expertise and valued counsel.
Such matters concerning the cavalry
rightly fall within your jurisdiction.
Yet they disrespect you with their silence!
Do you not concur, O Minister, that
their disobedience must reflect your own?
Is it not for you and you alone to
end their folly and rectify their course,
at mortal peril to your life? To climb
the stairwell to the Third, where chieftains reign,
and seize control of their divided ranks?'

So stood a beaten youth to plead his case:—
'O Ministers, your madness knows no bounds!
What business have I, a lowly pageboy,
with your cruel and petty games? You call me
Minister of War? A fine joke indeed!

How many scapegoats have held this office?
How many have you forced up to the Third
to broker the cavalry's surrender?
And not a single one returned. Tell me,
what happened to these men? Were they not killed
for angering the cavalry above?
I tell you now, I will not be the next.'

At this, the Grand Minister erupted:–
'How dare you question our authority!'

'What authority have you?' said the youth.
'Look closely at yourselves! Do you not see
how the ceremonial robes you wear are
but crudely tailored from your prison garb?
And what of the grand pews and benches of
the Court above? Instead you sit upon
the bare dirt! How desperately you cling to
ritual to pretend you still have meaning!'

His words shattered their mass delusion and
briefly they saw themselves as he described.
Enraged, they gave the apostate his wish.
The congregation tore him limb from limb
and once this furious bloodlust was resolved
did the Minister of Rites call order:–
'Who shall succeed our recently deceased?
In our endless wisdom do we deign to
recommence the infernal lottery,
among each of you fine candidates shall
we elect the new Minister of War.'

The Level descended into chaos
at such words. Those who ran or fought were killed.
The men remaining crossed the court to form

new coalitions and allegiances.
Not one among them sought the vacant seat
of power. With lowered eyes did each hope
to disappear within the shifting crowd.

The Prisoner from the Sixth observed them.
It was clear these ministers still mimicked
and craved their past lives in the Court above.
He could hear it in their voices, see it
in the way they jostled for position,
ridiculing those of lesser standing
and kowtowing to those of higher rank.

And summoning some aspect deep within,
his voice boomed and echoed throughout the court,
as though he were himself the sovereign.
They turned their attentions to this stranger
who seemed to grow in stature as he spoke.

'Ministers, once I knew you to be wise,
but it appears it is no longer so!
This lottery is a fine distraction
indeed, something to occupy your thoughts
while the true question remains unanswered.
Amidst your petty squabbles did you think
to ask yourselves what fate has found us here
in exile? Were we not true and loyal?
Why then did our Emperor cast us out?
Long have I pondered on this mystery
and now at last the answer do I hold.
He had no reason but that He feared us.'

A murmur made its way around the Court.

'Ask yourselves, why did He separate us
Level from Level? Man apart from man?
Was it not because He understood that
together we have the strength to best Him,
unseat him from His throne and make it ours?'

Their flame of hate was now ignited full.

He could not tease apart the motives of
the guards, who seemed to laugh and jeer along.
Yet, having begun, he now continued.

'Ministers, discard this senseless ballot!
For in it, you may only foster fear
and weakness. Choose not those unwilling fools
who hide among the shadows and the crowds.
These men cannot hope to win an army.
I shall journey unto the Third and bring
the wrath of Hell against our Emperor.
Far did we fall, but further shall we rise!'

They removed the ceremonial garment
– reduced to tatters and stained with crimson –
from the body of his predecessor
and draped him in this uniform to mark
his appointment as Minister of War.

The Minister of Rites took the floor and
brought an end to their cowardly congress.

～

He was escorted by the guards unto
the clamour of the Third, where he beheld
the salt mine in its full operation.

121

Its cavernous spaces dwarfed the Levels
below, for the miners had carried out
their most ambitious excavations here.

Generations ago, it had been the
predecessors of the cavalry who
built the vast fortunes of the new Empire,
for it was they who discovered the place
where the first shafts of the mines would be dug.
Traversing through that newly conquered land,
they found their horses licking at the stones ...

Along the way he passed the boy-miners
who had been born upon the Fifth, cast out
by virtue of their unwanted gender,
and put to meagre use upon the Third.

Further down, working the striated walls
were rows of listless men, each with one hand
in chains, the other free to mine the salt.
The guards led him to a corpse still shackled,
dragged it away, and locked him in its stead.
It was by now their standard procedure:
as the miners expired they were replaced
by able-bodied men from down below.

What agony, to have made it so far
only to be returned once more to chains!

So the lottery had been but a joke,
for he looked around and saw that each man

here wore garb identical to his own.
Were they all the Minister of War, then?
The remnants of the cavalry, he thought.
Years ago they would have swung their swords at
enemies in battle. Now, instead, they
swung picks at veins of salt upon the wall.

The miners murmured prayers as they laboured.
With every strike they feared they would release
the evil spirits hiding in the walls
and be expunged amidst the wicked flame.
For this reason, the guards dared not venture
near, except to drag away the bodies
of those who had expired from overwork.

Unsupervised, the Prisoner daily
chipped away at his shackle with the pick,
but the tool was dull, the shackle too strong.
The other miners ignored his attempts,
offering no comment or counsel, for
each man had gone through his own such cycles,
of hope and dreams of freedom, then despair.

In frustration, he cursed the worthless pick.
This was the wrong tool for such work. But no,
perhaps he had chosen the wrong object ...
for though the chains were nigh unbreakable,
his wrist — that shackled hand of his — was not.

He steadied himself, took time to observe
the comings and goings of the Level,
and, settling on his gambit then, he swung
the pick's blunt end with force to maim his hand.
But that first blow lacked sufficient courage,
and feeling his bones splinter, and hearing

his own screams escape, he nonetheless knew
he had not done enough to slip the bonds.

The others observed in silence as he
crushed his hand beyond all recognition,
and through streams of tears and ragged gasps he
tore his mangled hand free from the shackle.

He did not then take flight but lingered in
that place, and his neighbours, though greatly roused,
shared looks of confusion, and finally
addressed him; but in white-faced agony
he gave them no answer but rather steeled
himself, fought off his pain and exhaustion,
and awaited the arrival of the
two eunuchs bearing food. Against any
able-bodied foes he would stand no chance
— so weakened and hobbled was he — and yet
against these blind eunuchs he did great harm,
rendering the first one unconscious with
savage blows, while the other desperately
wrestled the pick from his weakening grip.
And seeing that he lacked sufficient strength
to emerge victorious against his foe,
the miners hurled their picks and blocks of salt
to render what lean assistance they could,
that the Prisoner from the Sixth might gain
a slim advantage, and in the final
frantic struggle he choked the eunuch dead.

He dressed himself in the dull robes of the
one less bloodied, and shared a silent look
with those complicit in his violent act,
before venturing into the cavern
in disguise, no one but they the wiser.

He trailed behind some eunuchs who ferried
blocks of salt towards the upper Levels.
As he passed through the door to the Second,
the guards posted there barely acknowledged
this eunuch with the limp and mangled hand.

~

He ascended to the Second Level.
Here, the battle engineers toiled on raw
materials brought from the surface to make
grand weapons for the Imperial Army.

Through their work in times of war they became
favoured inmates of the prison, and were
left to their own devices by the guards.

But in times of peace their attentions turned
to crafting curios and automatons
— birds, music boxes, simulated men —
for the amusement of the Emperor.
The Prisoner from the Sixth approached them
and overheard their worried mutterings.
Of late, the Emperor had become bored
with these toys and demanded something new.

The Prisoner from the Sixth observed each
of their designs. These men had such talent,
yet they lacked the spark of inspiration
that might catch the Emperor's attention.

He offered them the answer: construct an
automaton that had the skill to play
the game called Matriarch's chess:– 'Imagine
a machine brought to the Imperial Court

that could defeat player after player,
indeed perhaps even the Emperor,
for I know Him to be a connoisseur
of the game. Build this and I promise He
will not be able to resist its charms.'

They saw that he made sense, and in the end
consented to build the automaton.

He described his vision. In time they made
it to his precise specifications:
Two thrones faced one another across a
chessboard. The challenger's throne was empty.
On the other throne sat a clockwork man
whose features exuded fierce intellect.
Inside his chest a hollowed space was carved
to house the pieces and to demonstrate
that no man of flesh and blood hid within.

But they struggled to imbue such complex
rules into the machinery, and soon
they became frustrated with their progress.

In truth, their failure was by his design,
for they had relied on his expertise
to create and implement the logic,
and subtle errors did he introduce,
so that when it came time to test their skills
on the machine, they were disappointed.
Even they could easily defeat it.

Slyly, for he knew how they would respond,
he wondered aloud whether it might be
better to abandon this ambitious
task, settle for some simpler offering.

But they had already become seduced
by the image of this automaton
and refused to entertain the thought of
lesser gifts to offer the Emperor.

Now did he reveal his true intentions,
the subtle pathways along which he had
guided them. He courted their impatience
and knew that he could make them see his way:—

'Years may it take to perfect its knowledge
of the game. Yet you shall be rewarded
if you faithfully follow my design
to build a second iteration now,
for a failsafe within will ensure the
machine is ready not in years, but weeks.'

They gutted the machine but left its shell
intact, following now his instructions
without question, strange though they may have been …

The battle engineers came together
to marvel upon its assembled form.
The automaton was of larger make
and more ornate than they had built before.
Its mysterious innards fashioned from brass
and clockwork gears forever in motion.

But when they came to test this new machine
they found it immeasurably worse than
their past creation. It was inert and
remained so, refusing to come to life,

for the complex circuitry led nowhere
and was a misdirection, of a kind.

He uttered these words to the engineers:—
'Discard not this machine of finest make,
for it is not broken, nor have you erred
in its creation. Observe its secrets!
The concealed space I have unlocked within,
with board below to match the one above.
And here the cranks and dials to operate
the every move of the automaton.
And there the place where rations might be stored
to prolong the chances of survival.
And lo, the narrow crawl space down below
where a man of wasted frame might deign to
brave its suffocating quarters, and be
the final piece of the automaton.'

By what method did he contort himself
into such impossible positions
to fit into the hidden space inside?
Only now — concealed within the slab — was
the automaton finally complete.
Entombed within, he controlled its movements
with such precision. Challengers came forth
but none could best him. This was the level
of skill that they had failed to replicate:
an unbeatable machine that would not
go unnoticed in the Imperial Court.

Like pallbearers in a grand procession,
they carried this automaton — and he
in it — up the stairs leading to the First.
There they left their false offering for the

obsequious eunuchs to discover:
a gift worthy of their cruel Emperor.

The eunuchs of the First Level of Hell,
with ink and awful parchment, continued
in the digressive ways to which they were
most accustomed. Dear citizens, they wrote,
when we were taken to the inferno,
we could not curse or cry, for dumb and blind
had we been made. We loathed the Emperor
at first, but later understood Him wise!
In the Imperial City we were meek,
but here, we might wield power absolute!
Then did we come to accept our new lot
as wardens of the Six Levels of Hell.

But much has changed for us in these years hence,
and one by one and Level by Level
the inmates overthrew our governance
and we fell into familiar patterns
of submission and obeisance until
we were reduced to worthless errand boys.

The ink from this missive is made from blood;
the parchment, human skin. Do not judge us!
There was no other choice. For we must write
to tell you of the latest happenings.

Lately have we come into possession
of a gift from the engineers below.

An object of such great beauty that it
has once more restored meaning to our lives.

Sightless as we have become, it took some
time before we understood its nature.
With our hands we explored its surfaces.
We studied its clockwork mechanisms,
inspected its inscrutable innards
until a clearer picture of it formed:
an automaton made for playing chess!

Each took our turn to challenge the machine.
Yet none was able to claim victory,
for our opponent played with furious guile.

Further did we test its understanding
of the game. We moved a piece in error
in order to observe its reaction:
reaching out a hand, it undid our move!
We must admit, some fled the site in fear.

Our fright replaced by curiosity
we attempted conversation with it
to gauge the level of its intellect.
But speech is beyond its capacity.

Now we petition the Imperial Court
to accept this offering as something
worthy of the Emperor's attention.

Gladly do we offer this opinion
without dissent, for long ago did the
eunuch Sima Qing depart from our ranks.
We do not know where he went. Good riddance.
Were he still among our number he might

have uttered some thought-provoking rubbish,
designed, as always, to undermine us.

All this we swear by infernal decree,

The corrupted Order of the Eunuchs.

22

Airspace above the Philippine Sea, en route to Port Man Tou, China

On the plane, I awaken to find Yuan asleep, her head on my shoulder. How long have we been like this? I want to adjust my back but can't bear the thought that I might wake her up and bring an end to this intimate, if unintended, position of ours.

The rhythm of her sleep is intoxicating.

I observe the flight path on the screen in front of me. The information cycling through, first in Chinese, then English, of altitude, speed, estimated arrival time. Only two hours to go.

My head is spinning, and the hangover isn't helping. I try to take a swig from my bottle of water without disturbing Yuan.

'Oh. Sorry,' she says, lifting her head from my shoulder with an embarrassed look.

'Don't be,' I say. 'In fact, *I* should be the one apologising to you.'

'For what?' she asks, cautiously.

'I fucked up at the party. I should've defended you.'

I hand her a new bottle of water, which she takes gratefully.

The look she gives me tells me we're okay.

'This all feels so surreal,' I say. 'Three days ago I was in Sydney, wallowing in jobless solitude. Then I meet you, and it feels like I've known you my entire life. And now, I'm flying across an ocean, bound for China's most infamous ghost city.'

'You know,' she says, looking out the window, 'I have always had this silly thought that maybe, somehow, every city is the same. So when you go from one place to another, it's simply an illusion of flight. The take-off and landing is a simulation. In reality, you've never left the ground, or maybe you have, but are simply flying around in circles for hours, waiting for the new city to "load".'

'Is this why all airports look the same?' I ask.

She nods significantly. 'See? It takes longer for international flights because the city needs to undergo a more drastic change. But domestic flights are quicker. Why? Because the streets and buildings are already similar. They need less time to change.'

Hours later we see it, shimmering in the distance. Port Man Tou. The ghost city.

I don't know what I was expecting. It looks real. Like a real city. You wouldn't know it was a forgery from the topography alone. It has the same patterns and shapes as any other urban sprawl, the same concrete DNA. Only there are no cars, no traffic. The roads look perfect, barely used. The city, pristine in its ruination.

As the plane makes its gradual descent, a dull pain creeps into the back of my eye. I do my best to ignore it.

The pain gets worse.

I'm fine.

Suddenly, it feels like my eyeball is about to burst. I clutch my head.

'What's wrong?' Yuan says, her mouth forming concerned shapes.

'My head,' I say, redundantly. The pain is worsening by the second, making me stupid.

'A migraine?'

I shake my head. Worse than a migraine.

She rings for assistance but no one comes. The flight crew must be strapped in for landing.

'Don't worry, it's not that bad,' I say, but the pressure is tremendous.

It feels as if my head is being squashed. I let out an unintentional moan, which draws stares from other passengers, and then, as nonchalantly as possible, I scream.

An involuntary laugh escapes me.

'Has this happened before?'

'Yes, sometimes, in planes. But never this bad.'

Yuan prises my hands away from my head and replaces them with her own. She leans close and, in my delirium, I think she is about to kiss me.

I wonder if I'm going to die.

She touches my temple. 'You have too much pressure inside your head.'

'Pressure?'

'En. Useless things. Worries and secrets. There's only one way to release it.'

'What is it?'

'You must tell me something true. A secret, or a story you've not told anyone before.'

She is full of pensive theories like this.

'That doesn't sound … medically … uh …'

The pain has crossed from the left hemisphere to the right. The whole sphere.

'Please,' she says. 'It's the only way.'

And in the penultimate moment before I black out entirely, she leans in closer to accommodate the murmur of my lips. I am distantly aware of the scent of her, the shape of her ear. Why did I speak, and for how long, and what was it that I said? Surely it was a betrayal of sorts, some ghastly catalogue of all my fears, but the pain is loosening, ever so slightly, as I lose myself in a tangle of whispers, and the painlessness of dreams.

PART II:

A SIMULATED MAN

Whereon for different cause the Tempter set
Our second Adam in the Wilderness,
To shew him all Earths Kingdomes and thir Glory.
His Eye might there command wherever stood
City of old or modern Fame, the Seat
Of mightiest Empire, from the destind Walls
Of Cambalu, seat of Cathaian Can
And Samarchand by Oxus, Temirs Throne,
To Paquin of Sinaean Kings ...

—John Milton, *Paradise Lost*

23

THE ARMPIT OF THE ARMPIT

Long ago, before the village called Min Qiang was known as the armpit of the armpit, there lived nearby a mountain of great renown.

Monks came from afar to see it, to bask in its glory and learn from its wisdom. In the course of their worship they built a temple so their chants would better carry off into the surrounding valleys. They chanted and chanted until the earth below them sank deeper and deeper, steadily accumulating water from the ground until the temple (filled with such treasures and rarities) was submerged beneath a newly formed lake.

The few surviving monks retreated to higher ground, and built an empty replica of the temple. But they were further now, from the mountain, and their chants did not carry well over the water. At this disappointing distance, the mountain seemed to lose its stature and no longer inspired them to chant its praises. Eventually the sect lost purpose and scattered to the wind.

It was here, by the lakeside, that the first villagers built their homes alongside the ruins of the temple. They established farms, which thrived on the fertile steppe.

In the shade of ruins they told tales of what the temple might have been, and taught their superstitions to their children. By the time the story was repeated by the village gossip Yang Ying (who, of all the villagers, bore the most resemblance to my mother), no one knew that there had ever existed another temple at the bottom of the lake. The details had been lost in the telling and retelling until, transfixed by her version of events, they knew only the empty replica in their midst, and thought it true.

In winter months, when crops refused to grow, the farmers thought they might try their luck as fishermen. And so, with rods and nets, they walked across the frozen surface of the lake, divining where they might best break the ice and sink their nets to yield a greater catch.

They seemed to understand the newness of the world, that no one knew much more than any other. Every man had a hundred or more criticisms of his neighbour's amateurish technique, but when it came to the topic of their own pitiful yields, they stammered and shouted obscenities. Arguments broke out. The men fought, and this turned them away from one another. The frozen lake hummed with discontented murmurs, the men muttering under their breath, quietly cursing the others, berating themselves, or else pretending to win arguments their wives had long ago already won.

Ah Gong – the village elder and the least skilled of the fishermen – watched his neighbours with suspicion. He wiped his nose and conjured wild theories to explain his failure.

Still, the fish continued to elude their nets.

Back in the village, it was the wives – who held no grudges and spoke constantly to one another – who determined that each man's technique of fishing was much the same. They chided their husbands for their foolishness and forced them to reunite.

But Ah Gong's wife – Ai Leng – was dead or dying (he was not quite sure which). And so, with no one to chide him for his foolishness, he remained alone, separated from the others. Oh how he blamed her for that.

In coming winters, the men began to bring their nets together in small and sheepish conglomerates. The following years brought them better yields, and they drank and enjoyed each other's company and took turns telling crude jokes. And so the days seemed shorter; the cold did not sting so bitterly.

Ah Gong watched the others. He wondered what they could be talking about out there. He squinted across the lake belligerently, paying close attention to the movements of every man's lips, and at this distance, amidst the hallucinating cold, he saw lines and characters written in the steam of their wintry breaths, and even tried to read them. They were talking about him, surely.

In time, like all determined men, they came to master their craft, and grew to trust their deepest superstitions. Now, Ah Gong watched as they trekked across the lake in practised silence, communicating in simple hand gestures so that their voices would not carry and alert the fish below. He saw them kneel by the edges of the ice in prayerful positions. No longer did they drink, but instead sprinkled their liquor towards heaven and earth.

At day's end they dragged their nets from the water to find them fat with fish, solemn in their writhing masses.

I don't know why I lied to you that day, at the Rocks, but I did visit my ancestral village a couple of years ago, during a solo detour after a trip to the States with friends. I took a bus there. It wound its way along the perilous mountain roads. Each turn was sharp and frightening. I felt as though we would fall right into the valley. Then I got to Min Qiang and found there was nothing there for me. I walked around the village, ate stale food at the canteen. I was twenty. I didn't know how to speak to anyone or announce myself to distant relatives. I asked around in broken Mandarin, but everyone responded to me in the ancestral dialect, of which I am even less fluent. In the end I couldn't confirm my childhood vision of the gigantic hi-fi in my grandmother's cousin's home. Everything was different from what I remembered. Nothing was familiar.

The thought of making the return trip in that bus was too much for me, so I caught a taxi back, despite the exorbitant cost. I had an irrational fear that the driver would rob and abandon me in rural China. Despite this, I fell asleep in the taxi and awoke to incessant honking. We were stuck in a narrow street behind a crowd of people, dressed in white robes of mourning, bearing a coffin on their shoulders. There was no way to pass. I asked the driver to stop honking, but he didn't understand, and caught in that moment (for I was still half in dream) I thought I saw my grandmother standing among the crowd.

I thought I saw her smile.

In the dying days of winter, there came to the village a man and his infant son. This man introduced himself as a farmer from the Hunan province, but it was obvious even to the dullest villager that this was a fabrication, for his accent marked him as a city man from the north, and this is what they called him – Northerner – whenever word of him cropped up in gossip and conversation.

He bought a plot of land on the outskirts and set about tilling the soil in preparation for spring.

It was soon clear to everyone that he knew next to nothing about farming. Yang Ying, the village gossip, had even heard a rumour that the Northerner had once mistaken a plough for a hoe. And then there was the way in which he had reacted to word of the coming drought in spring. He did not join the other men in their chorus of moaning despair, his eyes did not cast fearfully towards the sky, his lips did not murmur for the mercy of precipitation – instead he shrugged and remarked that he did not much care for rain.

The villagers watched him closely thereafter. Nothing escaped their scrutiny. There was something in the language of his body, an unintentional elegance to his every movement that seemed to confound the villagers on some deep but inarticulate level. They were particularly suspicious of those hands of his, rough and callused and stained the colour of the earth, as a farmer's *ought* to be – but not quite, not really. They were more the hands of a craftsman, a carpenter. An Artisan.

They watched as he built his abode at the apex of the land.

Swiftly, single-handedly – his son, too young to assist, but forever by his side – the Northerner was thoroughly absorbed in the world of hammers and nails and timber frames. Yes. He was secretly a carpenter. They were sure of it. Soon, his home was complete, a stately work on the slender hillock that overlooked his land.

Then came the farm.

The Artisan was surprised to find he did not miss the city or his old life there. Nonetheless there were times, strolling the fields, observing the sun's poetry across the landscape, that he longed for the comfort of a brush and his inks, or else some malleable piece of clay that he might mould into art. But the soil and the fields were his only canvas now.

The drought ended. Crops grew in the villagers' farms, though they were unremarkable and frail. And yet rumour had it that upon the Northerner's farm grew the most magnificent of crops. It was inconceivable that the stupid Northerner, who kept no hired hands, could manage the effortless creation that blossomed in his fields. In their disbelief, the villagers thought to sneak by the Northerner's property to see it for themselves, but they could scarcely find the time, for the season was precarious and their own farms required the utmost care and attention. They sent their children, instead, to spy.

The village children saw the Northerner's plot filled with thickened rows of dragon fruit, nashis, lychees, cantaloupes as big as a man's head.

They had never seen a finer farm.

In time, the villagers learned the truth of the Northerner the night that Ah Nong broke his front teeth.

Ah Gong, the village elder, had never been good with names, and so had called his son Ah Nong (which translates, literally, to *Little One*, because Ah Nong was the youngest and smallest of the six siblings). There were the two elder boys (whose names I forget), then the three girls in between – Zhao Di (*Summoning a Brother*),

143

Lai Di (*Bring a Brother*) and Qiu Di (*Begging for a Brother*). Several years later, when the six became seven, it was already too late. Though his little sister Ah Xing was younger and smaller still, Ah Nong was and would be Ah Nong forever more.

Ah Gong instructed his seven children to watch over the Northerner's farm. Ah Gong's daughters, who by virtue of their gender were deemed unfit to be educated, were assigned the longer morning shifts. Their brothers would join them after school each day, rushing from one end of the village to the other, to take up their dutiful posts and stare, transfixed, at the endless rows of magnificent fruit.

Everything the Northerner owned grew with lush abandon, yet he was never once seen to toil the land himself. Such a strange impression this made on Ah Gong's children – and Ah Nong especially – who watched him every day and had grown to regard him as some dreamlike icon of the land.

Ah Nong returned to this fence even in the hours he was not required to keep watch, hoping to catch a glimpse of the stranger in the distance nestling his infant son, ferrying the boy above the ground, urging him into laughter in ways his own distracted father never had. It seemed to him some better way of being. Ah Nong never forgot their joined silhouettes against the setting sun, though in years and decades to come, in scattered moments of grief, he would grow to misremember this stray image, recalling instead, and with most generous affection, his own departed father.

It was the girls who were the chief architects of the plan to trespass onto the property. Over the course of weeks, while their brothers were in school, they had loosened the soil beneath the furthest portion of the Northerner's fence by minute movements of their feet.

When the moon filled the night sky, the seven of them snuck out of bed and gathered outside in a solemn huddle, counting down the seconds. Together, they launched into a run, slowly at first – Ah Nong at the head of the pack – gathering speed and momentum until they were a difficult blur.

And though it would not exist for another eight centuries, they were reminded, somehow, of Apollo's namesake, of a rocket escaping earth's orbit, and one by one the siblings detached from their mass and peeled away like spent thrusters. First the two brothers, whose names I forget, and then Zhao Di, Lai Di, and Qiu Di too, until it was just Ah Nong and Ah Xing, hand in hand, and finally only Ah Nong, who alone scrabbled through the dirt and emerged on the other side.

Up close and in the moonlight, the fruits of the stranger's labours were even larger and impossibly rich with heft and colour. Ah Nong prised one of the fruits from the soil, took a deep and hearty bite, and felt his teeth break.

The boy had bitten into stone.

For the Artisan, who had not known (had never known) the first thing about farming, did not beat the drought by employing superior methods of irrigation or crop rotation, but rather, with the skills at his disposal, simulated an image of a farm. Carving the individual fruits from stone, painting them one by one in saturated hues, he had constructed a thing that was useless in its beauty, and beautiful in its uselessness.

Ai Leng had seen her own death in the street that day, the day of the funeral procession. She had caught sight of it from her window, the slow march through the old village bound for the cemetery at the outskirts of their world. The shiver and the moan that had stuck in her throat as the mourners, the pallbearers and the coffin passed along the dusty street below. Perhaps she had known the deceased. Something of this scene, at least, had seemed familiar to her, like a faraway bell, or some forgotten scent from childhood, but she had not heard any news of who had died, or who might have been sick, and she understood, suddenly, with dreaded certainty that the body in the coffin was her own.

And so she followed the procession, lingering far behind, for she

145

did not wish anyone to recognise her, seemingly alive and well, and cause a fuss.

From a distance, she watched as they lowered her into the ground. A child stared at the grave for a long time then burst into inconsolable tears when he was led away. The villagers returned to their homes in columns of grief.

Those with careless minds might well have been misled, for they thought they saw Ai Leng inside her home, sweeping the floor, preparing her children's meals, sewing dresses for other women in the village. So, from a distance, it appeared that nothing had changed at all, that she was indeed alive. She moved, she breathed, but no one in her family – not her husband, Ah Gong, or her seven children – could convince her otherwise, for they spoke as the living spoke, in a meaningless language incomprehensible to her.

The stranger, who had been exposed as an artist of considerable skill, was not vilified for his deceptions. In fact, the men of the village were relieved that his farming skills were inferior to their own. They were no longer threatened by the things he made. Thereafter, they accepted him without question.

The Artisan did not feel the need to conceal his talents any longer, and so – the farmhouse now converted to a studio – he spent his days chiselling humble mounds of stone into forms ever more sublime.

The Artisan's son, Lu Shan Liang, watched his father, suspended high above the ground, labouring over creation. His father was crafting a magnificent sculpture supported by beams and planks and scaffolding. Eventually, the stone began to resemble a dragon, with its completed body spanning the entire length of the cavernous studio. The Artisan chiselled its defining features in painstaking detail: the face, the fangs, the claws, and all its meticulous coils into which the father would disappear from the boy's sight for what seemed like hours at a time.

From the safety of the ground, Lu Shan Liang would listen for the soothing sound of his father's tools. Once, having lost sight of his father up there, hidden in some distant corner of the dragon, the boy was overtaken with the fancy that the beast had swallowed his father whole, and that his father – ever unflappable – was simply chipping his way back out, with calm and steady hand. The boy would often fall asleep listening to the rhythmic chiselling pulse, his fluttering eyelids keeping time.

There was a time when he wondered whether he would become, like his father, an artisan. The thought did not displease Lu Shan Liang as he hunched over his playthings, keeping a languid watch as his father climbed the struts above. He did not hear, or perhaps he heard but could not remember, the moment his father lost his footing – that panicked shout – nor did he see his father fall. He only recalled the sight of scaffoldings, the way they seemed to come apart in midair, forming inconsolable patterns in their descent. And so the boy was protected from the full anguish of the moment when his father fell from such a height and split his back in two.

The villagers came to nurse his father's wounds and bring supplies. They donated a wheelbarrow, crudely modified into a wheelchair. And they arranged playdates for Lu Shan Liang with their own children while his father convalesced.

The boy learned the layout of the village by riding on the shoulders of Lai Di. Ah Xing taught him nursery rhymes, and in this way he learned the local dialect. Upon being returned to his father he would babble endlessly about his day, the houses he had visited, and the colour of their roofs. No detail was too small for the boy, and in breathless gulps (for everything was beautiful to him) he would stumble over himself to describe the villagers' furnishings, and catalogue the smells of their cooking, the texture of their walls, and the symbols of the god they prayed to.

Ai Leng once sent Lu Shan Liang home with the gift of a tiny brocade sash, and both father and son studied this treasure and its intricate stitching. Later, the boy found his father hunched over a magnifying glass, marvelling at the sash's perfect and minuscule artistry long into the night.

Now Lu Shan Liang watched his father at his truest convalescence. With finer instruments, the Artisan turned his setbacks into art. Returning to the studio where he had fallen, he transformed each fragment of that immense and broken statue into remarkable miniatures – farm animals so lifelike in their detail, tiny wagons, chess sets, toys – which he instructed his son to give to the villagers and their children as thanks for their care and acceptance.

Remember the time Xu Bei wept for days upon learning of her husband's infidelity? Yang Ying, the village gossip, did.

All rumours made their way to Yang Ying's ears, none too small or large for her attentions. She was the source of all reputable news regarding the village, and when the villagers disagreed over differing versions of events (Who had snubbed Hu Li Bian/for what reason? Who had lost his entire life savings/doing what? Who was the secret father of whom?), they would come to her to resolve such disagreements.

Without hesitation, Yang Ying would settle the score at once (The parents of the child Zhou Wu Man/Gift of excessively stingy red packet ... Lao Da/Inappropriate investment in self-driving rickshaws ... Ah Guan, the chicken farmer from the west side, of Seamstress Cai's baby). All that passed from her lips was reputable, beyond doubt, and worth repeating.

She had a habit, too, of recounting stories immediately after she had just told them, eyes widening as she looped back to the beginning of the very same tale, the second telling somehow different, surer in its details or delivery, as though each story in its retelling had eaten itself, was nourished on itself, until the events she described acquired a greater weight – truth becoming fiction – and, emboldened, she would launch into these recitations, rarely repeating the stories in full (for everyone knew by now their rhythms, and could tell the tale as well as she) but instead furnishing them with unforgettable details that had escaped the first telling. Remember the time Xu Bei learned of her husband's infidelities and banged the table so hard that all the pots and pans flew *gok-gok-gok-gok-gok!* (the sound of pots and pans) into the walls and came crashing out the windows?

And then, in a conspiratorial whisper, she would gild the characters of her tales with greater eloquence, or purpose, or beauty – fiction becoming myth – and so attuned were the villagers to Yang Ying's momentum that even as these rhapsodies grew in complexity and length, strangely so did the stories seem ever more elemental. Perfected in the repetition. Remember how Xu Bei, by the very force of her fury, had caused a complete reversal in Ah Guan's luck so that, years later, at the gambling dens, *gok-gok-gok-gok-gok!* (the sound of ill-fated dice), he lost his entire fortune and fell into ever-deepening spirals of madness? Coincidence?

In time, the third and final version was the one the villagers would repeat to one another, until it displaced the original – myth becoming truth – so that each of the villagers, slowly shaking their heads, would swear completely by the tale, in all its unquestionable veracity.

Once, Lu Shan Liang returned home despondent, having overheard village gossip.

He had heard talk that his father's injuries were far graver than had once been thought. That the Artisan had caused deep and irreparable damage to his body, and could no longer stand for lengthy periods, much less remount the scaffoldings to resume his grandiose works.

Yes, it was true, his father told him. Never again would he carve mighty icons into stone, or frescoes that spanned the length of walls. But he whispered now a secret: *it is no tragedy.* If his art had changed then it was simply because *he* had changed.

These words came as a great relief to the boy.

But had the son been older, less delicate, the father might have attempted to articulate the difficult weight in his heart. Something about pain, its necessity, or how, on rare and bitter days, he knew that he deserved its fullest measure.

The Artisan continued in his new craft, and over the years constructed an impressive miniature of the entire village from nothing more than Lu Shan Liang's descriptions. The long dirt road that led to the school, the slender hillock upon which their own house sat, the barn where the children lit off fireworks ... a perfect portrait of the village, carved from wood and clay and other stray materials. In time, the villagers grew to revere the miniature's similitude, and once in a while they would even call upon the Artisan to resolve boundary disputes. When Ah Nong fell into the well, so did the miniature show that empty groove where the stone had loosened from his grip. And when Ah Gong had destroyed the statue in the village square in a drunken rage, so too did its miniature turn to rubble and dust.

Over the years, the miniature charted the infinitesimal decay in the corners of each home, the cracks that would widen over time. And if Lu Shan Liang had lifted the little roofs and inspected the villagers' homes, he might have glimpsed even smaller specks, proudly displayed on the minuscule shelves.

These were representations of the tiny gifts his father had made for each of the villagers once upon a time. These tokens – miniatures of the miniatures – which were near invisible to the naked eye, microscopic and impossible in their smallness.

The rattle of a wooden bell sounded throughout the village. The village criers circled the village, calling out Ah Gong's words:

Emergency meeting at village square.

Attendance mandatory.

Bring food.

The Artisan descended to the village square, cane in hand. Lu

Shan Liang was at his side. It was their eleventh winter in the village.

Very few were in attendance, for the villagers had doubts about the urgency of such a meeting. They knew well the restless and pitiful nature of Ah Gong, who in the past was known to have invented catastrophes or fictive troubles, calling emergency meetings for no good reason other than to slake his loneliness or any other of his deeper disaffections.

Today it seemed he had no false agenda. He told a story of how, while fishing, he had found a bloated carp of strange dimensions tangled in his net. He had gutted it to inspect its interior, and – look here – found an ornamented totem of finest make, waterlogged but well preserved, with a dozen empty compartments.

But what was it? And how was it that such an item existed at the bottom of the lake? Those in attendance muttered to each other. Perhaps a travelling merchant had years ago thrown the object into the lake, where it was swallowed by the fish? Perhaps it was a divine object placed in the fish's womb? Some thought it was a blessing. Others thought it a curse. Someone near the back said, with trembling voice, that it might be Art.

They had seen nothing like it before, and could only guess at it in aggregate.

The Artisan stepped forward. He took the object into his hands and reckoned with it. It was smooth to the touch. He traced its etched lines, appraised its ancient technique and craftsmanship. At times he let out a little smile, or a nod, as though in exploring each of the object's nooks and concavities, he were communing with its maker.

It cannot be used, he said finally, and showed them how the object's maker had secretly graded the centre of each compartment with perishable materials at odds with the finery of its remainder and the richness of the whole. Its imperfections were undetectable to the untrained eye. But the Artisan was used to dealing with such tiny dimensions.

The villagers were even more confused now, for the compartments, to their eyes, appeared flawless. They asked him what the object was.

It is a clock, said the Artisan, *used by only the wealthiest of lords and designed to tell the time by smell.* And they watched him as he returned with his son to their estate, and felt they knew him even less now than before, as though in solving the object's mysteries, he had only deepened the chasm of his own.

The villagers argued over the ruined clock, for they did not trust its presence and were unsure of its meaning. Some among them thought it best to throw it back into the lake, but Ah Gong understood it to be an icon worthy of his devotion. He brought it home, intent on comprehending its mechanisms, and came to lavish his attentions on it, ignoring Ai Leng and their seven children, spending his days in deep and studious contemplation of the clock, its beauty and its uselessness.

He attempted its repair and, by trial and error, filled its grooves with various lengths of burning wick and sticks of incense. To better orient himself to his new-found purpose, Ah Gong spent much of his day staring at the sun, devising a metric by virtue of its location in the sky, and in the lightless evening, by consultation with the stars.

Ah Gong replaced each stick of incense with tokens collected from the village so that the clock might burn of jasmine or sunflower or cut grass – these divisions of the day to which he assigned a different aroma – and though the villagers did not have a name for that most difficult and languorous stretch of afternoon, they came somehow to think of it as the hour of chrysanthemum.

In weeks and months thereafter, moved by the metronomic wafting of oats, or chicken or steamed carp, the households that lived downwind of Ah Gong would prepare their meals in perfect parallel, for their stomachs had begun to growl in synchronicity, and in the night their dreams would be filled with the soothing scent of barley, of boiled milk, of oak, the lake and the stillness of the mountain soil.

The villagers came to rely entirely on their regimented hours. They filled their day with appointments, endless errands and house visits, and – fearing the inevitable collapse of those prolific plans – they developed contingencies with others, formed tentative arrangements in case of cancellations, and at these gatherings they sniffed at each other unhappily, hiding their discontent at how much more fulfilling the busy lives of others seemed. They carefully curated their own tales in hopes that others would envy them as well, proclaimed their own accomplishments in louder boasts, exaggerated the talents of their children, as though by sheer volume or velocity they might be saved, but from what exactly they were not quite sure.

Like Ah Gong, they could no longer stand to be alone and, in the wasteful moments that went unwitnessed by others, they mourned the briefness of their days, and felt regret as they had never known before the merciless mechanisms of time.

Once in a while, Ah Gong would stop in his tracks and retch at a foul odour in the wind. Where had it come from? Was it real or just his imagination? He would take deep inhalations, one after the other in quick succession, in order to confirm that the stench existed. In the end, he would shake his head and walk away, convinced that his mind had simply played another trick on him.

But at home, where the clock resided, this awful smell was ever-present.

Of course, Ah Gong blamed the clock.

Every time he breathed in, he found fault with his family, and dreamed of leaving them. He disappeared to take long walks about the village and lingered at its outskirts by the well. He spied, on the horizon, another village and often imagined its aroma – pleasing, no doubt – and the happiness he might have found if he had lived there instead. The smell magnified. He plucked at grey hairs on his head, fearing his own decay. He bargained with himself constantly: if he fixed the clock, he told himself, he would take it as a sign to stay. If not, he would go, for there was not much time left, not much time at all, in which to live a good life. It seemed fair to him.

Failing to locate the maddening odour, Ah Gong thought he

might at least drown it out, and stuffed the clock's compartments with incense full to bursting until their centres collapsed and every scent began to intermingle. The villagers, who had become reliant on the clock, were no longer able to separate the hour or the day from its sensation, and a fog of confusion settled over them, in which past appeared as future, and future appeared as past.

So that in years past or perhaps years to come, Ai Leng, following her own funeral procession through the labyrinthine streets, would see a strange vehicle come roaring in its wake. It was like nothing she had ever seen. The yellow carriage moved, yet there was no horse to pull it. A cacophonous sound rudely emitted from it like some broken horn and, as the carriage passed her, she briefly glimpsed a young man in the back seat. She thought she saw him smile.

So that when agents from the Imperial City came (would come) to the village and burned down luckless Ah Guan's property, the villagers would glimpse the Artisan presiding over the farm's repair and proclaim – as he climbed the struts and scaffoldings with ease, as though his back had never split in two – that, truly, time heals all wounds, not realising that this was in fact Lu Shan Liang, the Artisan's son, grown into a man.

So that the villagers celebrated, with no apparent error, the wedding of Ah Nong and Yang Ying – though they had forever known him as a boy and she a woman – for there came a time amidst the confusion when, briefly, their ages were in perfect parallel.

So that when the villagers threw the clock into the lake to end the grand confusion as they had done before or would do again, they would find the clock once more in Ah Gong's house, safe and sound, as though it had never been swallowed by a carp and found, but been there on his shelf from the beginning.

And so it was not Ah Gong's failure with the clock that caused him to leave – for he had already left, would again leave, had practised leaving in his sleep and, in the recurring hours in between, had memorised the numbers of steps to take, in perfect gait, to reach the village's exit, where, in his last act before replacing this village for another, he saved his son Ah Nong from falling into the well. In

Ah Gong's mind he had crossed into this other village so many times before that when the moment finally arrived, it hardly seemed real, was perhaps already ruined, some desperate ache that he could but barely articulate.

Did he find peace there – with his new wife, his new family – or succeed, at least, in escaping the scent of his senescence?

How the fuck should I know.

Time and memory failed them, so that they each carried with them different versions of events. There were those who recalled the moment Ah Gong saved Ah Nong from falling into the well without remembering that it was the sight of his father passing that had caused him to fall in the first place.

And Ah Nong found this recursive loop only magnified in years and decades to come, unable to prevent his own sons – my brother, me – from falling into different, deeper wells of their own.

Thus, amidst time's grand confusion, not even Yang Ying could quite explain the complexities of how a merchant barge bound for Jing Hang Canal – so read the manifest – had strayed so far off course as to appear, run aground, on the banks of the Min River. Its cargo – hundreds and thousands of books – had spilled upon their village shores. The villagers gathered at the riverbank to bear witness to the strange phenomenon and exchange exhaustive theories. The best Yang Ying could do was to look up at the sky and mutter that the span of autumn that year had seemed especially and inordinately long.

They made a library inside the ruins of the temple on the outskirts of the village. Books filled the hallowed shelves.

The villagers frequented the library, studied the maze-like stacks. And slowly, over time, they forgot Yang Ying's stories and came to rely less and less on gossip, instead revering the sheer volume of knowledge that was suddenly within their grasp.

Lu Shan Liang, too, was drawn to the library. It was his fourteenth year in the village.

His heart would dip and soar unbearably as he read the thrilling and adventuresome tales, scientific texts, even dour taxation logs. But the subject that most captured his imagination was the Imperial City itself. And the more he read, the more he seemed to see a deeper imprint of the city, so that in the embers of sunset, with the dust motes dancing among the stacks, Lu Shan Liang could close his eyes and see a shard of the city itself, the outline of a street or building, the tentative shape of the skyline at dusk.

Lu Shan Liang saw these patterns ever more vividly in his dreams, and in his waking hours he attempted to map these visions. But they were incomplete and made no sense. Only a handful of lines might survive his understanding, leaving his sketches frustratingly barren, overrun with dark and yawning gaps.

How was it that each book, authored by a different scholar, nonetheless appeared to have been written by the same hand? That same distinctive hand that swept the pages of books as varied as composition, or language, or chess. Though he could not explain why, he became convinced that every one of those books had been written only for him. Often, he found himself in tears for no good reason.

He returned to the library frequently. Each book was a clarion call. And when he traced the words, their fine calligraphy, he was overtaken by some immeasurable yearning.

Once, he happened upon a book within the library that began, *Every now and then a landmark is revealed to be a fallacy after all* ... and it occurred to Lu Shan Liang that every book was a secret map. In a daze he went home and unfurled his sketches, much surer of their contents now, returning to those once-empty spaces and filling their coordinates with all of his deepest longings and lassitudes.

With each book he read, the grander his sketches became, until they no longer represented the Imperial City as it currently was, but instead an Imperial City of his own creation that he might one day build, each blueprint drawn in thick strokes of ink that, when viewed from another angle, seemed somehow like a poem, as though the city itself were made purely of words and language.

Draughts would whistle through the floorboards of Ai Leng's house, and on hands and knees she would locate the holes and repair them, for she now knew that a wind had blown forever at her husband's back, and that it too, one day, might find her children. Already she had noticed their restlessness, the gusts and gales that followed in their wake, which only seemed to quieten when she embraced them. But there were those of them who resisted being held, or else had grown too old for such comforts, and they moved about the house in such a way that squalls began to form, and in their inclement moods the eldest ones would bicker endlessly. If one entered the room, another would leave on cue, and the youngest of them – Ah Nong, Ah Xing – were swept along these currents, causing them to dance about the house to find a quieter corner, and over time, in an almost-choreography, the siblings learned each other by their footsteps.

Ai Leng scraped together what little she had and spun threads of gold like gossamer, so thin they were barely able to be seen, and in their sleep she tied this thread around their ankles in hopes that they would never stray too far from one another, or scatter to the wind. And indeed things calmed. The children became close in proximity. But every so often, in the wrong light, they would detect a telltale glint, and soon their talk became gilded by the topic of money, how they might earn it, and dreams of what far-off places they might go to strike it rich.

Now she spun a different thread, with which she imbued a word, a feeling and a name, each of these things that once existed but no longer, and by whose very absence brought sharper definition to this world. She removed the gilded thread and attached this newer strand, impossible of length, to their sleeping ankles, and so strongly were they bound that when the clock's compartments collapsed and time began to skip and moments replay, when they goaded Ah Nong onto the stranger's land to steal a piece of fruit, they did not peel from him or break away but ran with him as one, and when he fell into the well, so inseparable were they that they were swept along from every corner of the village until they converged upon that well with ropes and threads to pull their brother out.

The Artisan had been busy in his workshop, studying the newest cracks and fissures upon the village miniature's well, and so was not aware when the visitors arrived at the house. There were ten of them, young men. Their leader, slightly older than the others, wore a robe that marked him as an agent of the Imperial City.

His son had let them into the home quite willingly, for in this life the boy had known no fear or earthly suspicion, but now seemed deeply aware of some crucial mistake, for the leader of these men had refused Lu Shan Liang's offer to go fetch his father from the workshop, and instead had grilled the boy with strange questions while the others fanned about the house, upending drawers and cabinets.

Eventually, the commotion drew the Artisan back to the house. Lu Shan Liang's face flooded with relief.

The Artisan trembled when he saw their uniforms. He asked the men what they were doing. The leader explained that he and his men were travelling acolytes who went door to door, expertly rearranging furniture according to the principles of feng shui. *Free of charge*, he added.

Father and son watched as the men ransacked the house and kicked at the walls, occasionally emerging to place certain items on a clearing upon the floor: inks and brushes, miniature chisels and clay. They were searching for evidence of artisanry.

The leader returned from the workshop holding one of the Artisan's miniatures.

It was over, then. They were here for him.

With an outward calm that belied the panic of his heart, the Artisan explained that his miniatures were merely a hobby and that he was but a humble amateur.

The Artisan withstood the leader's piercing stare. He regretted deeply that in years past he had not sat his son down to tell him the truth, to warn him that this day might come, to plan their escape. How would he save his son?

Finally, the leader pointed at the inks and brushes on the floor. *And these?* he asked.

After a moment's hesitation, the Artisan spoke truthfully. They belonged to the boy. He explained that Lu Shan Liang aspired to be a cartographer, or perhaps an architect. The Artisan seemed embarrassed – and all the more for being in the presence of his son – that he did not know for certain. And the leader (perhaps he too had a son?) seemed to soften at this stumbling admission, its distance and honesty.

Indeed they found the boy's sketches, entire sheaves arranged haphazardly on the floor, not only maps but also blueprints and designs.

The men inspected the suspect materials. By now they had abandoned their ruse, for they spoke freely of the Emperor and their task. To them, the father's miniatures were ugly, unimpressive (for they had mistaken the shabby exteriors for poor craftsmanship, not understanding that each model was perfect in its imperfections). But the boy's sketches – his line and eye for detail – seemed to them like art.

The leader delivered his verdict. The boy, though clearly talented, was far too young to be the one they sought. And as for the father and his miniatures, he repeated the Artisan's own words. *Merely a hobby. Only a humble amateur.*

The agents moved on to other houses and other villages.

That night the Artisan pored over each of his son's embryonic sketches, shaken by the scope and accuracy of the city's re-creation, the hidden network of yearning that the boy had coded, unknowingly, into the fabric of his work. How the father's heart ached with pride, and perhaps regret, when he regarded these designs laid out before him (for he once had thought that he could, with sufficient grace and love, shield the boy entirely from the perils of this world).

He asked his son, *Who taught you the shape of the Imperial City?*

I read it, the boy responded.

In which book?

All of them.

In a quiet voice, the Artisan forbade his son from ever stepping foot inside the Imperial City.

In their official report, the agents proclaimed that there was no evidence of skilled artisanry in the village known as the armpit of the armpit, that it was populated only with hobbyists and talentless amateurs.

No arrests were made, none executed.

It was noted, however, in the leader's disinterested prose, that a farm belonging to a certain farmer named Ah Guan, from the west side, had been burned to the ground for the heinous crime of harbouring chickens.

24

Port Man Tou General Hospital – Yingbin Road, Canton of Western Facade

I come to in a hospital bed.

A windowless room. Fluorescent lights. No clocks, no clues as to the time of day.

Tubes run from my arm to a drip that (I notice later) isn't dripping at all.

A poster on the wall reads, *Port Man Tou, China: The City Where Anything Is Possible!*

The door opens. A harried man in a white smock enters. A security camera tracks him to my bedside.

'感觉好点了吗?'

'I don't speak Chinese.'

He tsks at his clipboard, then switches to English.

'Yes, yes, we've all heard about you. You are the bad Chinese who refuses to speak his own language. I asked you, in Mandarin, if you are feeling better.'

'Um. Is that camera filming us?'

He jots down something on his clipboard.

'Good. CT scan has ruled out aneurysm. I have ordered a comprehensive metabolic panel. We should have your results in twenty-four hours.'

I suddenly notice a piece of cotton taped to my arm.

'Do you have a history of migraines?'

'Not really.'

'How many fingers am I holding up?' He flicks me the middle finger.

'One.'

'On a scale of one to ten, rate the pain you are feeling in your head. One being the highest, no, I mean lowest. Also, if you prefer, you may use a scale of five.'

'Five,' I say.

'I see,' he says grimly. 'Five out of ... five?'

'Ten.'

'I see.'

'Is that supposed to be dripping?' I ask.

He looks at the tube in my arm, then at the drip that isn't dripping. He ignores the question.

'How did I get here?' I'm suddenly very aware that I'm wearing nothing but a hospital gown.

'Ambulance. Straight from the tarmac. Very big scene, apparently. Very expensive. Caused many delays at the airport. Things would be very difficult for you if you weren't friends with The Director.'

I'd feel embarrassed if I wasn't so confused. 'I was travelling with someone. A friend. Is she here?'

'I don't know.' A long pause, another look at the clipboard. 'Well, you seem otherwise lucid, besides the tendency to ask ridiculous questions. But that might have something to do with your anxiety problem. Perhaps this is the reason for your "episode" on the flight? Were you seated next to any white people? The initial test results show that you suffer from crippling Anglophobia.'

'I think you mean Taikophobia.'

'No. No, no, no. "Also Anglophobia". See?'

The doctor shows me the chart. It's true.

He seems to glance at the camera.

'Well, unless you have any more stupid questions, I'll prepare you for immediate discharge. Here is a prescription for headache medication. It is written in Chinese. Have some self-respect and learn your native tongue. Also, Port Man Tou General Hospital employs some white doctors. Specialists. So if you pass them in the hallway, just avert your gaze and you should be fine.'

A nurse brings my clothes and personal effects. I'm escorted to a waiting room and told someone will pick me up. I switch on my phone and manage to find an unsecured network called PORTMANTOU_FREEWIFI. My phone pings. I have mail.

To whom it may concern,

Have you been let down by the big-city dream? Long commutes? The grind of the 9 to 9? The near-toxic levels of air pollution?

Then why not try a change of scenery?

Port Man Tou, China: The City Where Anything Is Possible is a lakeside metropolis in Inner Mongolia, situated on a tract of land equidistant between Manzhouli and Baotou.

Perhaps the name of our fine city rings a bell? Recently, *The New York Times* ran a piece entitled 'The Infamous Ghost Cities of China', which accused our government of building empty cities all over the countryside in order to maintain an aggressive GDP. Included in their exposé were photos of the empty roads and shopping malls of Port Man Tou.

Take a look. We have attached these photos for your reference.

And while we have your attention, perhaps you have heard of The Director, Baby Bao? Recently the *LA Times* listed him in an article entitled 'The Top Five Chinese Auteurs to Watch'. Surely you have seen his latest movie, *Death of a Pagoda*?

Indeed, those of you who have watched *Pagoda* will recognise this hospital as the exact one where the character Mao Wen Bo was taken, following his heart attack. The ambulance that arrived on the scene was real. The hospital was real. The doctors and nurses who saved him were real. But they are also actors. They have signed contracts agreeing to this. Baby Bao has complete access to every inch of Port Man Tou.

Slowly but surely, Port Man Tou is growing. Baby Bao's last two films were shot here entirely. Villagers from nearby have even migrated to Port Man Tou, having sensed the city's boundless opportunity. They have become its first citizens. They are employed in catering and set design. They are paid a salary. There are bus routes and grocery stores with real food. There is a school for children. But Baby Bao needs more. He needs extras. He needs you to fill the city. Because if Man Tou is a bun, then the people are the filling.

By official decree,
The Department of Tourism

Hospital Entrance – Yingbin Road, Canton of Western Facade

Outside, a handful of people are seated at benches near the entrance – families of the infirm – but I do not see Yuan or Baby Bao among them.

Is anyone coming to get me?

Instinctively, I check my phone. Nothing happens. I try my web browser, but it's blocked. A creeping panic sets in.

I am about to go back inside to find someone who can speak English when I hear a scream.

'是他!'

An elderly lady with a walker points a trembling finger at me. People rush out to see what the fuss is about.

'是 #BadChinese!' a teenager yells, brandishing his phone.

Someone grabs my sleeve. I yank it back. A crowd gathers, phones held high. A security guard approaches but all he wants is a selfie with me.

I manage to power-walk my way out of the crowd. They follow me up the ring-road.

'Go away!'

They laugh and cheer at my English.

I break into a run. Some give chase.

What the fuck is my plan here? Keep running?

A sleek black Bentley limousine pulls to the kerbside. The tinted window rolls down. There is Baby Bao, choking on his own laughter.

He opens the door and slides over to let me in.

The limousine speeds away, leaving the mob behind.

'Did you enjoy your hospital stay?' he asks.

It takes me a moment.

'Wait. How are you speaking English?'

'You are amazed, right? Your mind is doing somersaults, right? You are wondering why did Baby Bao go through all the unnecessary ceremony of hiring an interpreter? You are wondering, is this the reason why we understood each other so perfectly at the Teahouse Pavilion? Or is it possible that Baby Bao cannot speak English at all, and has hired a bilingual double to portray him in this scene?'

I examine him closely. He looks the same as the last time I saw him.

'What the hell *was* that just now?' I ask.

Baby Bao slaps my knee vigorously.

'The panic on your face! You can't teach that in an acting class! Look, someone has uploaded a video. It's already going viral.'

He shoves his phone in my face and plays the video.

I look like such an idiot.

'We had an official welcome prepared for you yesterday on the tarmac. But in retrospect, having the citizen-actors discover you organically was much better.'

Baby Bao says something to the driver in Mandarin and the limo pulls over.

'Come. We are only a few blocks from Bao Tower. Let's walk the rest of the way so you can see the city up close.'

We step out of the limo and into the scene. It is truly a sight. The towering high-rises. The cars honking. Traffic crawling. The streets surging with people talking on mobile phones, buying snacks from kerbside vendors, jaywalking. This place is real.

165

Suddenly it is harder to reconcile Port Man Tou with the pictures I have seen of other ghost cities.

'Where did all these people come from?' I ask.

'They are citizen-actors. They live and work here. Don't worry. They are under orders not to make eye contact with me. As long as I am around they will not bother you.'

I point out the kerbside vendor. 'Is that real food?'

'Yes, of course.'

'And those people standing nearby, are they eating or acting?'

'They are eat-acting.'

Baby Bao buys me a fried fish skewer from a vendor. I take a bite. It tastes the same as in Chinatown back home.

'And now *you* are eat-acting.'

Suddenly, I can't chew normally anymore because I am thinking too much about it.

'Is there a camera somewhere filming this?'

Baby Bao laughs – 'Hahaha!!!' – which doesn't answer the question.

Then he says, 'There is a camera somewhere, filming something in every modern city. A microphone somewhere, recording something. The UK has one CCTV camera for every eleven people. In Port Man Tou, we have eleven cameras for every person. But soon you will forget all about it. The city will seduce you. You will find that it is as real as any other. See the movie times outside that cinema? They are real. We can go and watch a movie right now.'

He runs across the street, picks up a newspaper from a stand, and runs back. A car almost hits him but he doesn't bat an eyelid. 'See? The newspaper is real. Everything is real. The city is real.'

'It's real and it's not,' I say. 'It's both.'

Baby Bao nods.

We approach Bao Tower. It dwarfs the other high-rises. A digital clock at its apex displays the time and date.

'Jesus. It's *July*? Was I in a coma for a month?'

'The clock is wrong. The clock is always wrong. You were only in hospital for a day.'

'Oh.'

'Now, you will report to me every morning, here at Bao Tower. We will go over the day's agenda: investment meetings, press events, ribbon-cutting ceremonies. It will be very busy, but there will also be time to explore the city.'

'What about Yuan?'

'I'll have my driver take you to her after we're done here. She lives and works in the Canton of The Unwritten. She does translation work for the Department of Verisimilitude.'

'What do they do?' I ask.

'The Department of Verisimilitude exists to make sure every inch of the city is believable. For example, the fish skewers you ate. They were real, right?'

'Right.'

'And the vendor who sold you the skewers. She was real? Believable?'

'As far as I could tell.'

'And the cart with all the skewers. Anything suspicious about it?'

'No. Nothing.'

'And the general atmosphere? The street, the buildings.'

'All believable.'

'Good. Then if you are questioned by the Department of Verisimilitude, you will have nothing to fear. There is nothing to report. But if, for example, you see actors in the Canton of Western Facade, leaving their scripts lying around, or even walking around the canton, reading, rehearsing, with scripts in hand, *that* is a reportable offence. But enough of that. Come, let me show you my base of operations.'

Bao Tower – Daqiao Road, Canton of Time's Uncertain Arrow

We step into an opulent building, with smoothly polished marble floors and chandeliers hanging from the ceiling. Baby Bao calls for the elevator. I follow him in.

A security guard greets us on the eighteenth floor. He is ancient and wrinkled, and after he buzzes us into the main concourse, he settles back on his chair to nap.

'When Port Man Tou was built,' says Baby Bao, 'the villagers who lived on the land were displaced. That man was one of them. For years, they were the only residents of the city. They languished in the modern world. When I became Director, I made sure to employ every one of them, to bring the old China into the new. Those villagers are part of the Chinese middle class now. Don't *they* deserve a middle-class job?'

The entire eighteenth floor is a honeycomb of computer monitors, each showing a different image: footage of an empty street, surgery in an operating room, a fistfight in a bar, the lush and opulent set of some ancient dynasty, the construction of as-yet-unfinished cantons.

Blank-faced technicians silently scrub through footage, marking down timestamps.

'You monitor the entire city?' I ask.

'Almost. Due to budget constraints, a few cantons remain unmonitored. The lake, obviously, cannot be surveilled for logistical reasons. But all citizens think they are being recorded. My doubles maintain a presence to ensure they continue acting naturally.'

'How many doubles do you have?'

'Several. Some I even allow to direct a scene once in a while for authenticity. But the doubles are untrained in the art of filmmaking. The quality is absolutely terrible. The framing is not right, the coverage non-existent. But do you know the funny thing? My assistants do not dare to criticise me. They say flattering things like, "Oh, Director, how masterfully you have created that perfect simulation of bad art!" Look, here is one of my doubles now.'

On one of the screens, we watch as a Caucasian journalist soundlessly interviews a sharp-suited Baby Bao. In the background, rickshaws run alongside motorised trams. River ferries traverse the Bund. People walk the streets, the men in zhongshan suits, the women in glamorous cheongsams.

Baby Bao continues, 'As you can see, the Canton of Western

Facade was modelled on the Shanghai of the thirties, when it was known as the Paris of the East. This was the golden age of Chinese cinema. Here, foreign journalists are free to roam the canton. They reside in luxury accommodation and are welcome to wander into the camera's frame. Their articles are always flattering. Their presence is very important for outside funding.'

We move on. The monitors display footage of police raiding a drug den. An emperor wearing golden-spun robes and headdress being attacked in the streets by men with swords. Teams crafting enormous buddhas made of bronze in cavernous backlots.

We take the elevator to the nineteenth floor. A team of editors sit before a panopticon of monitors. They peruse footage of themselves editing while others peruse footage of themselves perusing footage.

Baby Bao turns his gaze from them to me.

'Nothing is exempt. *Everything* is potentially part of the movie. If I so wish it.'

25

THE IMPERIAL ARCHITECT

One day, the Grand Prolonger of Autumn brought the Imperial Consort, Wuer, a sheaf of letters written in the hand of Yang Ying, which were addressed to her sister, the midwife Fan Mei, whose last known address had been the concubines' quarters in the Imperial City. Starved of material to read, the concubines had opened the letters but, finding them an interminably long catalogue of minor incidents in a far-off village, they sold the sheaf to the scholars, who were always in need of paper.

While perusing Scholar Ping's den for writing supplies on Wuer's behalf, the Grand Prolonger chanced upon this document. He read, with interest, the letter intended for Fan Mei, who had once belonged to Wuer's retinue.

Amidst the reams of petty village squabbles and grievances, one stray line struck him: the arrival in the village of a mysterious stranger with a young boy. He implored Scholar Ping to collect from the concubines any future letters addressed to Fan Mei.

As the letters made their way towards the labyrinth, so too was their course labyrinthine: posted by a woman in a remote village of the south, delivered to the concubines, sold to the scholars, passed in secret to the Grand Prolonger before coming, finally, into Wuer's trembling hands.

At first, the details she longed for were scant. Word of the mysterious stranger and his son comprised but a small fraction of these lengthy letters. It appeared that the stranger was reticent, and refused to mingle with the villagers. It was only some letters later – describing the delicious scandal of the stranger's outing as a fake farmer – that Yang Ying began to devote many words to the stranger and his son.

Her son.

His name was Lu Shan Liang. His first words: 爸爸 (*Father*). Yang Ying wrote of the villagers with whom he had consorted during his father's recuperation, and the boy's love of drawing.

Often, Wuer thought she would put pen to paper, write a letter to her son, explain herself and the choices she had made, but could never find the right thing to say, and as she wrote, the words seemed to have ideas of their own, and she would emerge from the room having written not a letter but the first pages of another book, some other tome in which to hide her longing and sorrow.

And so it proceeded: the Grand Prolonger of Autumn would come bearing letters and supplies, and the Imperial Consort would meet him with a stack of freshly written books.

Once, awaiting his arrival, she thought she heard the sound of someone fall as though from a great height. Emerging from the heart of the labyrinth, she found the wall of the Endless Corridor split in two.

She studied the wound then. Its repair was not beyond her. She recalled an illuminating detail from the pages of General Meng Tian's *Diary of the Long Wall*: how a section built with sticky-rice mortar had survived a major earthquake, where others had collapsed; its precise recipe illuminated in *Annotated Poisons, Elixirs and Sundry* by Wang Tao; and the tools and techniques she might require in *Treatise of Architectural Methods or State Building Standards* by Li Jie. She arranged for the Grand Prolonger of Autumn to bring these materials to her, and she set about mending the deepest cracks and fissures.

In time, Yang Ying wrote of the Artisan's declining health. He had become weak with consumption, the sum of his world reduced to his bed and the makeshift studio Lu Shan Liang had built beside it so that the Artisan might complete his master work, the self-portrait he called *A Simulated Man*. In her final letter, Yang Ying told of the Artisan's passing, and how his boy – now a man – could not be swayed by the others to stay in the village, for he sought to find his own way in the world.

Architecture was a dangerous field, he said, looking for a clean glass. Believe him. He should know. He was, after all, the Imperial Architect.

Buo Guong liked nothing better than to drink and pontificate. To be sure, he could drink without the pontificating. Likewise, he might at times pontificate without all the drinking. But together? *Well*, he told his new apprentice, Lu Shan Liang, *I like nothing better.*

And what better place to do both at once than the Phoenix Tavern – closed for renovation – as he pilfered the bar for more wine and left his team of labourers to their own devices.

He came, he said, from a long line of architects. Take his father, the venerable Buo Jiong, who had built temples and gate towers. Or his father's father, the illustrious Buo Hui, who, during his time as Imperial Architect, had designed the Emperor's palace. Unfortunately, it seemed the line would end with him. He was the father of eight girls. A soothsayer, a palm reader and an acquaintance who dabbled in astrology had each informed him that the ninth, were he and his exhausted wife to have a ninth, would also be a girl. Nothing but girls. *Forget it! No more children! What's the point?* He poured himself another glass.

He was saying something about danger. A dangerous field, architecture. *How so, I hear you ask?* (Though Lu Shan Liang had asked nothing of the sort.) Consider then, Buo Guong continued, that each Imperial Architect before him had been executed in the course of carrying out his sworn Imperial duties. His father, for having assisted in the construction of the labyrinth. His father's father, for knowing too much about the secret layout of the Sagacious Emperor's Imperial Tomb.

Buo Guong had long ago realised the secret to longevity as Imperial Architect, and with no son of his own to pass on such sage wisdom, he decided his apprentice Lu Shan Liang would do. The secret was simple: *Curb your ambition! Aim low! If the Emperor, on some tyrannical whim, orders the building of a grand and expensive monument, simply persuade His advisers that such an extravagance would be too costly. Or else see to it that the paperwork is lost. Finally, blame your labourers for your own failures. Eventually, people will lose interest, the project will falter, and you will come through unscathed.*

In his two decades as Imperial Architect, Buo Guong had completed not a single major work in the Empire. Not one! Only trivial renovations in brothels and taverns such as this.

No building or structure – no matter how grand or everlasting – is worth death, he said.

Lu Shan Liang, unable to hold his tongue any longer, pointed out the slipshod wall the bumbling labourers were erecting. The material was made of rammed earth, which could not properly bear weight. Without a dougong to brace the wall and ceiling, its collapse was imminent.

Dougong? The Imperial Architect shrugged. Ever since the burning of the books, those terms had been lost to the ether. The apprentice drew a sketch of the structure, all horizontal beams and interlocking brackets. *Oh, that,* said Buo Guong. And he promised the young man that he would see to it that the labourers construct such a thing, but in truth he forgot about it almost immediately.

26

Efficiency and Relaxation Apartments – Fuxing Road, Canton of The Unwritten

Yuan is waiting in the lobby as I arrive in the limousine. She stands and walks quickly over to the entrance and gives me a long hug. The doormen exchange looks with each other.

She pulls away. 'Are you feeling better?'

'Yes. I'm still a little disoriented, but I'm not sure if it's from the drugs or just ... getting a mini-tour of the city from Baby Bao.'

The limousine drives off.

'Wait,' she says. 'So you get a limo and *I* have to take the train? What's that about?'

'I'm an invalid, remember?'

We go to the reception desk to check in. It's quick and painless, the service impeccable.

'So, are the receptionists actors too?' I ask Yuan on our way to the elevator. 'And the bellboys?'

'I don't know.'

'Did you know Baby Bao can speak perfect English?'

'What? I didn't know that! But, come to think of it, I'm not surprised. It's just like him to act more important by hiring an interpreter he doesn't need. By the way, you're not to call him that. We refer to him at all times as "The Director".'

'Well, The Director says you're to be my guide and interpreter in the city.'

'Good. It's creepy being here alone.'

The elevator doors open. I swipe for the sixteenth floor. Yuan swipes for the twelfth.

'Okay, I'm going to wash the hospital stench off me. Give me fifteen minutes, then we'll meet back in the lobby?'

'Actually, I want to see what your room is like. Just call me when you're done. Room 1264. Then I'll come over and we can work out what we want to do today.'

Fifteen minutes later the doorbell rings. It's Yuan.

'Hey, come on in,' I say.   •

She gasps. 'Your room is huge!'

The room *is* luxurious: king-size bed, ensuite facilities, kitchenette and separate living room.

'Yours isn't like this?' I ask.

'No. Mine is just a one-room studio, a quarter of the size, no kitchenette, only a bar fridge. Even my furniture is shabby. Let's swap apartments.'

'Not after that glowing endorsement,' I say, following her into my bedroom. 'I figured they would put us up in identical rooms.'

'Only the best for #BadChinese,' she says.

She wanders into my ensuite.

I lie on the bed and switch on the TV. News, sports, movies. Everything seems real enough.

'Hey,' I call out.

'Yes?' She peeks her head around the corner.

I switch off the TV and look at her.

'What was it I said to you? On the plane? Before I blacked out?'

She sits on the edge of my bed. 'You don't remember?'

'No.'

'You really don't remember?'

'No. Tell me. What did I say?' I am suddenly fearful of what embarrassing information I might have armed her with.

'You told me ...' Yuan stands up abruptly and paces a few steps away, then turns around and looks me in the eyes. 'You told me you have ... fallen in love ... with ...'

My heart is in my throat.

'With?'

'... with ... wearing women's lingerie. So soft and lacy.'

She snorts at her own joke. I hurl a pillow at her. She catches it.

'Actually,' she says, 'you told me about the time you went to visit your ancestral village, as an adult. You were in a taxi, stuck behind a funeral procession, and you thought you saw your grandmother smiling at you.'

My mouth falls open.

'What's wrong?' she asks.

You weigh up the things of you that mean something. And impart them with care. The details, I mean. The embarrassing stories. The truth behind complicated events. Dreams. Even among my great friends there are different tiers of intimacy. Same as anyone. Yuan and I have known each other for only days. Surely it's the ones who've known you longest – years, decades – who would know you best, who might hold the most complete map of you.

Yet it is not always so.

'I ... I've never told that story to anyone. Not even my parents. Nobody knows but you.'

'Why not? It's lovely. There's nothing embarrassing about it.'

'I went there to learn about my family. I thought it would feel like going home. But it didn't,' I say, surprised to find a lump in my throat. 'And I came back feeling ...'

Her face softens, and she takes a step towards me.

The doorbell rings.

'I'll get it,' she says, throwing the pillow back to me.

I hear her open the door; no words are exchanged. After a moment, Yuan returns.

'There was no one there, but this was left under the door.' She holds up an envelope.

I take it. I almost laugh. It's the same postmark, the same pattern. I open it. It's all typed in Chinese.

'Did you mean what you said in Sydney?' I ask her. 'That you'd teach me Mandarin?'

'Of course.'

'Can I take you up on that offer now?'

I show her the card.

She translates it. 'You're invited to a red carpet event, tonight at eight, for the Chinese premiere of *Death of a Pagoda* at the Port Man Tou State Theatre. There's a phone number here for the costume department so you can come appropriately attired.'

'Does it say if I can bring ... a date?'

She attempts to hide a smile. 'En. See here? 同伴. That means "guest".'

'I think "date" sounds better. What do you say? Will you go with me?'

Port Man Tou State Theatre – Nangua Road, Canton of Eternal Ruin

Our limousine slows to a crawl, stuck behind a row of others. Yuan and I can hear the crowd gathered around the entrance to the Port Man Tou State Theatre. The streetlights are draped with banners advertising tonight's event.

I can see the theatre now: a towering piece of brutalist architecture with a stone-grey aesthetic that makes it look incomplete.

We finally round the corner. The red carpet is in view. I press my face against the tinted window for a better look.

The Director alights onto the red carpet. He wears a shimmering gold tuxedo and his trademark sunglasses. The crowd goes wild.

177

He is joined by two models wearing identical black gowns with plunging necklines. The Director makes his way down the red carpet, an arm draped around each model.

'I shouldn't have worn red,' Yuan laments.

Her gown is a figure-hugging, strapless wonder with matching stiletto heels. Her hair is done up in a glamorous bun.

'You look amazing,' I reassure her.

'That red carpet is going to swallow me up. But thanks. Your tuxedo is very sharp, though maybe you should take off your glasses before we get out.'

'You think?'

'I can't remember ever seeing someone on a red carpet wearing glasses.'

A chic-looking couple emerge from the limousine in front of us.

'They look familiar. Who are they?' I ask.

'Mao Wen Bo and Gu Ting Ting, The Director's leading actors,' Yuan says. 'I wasn't expecting to see them.'

'Why not?'

'When they failed to join us in Sydney for the world premiere, all sorts of rumours went around that they'd displeased The Director and had been re-cast.'

'Re-cast?'

We're moving now.

'Glasses,' she reminds me.

I take them off, put them in my pocket.

My heart is racing.

'Have you ever done anything like this before?' Yuan asks.

'No. You?'

She shakes her head.

I give her hand a squeeze. She holds mine tightly.

The limousine pulls up to the red carpet. An attendant opens the door. I step out and am immediately blinded by flashes. I offer Yuan a hand and we make our way through the gauntlet. Another attendant points out where we need to stand for the press. The disorienting flashes never stop. I force a smile, but Yuan is a natural, with one hand on her hip, a demure smile for the cameras, even slowly turning her head from left to right to ensure that everyone can capture her best angle.

Further down the red carpet, a reporter shoves a microphone in my face.

'您的父母以你为耻吗?'

'What?'

Foyer, Port Man Tou State Theatre – Nangua Road, Canton of Eternal Ruin

The pre-show crowd mingles in the foyer. Everyone has a drink in hand as they busy themselves with animated conversations, while at the same time tracking The Director out of the corner of their eye.

'Look,' whispers Yuan.

'I can't see that far without my glasses.'

'Baby Bao just whispered something to Gu Ting Ting. Maybe the rumours aren't true.'

'What if they *are* true?' I ask.

'Then it's likely that they're here for appearance's sake.'

'You were saying something about them being re-cast in another film?'

'No. Re-cast in the city itself. They could find themselves working on a farm tomorrow, or sweeping the streets. Re-casting is a form of punishment.'

An attendant tops up our champagne.

'We should change the subject,' she whispers.

Baby Bao weaves through the crowd. Even at this distance I can tell it's him because of how his suit glitters in the light. He approaches and slaps me on the back. He speaks in Mandarin, presumably for the benefit of eavesdroppers. Yuan falls effortlessly back into her interpreter role.

'*Xiang Lu! You look silly without your glasses. Put them back on. How do you like the festivities? Get used to this. There will be many such events for you to attend in your capacity as the infamous #BadChinese. Drink up, both of you! That's an order!*'

The three of us drain our glasses.

He snaps his fingers and the attendant returns with the bottle. Baby Bao lifts his glass and guzzles his champagne.

'*We shall continue this later. I need to schmooze. As do you. Look, that waitress at the bar is sneaking a photo of you. My spies tell me she has a boyfriend but he doesn't treat her well. Go for it!*'

I say nothing, and instead exchange a glance with Yuan.

'*Ah, and over there, see that old man? A very important investor. He is the CEO of a major beer brand. They have breweries all over China. I'm in the process of lavishing my attentions on him, making him feel like a VIP in the city. To what end? Come on, guess.*'

'You're negotiating a deal for product placement?'

'*More than that! You must think bigger!*'

But Baby Bao falls silent as he watches Farmstrong Tian approach the investor. The two men shake hands. Farmstrong says something. Both men laugh. Baby Bao, infuriated, outlaughs them, as though I've just told him an outrageous joke. All eyes in the room are suddenly on us. Baby Bao raises his glass to me, then waltzes off.

Yuan goes to the ladies' room. Meanwhile, the lights dim for us to take our seats. I wait for her as people file into the cinema. Yuan returns, and we make our way towards the doors.

'不好意思.' The waitress from the bar approaches, phone in hand. '可以合个影吗?'

I look to Yuan for the translation. She remains silent.

The waitress mimes a selfie with me.

'Oh, sure.'

She snaps a photo and writes down her number for me. Yuan stares at her incredulously.

We head into the cinema.

'So. Are you going to call her?' Yuan asks in a neutral tone.

In the lightless corridor, head spinning from champagne and the scent of Yuan's perfume, I muster all my courage and answer her question with a kiss.

27

THE TASTER TO THE TASTER

In the earliest days of his appointment after the Poisoned Banquet, when the memories of begging in the streets were still fresh in his mind, the Taster to the Taster would allow himself only a morsel of the Emperor's dish, as was the custom. But how he savoured that bite! Crispy pork cooked to perfection, the delightful crackle as he slowly chewed, then a sip of the Emperor's heavenly wine to swish about his mouth. One bite per dish, one sip per drink, three meals per day (or more, or less, to match the Emperor's whims). It was enough to sustain him. He no longer ate the food of commoners, and though his stomach growled at the sight and smell of congee and steamed buns prepared in the servants' quarters, he never joined his colleagues, for he had developed a palate for Imperial Cuisine that he could not bear to relinquish.

Once, by accident, he took two bites, and was thrilled to find that no one had seemed to notice. After this chance discovery, he continued brazenly in this manner.

It soon became custom for the Imperial Kitchen to prepare a (small) bowl for him at mealtimes, which, over the years, and at the Taster to the Taster's insistence, grew in size and scope until it rivalled the Emperor's portion.

Was it the richness of the food that had caused the Taster to the Taster to acquire the Emperor's mannerisms? The veneer of boredom, the same withering sneer when a dish was not to his liking. Often, he sent dishes back to the Imperial Kitchen, judging them not fit for his own delicate palate, much less the Emperor's.

One day, though it might have been a trick of the light, the Emperor glanced across His table and was enraged to find the Taster to the Taster's portion even bigger than His own. Consequently, the Emperor ordered the Taster to the Taster's next meal be seasoned with a healthy dose of lye.

The lye burned the Taster to the Taster's tongue beyond repair, and thereafter his tongue seemed constantly aflame, never to be rid of the acrid taste. He sought out tonics and salves, but to no avail. Even the slightest movement in his mouth would induce excruciating pain. He even considered removing his tongue entirely.

Still, he was forced to continue in his sworn duties, though he could no longer discern the difference between a mouldy crust of bread and the Heavenly Loaf from the Imperial Kitchen. Yet, over time, his skill as Taster to the Taster improved.

True it was that food had lost its pleasure for him but, amidst his constant pain, the Taster to the Taster had chanced upon another method. In each morsel of food, he learned to detect textures, and deeper patterns. By accident, he had found art in the wound, and thereafter he pursued it like a distant signal by which he might survive.

Each bowl of rice was distinct from every other, for in the subtle modulations of the coarseness of the grain did he know the passing of the seasons.

Such became the refinement of his palate that the Taster to the Taster could discern, from a single sip, the age of the turtle used in the broth. Over the course of months, singularly aware of the ever-increasing smoothness of the broth, he seemed to grasp – long before the harvesters did – that the turtles were getting younger. How was this so? The Taster to the Taster was captive to the walls of the Imperial City, and could not have known their patterns of migration. And yet he tasted worlds beyond his world.

On any given day, as soon as the food entered his mouth, he knew which of the four chefs had prepared the Emperor's meal.

There was Chef Dong, kidnapped from the east, who excelled at bringing out the natural essence of foods. Chef Nan, annexed from the south against his will, whose insistence on spices could either ruin a dish or elevate it to pure perfection. Chef Xi, snatched from the west, who salted his dishes with homesick tears.

But the most impressive of them was the Imperial Chef Bei, local to the north. He had come of age during the famines of yesteryear, when food and grain in the Imperial City were in short supply. In those days, as a young apprentice chef, he had been inspired by the infamous tale of the Emperor's Outer Feast, and set his life's work to re-creating it, to coaxing out an impressive spectrum of taste from the humble bean curd and fashioning it into a dish of endless delights. He had sought to perfect not only the look of his tofu-forgeries, but also the taste. Naturally, Chef Bei was skilled in all the disciplines, and could prepare any dish the Emperor so desired. But once in a while, he would serve up exquisite combinations – roasted duck, twice-cooked pork, lamb hotpot – only to reveal by meal's end, and to the Emperor's roars of laughter, that it had been tofu all along.

The Taster to the Taster recognised the dishes by Imperial Chef Bei from the intensity of their flavours, the telltale frenzy of the skillet that betrayed some bitter nexus (indeed, Chef Bei's father, once a successful poultry farmer, had died in shame and squalor after the Emperor's edict banning all chickens from the Empire).

Chef Bei's dishes were so clearly superior that they provoked a jealousy in the other chefs, who became obsessed with attempting to uncover Chef Bei's methods. Only the Taster to the Taster, with his ruined tongue and its new-found knowledge, understood that the wellspring of Chef Bei's culinary genius was a deep and unforgiving hatred of the Emperor. The Taster to the Taster's heart quickened whenever he discerned that the day's meal had been prepared by the Imperial Chef himself, for each spoonful seemed somehow fraught with emotion and murderous desire. Each meal tasted better, knowing it might have been his – and the Emperor's – last.

The Taster to the Taster's ruined tongue began to speak in riddles that stirred the ears of the Emperor's advisers. To some, he would whisper: *The world is not without its reasons.* To others: *The world is not without its treasons.*

In time it became clear that the Taster to the Taster's murmurings were not meaningless babble, but instead some signifier of a latent talent for prognostication.

Sipping a thick and flavourful broth, the Taster to the Taster spoke of the arrival of a certain Manchurian, whose feats and exploits would soon occupy the thoughts of all who set eyes upon him.

Chewing on a single grain of boiled rice, he intoned, as though in a fever dream, a vision of an immense monsoon that would engulf the Imperial City.

The Emperor's advisers paid close attention to the Taster to the Taster's painful divinations and attempted to interpret his deepest and darkest portents.

Inside a perfect red bean bun, the Taster to the Taster detected a terrifying numbness that previously would have been lost to him had he retained his sense of taste, and from the pitiless void he was compelled to describe a hermit on a mountain who, after years of satisfying isolation, came to realise that there had been, in the mountain's deepest pockets, a thousand other hermits.

After much scrying and astral consultation, the Emperor's advisers announced their interpretation: *By the next full cycle of the zodiac, the Emperor will die one thousand deaths.*

28

Ministerial Office Complex – National Road, Canton of The Unwritten

I sign the visitors' log while the receptionist telephones Yuan. I fill out my details in English. It occurs to me that I have even forgotten how to write my name in Chinese.

Yuan arrives through the swipe door. She is wearing a smart blouse and flats and has her hair in a ponytail. She gives me a quick smile, but when she speaks it's all business.

'Hello. You're late.'

'I had to stop by Costume for a suit and tie.'

'You didn't pack one from Sydney?'

'I ... forgot.'

'You're such a *boy*. Though I'm impressed you know how to ask for a suit in Chinese.'

'Actually, I don't. I told them in broken Mandarin I am "going to work" and "have no clothes". They figured out the rest.'

The receptionist hands me a lanyard and says something.

'She says you'll have to make do with a guest pass because you're coded under Social Media and Marketing,' Yuan says. 'You'll have to sign in whenever you visit and return the swipe card at the end of the day.'

Yuan swipes and we enter the ground-floor office. Where Bao Tower's offices were modern and spacious, the ministerial offices are drab. The cubicle walls are shoulder-high and packed tightly together. Young secretaries cart around trolleys filled with paper.

'There's email here, but it's rarely used,' Yuan explains. 'Most of the correspondence is paper-based.'

I notice workers peeking over the cubicle walls to observe us. They duck down when they see me seeing them.

Yuan's desk is messy with papers. There is a backlog of documents for the translation teams to review and approve: parliamentary cables, today's edition of the *Port Man Tou Tribune*. On the cubicle wall is a map of the city, collaged out of A4 paper.

I put my hand on her waist.

'Not here,' she whispers. 'There are cameras everywhere.'

I look up. She's right. I put my hands in my pockets.

'So where's my desk?'

'You don't get one. I'll find you a chair later.'

There is a folder marked 重要 on Yuan's desk.

'This one is urgent,' she explains. 'An official communiqué from The Director needs to be vetted before publication. Hmm. But a page is missing. We'll need to check the mailroom.'

We head towards the elevators. A group of salarymen–actors lapse into silence as we approach.

The elevator arrives. They hold the door open for us, but do not enter. The doors close.

Outside the mailroom, we watch a dozen or so elderly women slice open envelopes, datestamp the contents and sort them into piles. They sit shoulder to shoulder on a communal bench, wrinkled and rail thin, wearing identical short-sleeved purple paisley blouses and latex gloves to ward off paper cuts.

Yuan sighs. 'The missing page is in one of those piles.'

She enters the room, but I remain in the hallway. She looks back at me, quizzically.

'I can't go in there,' I say.

'Why not?'

'They all look like my grandmother.'

Dear future citizen-actors of Port Man Tou,

Welcome! Likely you spent the long bus ride here speculating: is Port Man Tou a real city or a series of sound stages and exterior film sets designed to look like a real city? The answer is: both! Port Man Tou is a film set within a city within a film set. The traffic lights work. The elevators work. The telephones work. Try them if you wish!

All on-set facilities have been relocated to maintain authenticity. The wardrobe department has been moved to the shopping mall, where it appears to be a clothing store. Craft services can be found at our many kerbside vendors. On-set catering has been moved to restaurants.

Those of you who pass the initiation process will be granted citizenship, and soon you too will be jaywalking the streets and spitting at the sidewalks like a true local. If, perhaps, you choose to stay long term, you will be eligible for free housing in one of our many luxury apartments in the Canton of The Unwritten. Once you have mastered the art of background acting, you will be given more complicated roles subject to approval from central casting. Who knows? You may become bus driver–actors, or chef-actors, or office worker–actors. The sky is the limit!

Here, in the Canton of TU, there are no scripts. Instead, The Director films everything and every person. And in the editing bay, he will find the narrative. But where are the cameras, you may ask? Where are the microphones? Where are the cast and crew? They are everywhere!

Improvisation is highly encouraged. Let us say, hypothetically, that The Director requires a scene in which a bookstore is burned to the ground. He might employ an assistant-actress at said bookstore. Now the bookstore owner–actor might be a horrible person who makes the assistant-actress's life a living hell. The owner-actor might verbally, psychologically and sexually harass his assistant-actress, shout obscenities at her until, one day, the assistant-actress burns down the bookstore out of spite.

Or, perhaps, The Director will see to it that the bookstore owner–actor never quite has enough money to survive. His wife-actress is embezzling his savings. She is cheating on him, perhaps with The Director himself. The Director might have his producers enquire incessantly about a certain book. They must locate this book, for it is very important to them. Eventually, the bookstore owner–actor finds it on his shelves. It is a manual on how to profit from insurance fraud. The next day or the next month, the bookstore mysteriously burns down. And when it happens, The Director will be there to film its demise.

So many intriguing things happen in Port Man Tou. Day to day, each citizen-actor is free to improvise their role. The owner-actor is free to burn or not burn down his bookstore. If he does not burn it down, The Director will simply conclude that the movie did not require such a scene. Everything is permitted.

So remember, new arrivals: anything you say or do might lead to a pivotal scene in the movie. Even a lowly extra may become, through word and deed, the leading man or lady in this production.

Please remember to sign and return your Release and Waiver of Liability Agreement.

By official decree,
The Department of Immigration

29

TONG LI MO THE DAOIST

Tong Li Mo had never been the wisest of the Emperor's advisers, or the most obsequious, but he did understand the power of a good story.

To distinguish himself and gain the Emperor's favour, he fashioned a tale of his own obscure origins that would pique the Emperor's interest. Rumour had it that Tong Li Mo had been a Buddhist monk in a secluded monastery atop the Thousand Stairs to Heaven, famous for its steep and punishing ascent. He had been revered by the Order for his piety and dedication, attaining the rarefied rank of abbot before he fell – not from grace or favour but in the literal sense, from the top of the brutal and jagged and unforgiving stone steps. When they found him at the bottom of the Thousand Stairs (in some versions unharmed, in others near death), Tong Li Mo awakened to find himself no longer a Buddhist, but a Daoist.

It could not have been further from the truth. Tong Li Mo had never once fallen down a flight of stairs and had no great affinity for Buddhism, much less Daoism. Nevertheless, those in the Imperial Court dubbed him Tong Li Mo the Daoist, and the Emperor took to calling upon him regularly for advice.

And so, in the aftermath of the Taster to the Taster's ominous prophecy – *by the next full cycle of the zodiac, the Emperor will die one thousand deaths* – it was Tong Li Mo to whom the Emperor turned for guidance.

Tong Li Mo pondered. Finally, he explained to the Emperor that the only way to escape his fate was to find one thousand men to die in His stead. Greatly relieved, the Emperor sent forth Tong Li Mo to scour the outlying cities and villages for any and all men who bore a likeness to His own handsome and resplendent face.

In time, the Daoist returned with one thousand men in tow: some taller, some shorter, some with only a passing echo of His features, some who might be mistaken for Him at a distance, and some – four of them – in whom the resemblance was so uncanny that even the Emperor Himself was taken aback.

The Daoist brought in barbers to dye the men's hair and trim their beards. He ordered servants to bathe them with the richest scents of peony and white lotus. He instructed the weavers to weave a thousand suits of finest brocade, so that each man might appear as regal as the Emperor Himself.

Tong Li Mo educated the thousand men in the ways of the Emperor. He taught them how to speak as the Emperor spoke, how to curl their lips in laughter and cruelly inflect Imperial Edicts.

Then he commanded Buo Guong, the Imperial Architect, to design and build an opulent tower to house these false emperors. The Imperial Architect, blinking rapidly, asked Tong Li Mo whether such an extravagance might perhaps be too costly? The Daoist replied that the order had come straight from the Emperor Himself and that no expense was to be spared.

The Imperial Architect dithered and dallied and when the Daoist came to check upon the status of the project, the Imperial Architect admitted to having lost the necessary paperwork.

The Daoist had a copy sent to the Architect's office.

Weeks later, when interrogated as to why the work had still not begun, the Imperial Architect blamed his labourers who – sick of the rubbish that perpetually came out of his mouth – responded by promptly beating him to death.

The deceased's apprentice, Lu Shan Liang, was appointed Imperial Architect.

Blueprints were drawn up and construction began. The tower was impressive even in its unfinished state, spiralling higher and more magnificently than any pagoda. Citizens of the Imperial City were mesmerised by its very structure and definition. They attempted to ascertain the number of storeys, but lost count when the tower disappeared into the clouds. A miserable group of servants were conscripted to operate the pulley shafts to spirit the emperors up and down at all hours of the day.

Within the tower, each of the one thousand and one rooms was grandly and identically furnished. The false emperors took up lodging there. It was even rumoured that the true Emperor, to better obscure His identity, had vacated His palatial suite and joined this complex of pretenders.

In the mirrored halls, each emperor humbled himself and spoke in deference to one another, in case that other emperor was secretly the Emperor Himself.

In order to avert suspicion, the Emperor took up this practice also.

It was not long before the Emperor came to rue this new predicament. The doubles were running amok, strutting the streets of the Imperial City with impunity, holding court, drinking His wine, spending His money, making nonsense proclamations.

Amidst the confusion, the true Emperor issued three Imperial Edicts:

1. That whosoever was caught impersonating the Emperor would be put to death.
2. That whosoever was caught falsely accusing the Emperor would be put to death.
3. That whosoever touched the Emperor would be put to death.

The full force of the disorder that followed was complete and unrelenting. Soon emperors were seen consulting one another in the hallways, teasing apart the language of these edicts and testing the waters of interpretation.

A faction of cowardly emperors, who feared for their lives, came before the Imperial Court and confessed their true identities. The emperor confessors reasoned that because they had come forth *themselves* – and therefore had not been caught, per se – they were exempt from death. The remaining emperors ordered an Imperial Magistrate to deliver their verdict: the first edict implied a retroactive operation; the act of confession was useless and, in fact, had aided their catching in the first place. The emperor confessors were put to death.

The blades of the Imperial Executioners ran red with the blood of these pretenders.

The remaining emperors, trapped and unable to confess or flee, sought to survive the bloodshed by studying the edicts for loopholes, intoning them at all times of the day.

Some neutral emperors avoided making trouble altogether, so as not to run afoul of the second edict. However, certain emperor accusers argued that the true Emperor would never have acted in such a passive or peaceful manner and that it was clear, therefore, that these neutral emperors had been imperfect in their impersonations. The neutral emperors had breached the first edict and were put to death.

The halls were thinning.

Eventually, the majority of emperors reached a consensus on the first edict. They understood it to imply that impersonation *was* permitted. Rather, the true crime was having been caught doing so. They adjusted their behaviours accordingly.

Only an elite handful understood the first edict to the perfect letter of the law: to impersonate was insufficient. Only by *being* the Emperor, by flawlessly embodying Him, personifying Him so completely, would they be above reproach.

One ordered the lake to be drained and filled with wine. Another ordered the wine-lake to be drained and filled with water. Perhaps these were even the same man. Some emperors were quick to accuse this emperor/Emperor, but at a makeshift trial it was found that the accused's actions, though suspect, were entirely consistent with the Emperor's famed inconsistency.

Thereafter, emboldened by each emperor's actions, a faction of amorous emperors sought fit to complete the illusion by taking what was rightfully theirs, or His. They came for the Emperor's concubines, bedded them, gave themselves entirely over to His pleasures and privileges. But the concubines, knowing intimately the true Emperor's length and girth and thrust, denounced each of the impostors. Thus, the amorous emperors were executed.

The citizens of the Imperial City secretly cheered each emperor's death. Nonetheless, they were disheartened, for each time one was slain, it seemed that there were endless more waiting in the wings.

In a terrible and most natural progression, one emperor/Emperor issued a fourth and secret edict, known only to him/Himself. Those who fell afoul of it – whatever it was – were to be put to death.

The remaining emperors, frightened and defeated, realised their only chance was to band together in force against the true Emperor. They convened in secret and announced, by Imperial decree, that the three edicts were hereby abolished.

They were put to death for having breached the fourth edict.

Five emperors remained: the one true Emperor, and those whose names were known only to themselves – Mountain, Dragon, Child and Trickster.

30

Port Man Tou Primary School – Canton of Print to PDF

On one of our rare days off together – me, from the humiliating #BadChinese public appearances that Baby Bao has organised, and Yuan, from her duties in the Department of Verisimilitude – we wander the streets of new cantons. We walk down a row of small shops selling leather goods, dried foods in see-through jars, fruit at a stall with a dusty parapet. Drying laundry hangs on the balconies of the tenants above. The whole block appears worn and weather-beaten, yet given the canton's infancy we know this cannot be true.

Though Yuan is off the clock, she cannot help but assess the accuracy of signage, peruse restaurant menus in windows, observe the behaviour of beggars for telltale signs of artifice.

We count the seconds on a traffic light.

'I was thinking,' I say, 'about how the city in which we live defines us – New Yorkers, Tokyoites, Parisians. The me who lived in Sydney is different from the me who lived in Brisbane and the me who lives here in Port Man Tou. And I am deeply nostalgic for all the cities I've lived in, Sydney especially so, because I chose it. Or it chose me. I don't know. I was always walking, savouring my solitude. Glebe, Ultimo, Newtown. I felt as though I was mapping new territories by my feet alone. Finding my very definition with every step. What if, on my first arrival in Sydney, I had explored Darlinghurst or Surry Hills instead?'

'Would you have been vastly different if so? I find that hard to believe.'

'Not vastly, but maybe in some subtle way. A few years ago, I was on a holiday with friends in Venice. We got hopelessly lost and ducked into a T-shirt shop to ask for directions. The owner was this wild-eyed bearded guy who wore his own merchandise and we spent a good forty minutes listening to him talk about the secret systems of the world. He had this theory about the angles and shapes of streets, the architecture of the city, the height of buildings and landmarks: that all of it was somehow deliberate and therefore conducive to modes of expression.'

'What does that mean?'

'For example, there might be a certain bridge whose very construction is such that an unhappy couple crossing it could only become more unhappy. And that logically there must exist an opposite bridge that, were they to cross it, might—'

'—make them happy? That sounds crazy.'

'Well, yeah, he was obviously nuts, or a fantasist, but there was something seductive about his notion ...'

I can't help but recall now the unpolished quality of his speech, like mine, easily jumbled, led astray, full of detours and belated corrections, as though he himself were so indelibly defined by the labyrinth of Venice and therefore living proof of his own theory.

'I bought a couple of shirts and left. He didn't change my life, I didn't change his, and yet I think of him whenever I walk the streets of a new city, and I wonder if he was right. To what extent does the city change us? What is its effect? Are the things that people think and say to each other, here in Port Man Tou, the same things that they might have said in Sydney?'

We come across a gated building. Maybe a hundred people stand around, arms folded, forming small groups and uneasy alliances, waiting for something to happen. Some silent congress. They look like the hushed crowds that used to gather around televisions in storefront windows to observe moon landings, the deaths of Lennon, the Fischers versus the Spasskys.

A security camera on the second floor of the building points straight at us. I stare deeply into it. I'm compelled to do this every once in a while, at CCTV cameras in malls and department stores, at train stations, at cameras inside banks, for reasons I can't quite articulate. Surely I'm not the only one.

I look around at the crowd of waiting people.

'Is this a school?' I ask.

'En.'

We have fallen into the same patterns, the same rhythms. And our wandering thoughts, our wandering feet, have led us to the very same landmarks.

I stand there, perplexed, wrestling with my déjà vu.

We pause among the crowd, caught in the back with the rest of the suckers who didn't care enough about their children to beat the traffic and secure prime positions in the gauntlet of mothers and fathers and grandparents. We roll on the balls of our feet, trying to get a glimpse – any moment now – feeling complicit in the hum of boredom and anxiety, wondering where the children are, wondering what's taking so long? I observe the crowd.

They seem real.

Finally, the kids begin filing out. The parents and grandparents perk up and scan the crowd for their own. We peel away from the mob, where the young and old have begun to pair together like long-lost atoms.

Once the crowd has dissipated, we enter the school grounds. No one is around. We walk hand in hand, looking through windows at the tiny desks and the blackboards smudged with chalk.

'You know,' I say, 'there was something I wanted to tell you in front of the school in Sydney, but we'd only just met, and it felt too intimate. Maybe intimate's not the right word, but it's the only word I can think of.'

'Tell me.'

'It was about when my mother used to pick me up from primary school.'

'The kiss and ride!'

'Right. There were two pick-up areas, our usual by the swimming pool and another by the tennis court on the other side of the school. For whatever reason, that day she arranged to pick me up at the tennis court instead. She explained it to me many times, making me repeat it so I would remember – "I'll pick you up where? Outside the tennis court. Not the swimming pool." So guess where I waited for her?'

Yuan looks confused, like it's a trick question.

'The *pool*,' I say. 'I waited for what seemed like hours, stubbornly, knowing she was waiting for me at the other exit, probably worried sick. I remember bursting into tears. Eventually she found me at the swimming pool.'

'But why didn't you just go to the tennis court?' she asks.

'That's what I figured out standing with you in front of the school in Sydney. It suddenly clicked, but I didn't say it.'

'Because it was … intimate?'

'Right. It only occurred to me then, all these years later, that – unfairly – I was testing my mother's omniscience … not expecting her to fail.'

Yuan nods in understanding.

Our footsteps echo around the empty grounds.

'Do you … want to have children?' she asks.

Uh-oh.

'One day,' I hedge.

'Long term.'

'Right. Long term.' I wince. 'You?'

'En. One day,' she says. 'But there's one thing I'm sure of. Not here. Not in this city.'

Dear citizens of Port Man Tou,

Today is an auspicious day, indeed, for on this day we welcome our newest citizen and the first child born in Port Man Tou!

Proud parents Xu Mei Feng and Jiang Ji Fa have given birth to a 7lb 8oz baby girl with the following name:

包 宝 宝 的 宝 宝: 包 宝 宝
Bāo Bǎo Bao de bǎo bao: Bāo Bǎo Bao

(Baby Bao's Baby: Baby Bao)

What bounds and strides the city has made! No longer is Port Man Tou the infamous 'ghost city' of the foreign press. Our apartments and offices are filling with tenants. Our streets are teeming with people. And now our hospitals are delivering our newest citizens!

The moment The Director saw the firstborn citizen and his namesake, he decreed a glorious prize be bestowed upon her, the terms of which he has instructed us to communicate:

1. All citizens in the canton where the firstborn came into existence will be granted free wi-fi. In the Canton of Free Wi-fi, you may now access the intranet completely free of charge.
2. The firstborn will be raised in one of the more affluent cantons, befitting her affluent status. The firstborn's parents will remain in the Canton of FWF but will be given generous visitation rights (twice per year) to meet with their beloved offspring. They may also search for any press releases mentioning their child via the intranet (see above).
3. The firstborn and immediate family members agree to license their image and likeness to The Director in perpetuity for his sole use and disposition. Said rights shall be used for promotional purposes, most likely.

The Director's glorious prize will be awarded upon final judgement of a lawsuit brought by the parents of the firstborn citizen, alleging that another couple in the Canton of FWF, who gave birth minutes earlier, are in fact more deserving of The Director's glorious prize.

The defendants have countersued on grounds of slander.

By official decree,
The Department of Social Services

31

CHILD

After the frenzied deaths of the emperor pretenders, the tower where the true Emperor hid fell into silence. Safe in this complex, He had watched in grim fascination as His own ranks were thinned until only a handful remained. Fearing for their lives, they too retreated to the tower. He watched them as they skulked about, watching Him, watching each other, waiting for something to happen.

He grew anxious and irate. Would He have to kill them Himself? What if they tried to kill *Him*? He missed His palace and longed to return and stamp His authority on the Imperial Court once more. How were His citizens faring without their Emperor's guidance and leadership? Poorly, no doubt. But He thought it unwise to descend before the prophecy was fulfilled and His safety assured.

The Emperor thought He might get to know these remaining pretenders and learn their weaknesses so that He might turn them against each other. He was frankly dazzled by their physical likeness. Yet, He found, they had distinct personalities, each with a trait recognisable as His own.

One had a youthful naivety, constantly pestering the others to keep him company, to play games with him, throwing childish tantrums when they refused.

Another was filled with melancholy, prone to bouts of silence, and was often found contemplating distant mountains and the landscape below.

One spoke with supreme arrogance, berated the servants and had a temper as fearsome as a dragon.

But they were mere fractions of Him. They could not recall their lives prior to their arrival in the Imperial City.

It was quite some time later and only by chance that the Emperor noticed a double He had not seen before. Gazing at the palace grounds below, He spotted a golden-coloured speck leading a fawning pack of dull-coloured specks. He rushed to a lower level for a better vantage point, but the pulley operators were lazy and slow, and by the time He reached the third-floor balcony, the speck below was long gone. Still, He knew what He had seen. All this time, some other tricky emperor had been ruling in His place!

Several hours later, camped on the balcony, He had His suspicions confirmed when He spied that same golden-robed doppelganger making His way from the concubines' quarters back to the palace chambers where the true Emperor had once resided.

Overcome with indignation, He rushed back to His doubles and informed them of the impostor in the Imperial Palace.

They descended the tower and strode into the palace, four abreast. A frightened guard admitted them into His chambers, where they confronted the one named Trickster.

Trickster scoffed. Only the true Emperor would rule without fear. And, as He was the only one who sat upon the Imperial Throne, He must therefore be the true Emperor.

The others, thinking Him reckless, returned to the tower to await news of His imminent death.

Days passed, then weeks. Trickster did not die, but instead thrived.

They watched jealously from the tower balconies as Trickster strode the Imperial Grounds with impunity. In fact, Trickster made sure to pass in sight of the tower wherever He went, in order to stoke their frustration.

Trickster knew that the only way He could truly survive the prophecy was by goading the others to put themselves in harm's way, and so once in a while He would ascend the tower to visit with them, recounting recent proclamations He had ordered, and cataloguing His numerous sexual exploits with the Imperial Concubines. Magnanimously, He invited the 'false emperors' to descend the tower and rule for a day in His place.

If they dared.

Dragon was the first to descend, and He returned that night exhilarated at having successfully wielded His authority without succumbing.

Child's turn came next. He deferred matters of State – book burnings, people burnings, Imperial Court petitions – and spent His time in search of playmates with whom He might jostle and roughhouse.

He would summon fearful generals or advisers, some unlucky lord or scullion from the nearby halls, to join Him in His quarters. There, they would laugh forcefully at His jokes, play at xiangqi and Matriarch's chess, patiently parse His new and whimsical rules (*Let one side be filled with shahs!*), and, though their skills far outstripped His, they would arrange to have their opponent obliterate them and end these stressful mind games once and for all.

Child heard many tales of the Emperor's past cruelties, and each time burst into tears, shocked and inconsolable, as though it were another man entirely who had debased His concubines, watched His father die, and banished His brother to the Sixth Level of Hell.

Once, bored of the usual offerings from the Imperial Kitchen, Child demanded a menu so that He might try a never-before-tasted dish. He perused the menu with deep intensity, as though He had found art in the maze of words and the spaces between each brushstroke. Finally (for He could not read), He selected a dish whose characters seemed the most striking and wondrous to Him:

猪妈妈为孩子哭泣

Mother Swine Weeps for Child

When Imperial Chef Bei emerged from the Imperial Kitchen to present the baby pig for slaughter, Child could not bear to see the poor beast killed. Its barely opened eyes and helpless grunts touched His heart. He cancelled the meal and took the piglet into His arms, like a dear and beloved friend.

Child christened His new pet the Imperial Swine and appointed it Chief Adviser to the Emperor, the rank previously held by Tong Li Mo the Daoist, who was thus unceremoniously demoted to the role of Adviser to the Adviser.

The next day, the Daoist came before the Emperor to appeal this mad decision, not knowing that he was beseeching none other than Trickster.

Trickster, perfectly intoning the Emperor's forever-wounded pitch, reminded the Daoist that the Adviser to the Adviser was no longer of high rank and therefore forbidden from addressing Him in person. Tong Li Mo the Daoist must therefore direct any matters of import to his superior, the Chief Adviser.

The Chief Adviser grunted its apparent agreement with Trickster.

Tong Li Mo was made to prostrate himself before the Imperial Swine. On his hands and knees, he appealed to the pig's sense of logic and propriety: *Surely a swine could not properly advise the Emperor on matters of the State, a swine could not know nearly as well as Tong Li Mo the subtleties of the Emperor's moods and whims. And what of the Emperor's enemies*, he added delicately, *who might hear of such unusual developments, and perhaps ridicule Him?*

The Imperial Swine's heart was not sufficiently moved. It turned away from Tong Li Mo, more interested in a nearby trough of slop.

Tong Li Mo's desperate gaze flitted back and forth between the

Chief Adviser and Trickster, who took glee in having seen and heard a grown man address a pig as his superior.

As there was no further business, Trickster dismissed the Adviser to the Adviser from the Imperial Court.

In the weeks thereafter, the Daoist often encountered the Imperial Swine roaming the hallways and cursed it under his breath, for he was forbidden by law from ever passing his superior. Moreover, he became convinced that the Imperial Swine knew his daily movements for, increasingly, he seemed to encounter it on the way to his most important meetings and engagements.

In its slow and meandering wake, he wavered between following the swine – hoping it might make a turn and let him hurry down the path – and retreating, backtracking, taking detours that were so agonisingly lengthy that when he finally arrived at his destination, the committees had already dispersed, having made their decisions in his absence.

At times he found it in graceless repose in front of the sole entrance to the Imperial Court, asleep and unmovable (he was bitterly certain that the Imperial Swine was the reincarnation of his ex-wife), and he would attempt to wake the swine, shoo and cajole it to no avail. The Imperial Swine would simply smile at him before settling back to sleep, thereby preventing him from carrying out his courtly duties.

Once, while he forlornly navigated an alternate route through the northern wing, a petition was heard suggesting the removal of the Adviser to the Adviser from his lofty post. It seemed the running of the Empire had proceeded well enough despite the Daoist's frequent and unprofessional absences. With no one present to object, the petition passed unanimously and the Daoist was relegated to the faceless ranks.

In playful moods, Trickster would allow the Imperial Swine to sit upon His throne and rule as it saw fit. Trickster would play the humble servant, translating its squeals and grunts for the benefit of the members of the Imperial Court.

On the days that the Imperial Swine sat, farmers would come before the Court in droves. They reasoned that a swine, born and raised on a humble farm itself, would lend a sympathetic ear to their petitions for lower taxes. The Imperial Swine listened as the farmers' spokesman presented their arguments, and then it paused to consider its response.

It defecated on the throne.

Trickster declared this a good omen.

The farmers cheered. The order was given to lower the farmers' taxes immediately.

Rumour spread of the Imperial Swine's generosity, and the Emperor's ministers, seeking to add to their already-deep pockets, rallied together to bring their own petition before it.

Once again, the Swine defecated on the throne.

The ministers cheered.

However, Trickster, with a perfunctory glance at the stool, gleefully declared this a bad omen indeed.

The order was given to double the ministers' taxes immediately.

Thus, the Imperial Swine became the champion of the farmers – by constantly defecating in their presence – granting them ever-larger plots of land and greater sums of profit, while earning the ire of the ministers – by constantly defecating in their presence – stripping their power and status until they became nothing more than glorified beggars.

Made rich by the Imperial Swine, the farmers abandoned their lands and lived lives of leisure in luxurious estates. They mingled with lords and generals. They held soirees. To protect their political, financial and social interests, they joined the ministry.

The ministers, rendered destitute, moved to the outskirts of the city. They tilled the land and took up farming.

32

Garden Books – Hangjin South Road, Canton of The Unwritten

Baby Bao's driver ceremoniously opens the car door. Baby Bao and I step onto the kerb. This is my first book launch event and I am a ball of nerves. The place is packed with attendees. Christ. I linger outside. Perhaps I can make a run for it.

'Come inside. Stop being a baby! There is only room for one baby and that is me. Hahaha!!!'

He drags me inside.

Rows and rows of 'my book' accost my sightline. I had always wanted to be a writer but not like this – my pixelated ID photo blown up to fit the cover, the title *#BadChinese: The Authorised Biography* splashed across the front, with pages filled with ghostwritten words I did not approve.

I have been too embarrassed to ask Yuan for help in translating (even though she's not here today to interpret for the event, she has surely read the book – I saw a copy of it on her desk at the Department of Verisimilitude), and so have been attempting to translate the book myself, in my apartment, character by painstaking character, with an English–Chinese language dictionary. The progress has been slow, but the chapters I have been able to decode thus far have been reams of complete and utter bullshit, mixed with alarmingly personal anecdotes specific to my life that represent, surely, some egregious breach of privacy.

Chapter one is an unfortunate record of my intranet browsing history since arriving in Port Man Tou. In my defence, I didn't know they were tracking that stuff.

Chapter two is a comprehensive list of all the various malapropisms I've unknowingly uttered in Mandarin during media appearances in the context of #BadChinese.

Chapter three is filled with baby photos of me that I have no idea how Baby Bao managed to get a hold of.

I can only imagine in dreaded horror what the remaining chapters – once translated – will reveal to me. I'd burn the book, but there are thousands more in bookstores all over the city. *Fuck.* Maybe I should burn all the bookstores.

The Director leads me to the stage and sits beside me, playing the humble moderator and translator. He is holding a copy of the book, as though he wrote it himself.

What an asshole.

Then he takes the microphone and announces that I will be doing a reading. I try to refuse, but he encourages the crowd to goad me into it.

He hands me the microphone and the book. It is opened to chapter two.

I am confounded by the presence of pinyin under each line, hastily transcribed in The Director's hand. I read out the pinyin, but this phonetic crutch, far from making things easier, in fact achieves only the opposite. In front of the crowd, my slowly improving semi-fluency in Mandarin deserts me. I mess up even the easiest words, painfully aware of each of my failures of diction from the tuts and titters of the crowd.

Baby Bao dashes off once it's time for the book signing, citing urgent business. What follows is an hour of signings, small talk from the line of readers who are delighted at my lack of fluency, and selfies where they encourage me to imitate my fucked-up ID-photo face.

Finally, as the line reaches its last few stragglers, I can see the relief of an end in sight.

But, oh no. Yuan is here, the final person in the line. She's been here the entire time.

There is no hole deep enough for me to crawl into.

The penultimate book signee – an old grandmother who pinches my cheek – squints at my signature on the inside cover of the book and walks off, leaving only Yuan and, thankfully, a practically empty bookstore.

'Don't say a word,' I plead.

She honours my desperate request by holding back laughter.

'Can I get *my* copy signed?'

'If you want the author's signature, go ask Baby Bao.' I shake the signing cramps out of my hand. 'I've got to give it to him. He really found the perfect way to fuck with me this time.'

'What do you mean?'

I stand up.

'I always wanted to be an author. To write something good. Something true. About … I don't know, my family, everything that is important to me, but now it's spoiled by *this* garbage, and I won't be able to walk into a bookstore ever again – my safe space – and feel the way I used to.'

'Well, maybe you can write that true thing, that good thing, and publish it one day. Then you can replace *this* memory with something better.'

'Yeah. Maybe you're right. Let's get the hell out of here.'

'In a minute,' she says. 'I want to buy a few books.'

Yuan lingers in Chinese Literature. I wander over to the English section.

In the West, people browse bookstores with heads tilted sideways to read the titles. But here, there is no need for head tilting. The titles and author names are printed vertically along the spines. And I wonder: do literate Westerners statistically suffer more neck pain compared with their Chinese counterparts?

Here she comes, book in hand.

'What've you got there?' I ask.

'*Xibao* by Yi Shu,' she says.

'Ah! The book you borrowed over and over from the village library.'

'You remembered. How about you? Are you going to buy something?'

I scan the shelves, pick out Milton's *Paradise Lost*, and leaf through it.

But the book is blank: the pages empty, except for a single page at the front, a single line.

It reads: *How can you be sure she's not an actor?*

'What the ...?'

Yuan looks at me, confused. She takes my book, flips through the pages. All blank except that one page.

She opens her book. It's empty too. Except for a single line, in Chinese.

你怎能确定他不是演员?

Yuan begins to translate, but I already know. 'Let me guess. "How can you be sure he's not an actor?"'

A long period of silence and confusion.

Finally, I say, 'I'm not an actor.'

'I'm not an actor.'

I return her book to her. She returns my book to me.

'There's only one way to tell,' I say, slowly.

'Tell?'

'That you and me, we're not actors.'

'What is it?'

'We need to sleep together.'

She snorts. Not the best reaction for my ego.

'And how would that prove anything?'

Hmm. Hadn't thought that far yet.

'Well. See, the body doesn't lie. So ...' – nervous laugh – 'and, I mean, I'm a simple guy. I can't really multitask. Like, I wouldn't be able to act and, uh, perform, at the same time. That would be too much. So in that situation, if I was an actor, which I'm not, but if I was then you would be able to figure out that the jig was up pretty quick. But not too quick. Do you know what I mean?'

Yuan is trying very hard to maintain some grace and composure. But her lip is twitching: offended or amused, I am not sure.

'Hypothetically. Let's say I am an actor,' says Yuan, 'which I'm not.'

'Let's.'

'Then your stupid plan would only work if I found you repulsive and was a bad enough actor to let it show.'

'Do you find me repulsive?'

'After your suggestion? Yes!'

'This is just Baby Bao being Baby Bao,' I say. 'He's messing with us.'

'How did he know we'd pick these specific books?' she asks.

I have a hunch.

'I'm willing to bet every Chinese book in here is addressed to you. Every English book to me.'

I pick another title.

Empty. Except for the stupid line.

'Look,' I say, 'it's the same.'

'This one too.'

We go to the next aisle. All of the Chinese books are addressed to Yuan.

'What a fucking waste of paper,' I say. 'And what if we'd never even opened a book?'

'Come on.' She looks at me. 'Have you ever gone into a bookstore and not opened a book?'

'Good point.'

'Look,' she says, her voice suddenly a whisper. 'Over there.'

A man is perusing a book in the Business Bestsellers section. He seems engrossed.

'If all the books here are false,' she says, 'then he's not really reading at all.'

'What are you going to do?'

'I'm going to check his book.'

Yuan strides towards the aisle. Positions herself behind him as she pretends to scan the shelves. He glances at her and angles the book away from her sightline. She goes to the other side of him. He angles his book away again. She grows exasperated.

'不好意思, 请问你在看什么书? 看起来挺有趣的!'

He ignores her.

'我可以看一下吗?' she says.

'书架上还有很多本一样的书,' he snaps.

'我就要这本.' She grabs for the book.

'你疯了吧?!'

Yuan jabs a finger at his face. '哈! 我就知道这本书不是真书! 你是演员! 我是逼真程度调查局的!'

The man drops the book and runs off in fear. Yuan picks it up, opens it.

'Yep. Same as all the others,' she says, returning to me.

'What did you say to him?'

'I told him I'm from the Department of Verisimilitude, and I knew he was an actor.'

'Nice one.'

We end up buying the books. Why not? Mementos of this strange occasion. The cashier – an old man – has witnessed the commotion and looks wary, perhaps afraid that Yuan might report him too. He rings the total up on the cash register.

I take the cash out of my wallet to pay.

I am not used to seeing this money. Not RMB, but a new denomination – ฿1, ฿10, ฿20 – with the image of Baby Bao grinning up at me from the face of each banknote.

All bear his likeness in different poses. His mouth slightly askew, his eyelids caught mid-blink. His face an arc of amusement that seems to escalate according to the value of the note. The smirk of the ฿50 that breaks into an ever-widening grin as I flip through the ฿100, the ฿200, the ฿500, then into the four-figure notes, five figures, six, with his mouth mid-giggle, until I reach, finally, the ฿1,000,000 note, with his head rocked back in howling laughter and visible tears streaming down his cheeks.

Dear citizens of Port Man Tou,

Just a friendly reminder to residents of the Canton of Illegal Tender that the 'cut-off date' to convert your RMB to our new city-wide denomination (hereafter referred to simply as 'the Bao') is fast approaching.

From the paper mills to the printing works, from the testing labs to the streets, the launch of the Bao has been a resounding success!

Soon, banks and stores will no longer accept RMB as legal tender. The same goes for ATMs and vending machines.

Anyone caught attempting to spend or pass off any notes in RMB will be prosecuted. Crimes involving minor sums will incur a pecuniary fine (payable in Bao). Anything larger may result in capital punishment.

Officials from the Department of Finance will be making scheduled visits to each and every home following the cut-off date, in order to confiscate any remaining hoards of RMB. Please accept them into your homes and comply with their demands.

Nameless dissenters have levelled baseless accusations at the pre-eminent Director. They say he is a fraud and a charlatan who is cheating the citizens of Port Man Tou out of their hard-earned money, in order to keep his troubled productions afloat. Rumour has it that citizens have even been barred from leaving the city altogether. This could not be further from the truth! Any citizen is free to leave the city whenever they so please. The exit process is very simple:

1. Fill out a Temporary Departure form (standard fees apply).
2. Submit the form to your local cadre representative from the People's Investigations Bureau, who will make an assessment based on criteria, such as [redacted].
3. Provide the necessary sum ($100,000,000) for the security deposit, a generous half of which will be refunded upon your return.

By official decree,
The Department of Finance

33

THE MANCHURIAN

The Imperial Court had come into possession of an intriguing curio: a grand automaton, the likes of which none had ever seen. The eunuchs had arranged for its formal presentation after a thorough inspection by the Imperial Guards. Members of the Court were allowed to approach the automaton and marvel at its construction.

Two thrones of white marble faced each other over a boxwood and ebony chessboard with pieces carved by the finest ivory artists in the Empire. On one throne sat the upper body of a man made of brass whose piercing jade eyes and stately features resembled that of a Manchu lord. Henceforth in myth and song he would be known as the Manchurian.

The other throne was empty.

A compartment below the chessboard housed the automaton's whirring clockwork innards.

None stepped forth to challenge the Manchurian. So the machine began to play both sides. To those who might have doubted the machine's aptitude, it soon became clear that it could play, and play well. Members of the Court traded theories on the mystery of its operation.

Of course, the Court had seen its fair share of automatons over the years – birds that chirped and tiny wind-up toys whose actions soon became predictable – but none so impressive as this.

The game unfolded at lightning speed, white and black coming to blows, trading pieces. And all the while the Manchurian's jade eyes darted about, sizing up the Court and all its dimensions.

A fearful whisper spread that a demon or spirit inhabited the machine's innards. Scholars and other learned men of the Court were quick to scoff at this claim, but slow to proffer their own explanation, for fear they would appear foolish.

And when the Emperor sought their scholarly opinion of the automaton, including the mystery of its operation, they replied in riddles and rhetorical questions, intoning archaic words and portentous phrases that were even more mysterious than the mystery they were supposed to explain. Indeed, this was how they had survived for so long under the Emperor's cruel reign: by carefully choosing their words so that they were never right and never wrong, but forever nestled in the gulf in between – right in their wrongness, and wrong in their rightness – striving always for this, the height (and depth) of scholarly ecstasy.

They asked to further observe the machine in action before arriving at any hasty conclusions. This seemed reasonable to the Emperor, and He gave orders for the first match of the exhibition to begin.

The first challengers treated the machine as a simpleton.

They were soundly beaten.

When, in jest, the mediocre scholar Dao Ting Qiao mocked the machine by moving a piece illegally, the Manchurian rebuked the scholar with a shake of its head and returned the offending knight to its original position. A murmur made its way around the Court.

Men lined up to match wits with the machine: a rich farmer; a Court attendant; a visiting merchant.

Each was vanquished with grim ferocity.

Then the new Imperial Architect came forth to try his luck.

He was skilled, had clearly studied the seminal texts, and twice played crafty moves that appeared to give the Manchurian much pause. But Lu Shan Liang had not the killer instinct to capitalise. The Manchurian cast its commanding gaze upon him, redoubled its pressure, and he lost focus. Following a taxing exchange of pieces, the new Imperial Architect was soon dispatched.

He stood, and was much surprised to see the Manchurian offer its hand. The only time it had done so in the exhibition thus far.

As Lu Shan Liang grasped the Manchurian's hand, some trace sensation caused his heart to skip. If the young man had glimpsed his *true* opponent's face in, say, the scholarly gardens – impossibly, in some happier life in which this automaton never had cause to have been built – might he have marvelled at their resemblance?

Lu Shan Liang returned to the crowd none the wiser.

The Manchurian seemed to collect itself for a moment, before turning its head towards the throne and fixing its unblinking gaze upon the Emperor Himself.

Disquieted, the Emperor sought a reprieve from the automaton's unrelenting eye. So as not to appear ridiculous and cowardly, He instructed one of His advisers to circulate a rumour that the Manchurian's jade eyes could penetrate its opponent's soul and read the secret contents therein. As expected, the Court grew hysterical. A few courtiers fainted. Magnanimously, the Emperor ordered that the automaton henceforth be blindfolded.

The effects of the blindfold were immediate. Guided by the voice of an official, who announced the coordinates aloud, the Manchurian's speed slowed. It ruminated over tricky plays. Still, any opponent who thought he might have gained the upper hand was sorely mistaken. In the darkened fog of each game, the machine reverted to defensive stances and more careful play.

By day's end, the Manchurian remained undefeated.

They removed its blindfold. Once again, the machine turned towards the Emperor with cold regard, its piercing stare inscrutable to the last.

Word spread like wildfire throughout the Imperial City. By nightfall, every citizen – from the richest lord to the lowliest urchin – had heard of the dread machine that, with calm and expressionless visage, had come to challenge the Emperor and prove Him fallible.

The grand masters of the game came from all four corners of the Imperial City to match wits against the Manchurian.

The automaton faced Grand Master Hong's leaping knights, Grand Master Ouyang's free-flowing attrition, and Grand Master Zhang's diamond defence. To the untrained eye, the automaton appeared to struggle. Indeed, though the games were closely fought, it did not win a single match.

Yet Hong, Ouyang and Zhang could hardly share the crowd's enthusiasm for their victories. No one but the masters understood that they had been outmatched. The automaton had teased out their hidden weaknesses, flawlessly taken them to the very brink of defeat and then, inexplicably, relinquished its hard-fought advantage and allowed them to scrape out a win.

The Emperor announced to the Imperial Court that *He* would try His hand against the Manchurian the following morning. The results of the second day had spurred Him into boldness, for He Himself carried an unassailable record against Grand Masters Hong, Ouyang and Zhang.

In point of fact, only one man had ever defeated Him: the deceased Grand Master Ji, who had been summarily executed for treason, having dared defeat the Emperor in a game of chess.

Each night, the Manchurian was wheeled into the treasury vaults to repose under constant watch by Imperial Guards, to rule out foul play.

No one had yet determined how to turn off the automaton, and its gears continued grinding throughout the night as though the machine were constantly in deep thought, and incapable of rest. Indeed, it had been designed purposely so, to protect its creator within, who frequently spoke in his sleep, in muffled and melancholic tones.

Wuer. Wuer. Wuer.

But it was only a misremembered echo of some past life, some meaningless mantra. For only vengeance now could balance the ledger of his pain.

The moment arrived, and every impression was heightened and terrifying, as in a fever dream. From inside the automaton, Lu Dong Pu peered through the scopes and watched Him, in flowing robes, descend the throne and encircle the machine thrice, a smile playing across the Emperor's lips.

Did He suspect?

The Emperor sat.

It was a shock to see his brother's face so youthful still, untouched by time, as though the Emperor had somehow relinquished His heaviest burdens. A life well lived. And here *he* lay, atrophied, inside this instrument of hate, his eyesight fading, his breathing shallowed, mired in his own filth. He was dying, his body already a sepulchre.

The pieces were set. The game began. But he had not the ceremony to carry on, to dazzle his opponent with his superior skills.

There was no need to savour or prolong the pain.

It was the slightest of sleights, the way the automaton played its turn while, at the same time, releasing the hidden blade from the slab beneath the chessboard. The courtiers did not see, at first, what had happened, and when they *did* see, they did not understand. It only dawned on them when the Emperor cried out in fear and pain, His robes already soaked with royal blood, and His guards rushed the machine with weapons drawn.

Entranced, those in attendance watched as the Manchurian reached across the board, took the Emperor's shah into its hand and with inhuman strength crushed the piece into finest powder.

His guards attempted to rescue Him, but the blade had pierced His bowels and pinned Him to the seat. They attacked the Manchurian, hacked off its arm and head, tore its torso from the base. But finding no assassin hidden there, they turned their attentions to the slab below the chessboard, ran their spears and swords through the gears, punctured the sanctum within until the Manchurian's blood and filth pooled the floor of the Imperial Court.

The Emperor was dead.

So too, His killer.

The Imperial Traitor had earned his name.

34

Meeting Room, Bao Tower – Daqiao Road,
Canton of Time's Uncertain Arrow

A group of producers representing the national broadcaster NCTV have arrived from Beijing to meet with The Director. They're ushered into a conference room where Yuan and I have been waiting for the last twenty minutes. We shake hands and pose for a group selfie at their request.

The Director takes his place at the head of the table. A market researcher–actor in a white smock begins a PowerPoint presentation.

Yuan translates for me.

'*Welcome, honoured guests. As you know, we have experienced a surge of interest in Port Man Tou since the introduction of the viral campaigns featuring the #BadChinese. The leaked CCTV footage where he unknowingly eats spicy Sichuan food and ends up requiring medical assistance has been particularly popular on the national news and on social media.*'

I go red. Fortunately, the room is dark and no one can see my embarrassment.

'*This next slide shows interest in Port Man Tou, pre- and post-#BadChinese. Metro hotels are consistently at full occupancy as compared with this time last year, when many were empty. In fact, Port Man Tou has rocketed to an unprecedented eighth position in favoured domestic travel destinations. Last year, we were not even in the top five hundred. The city's Mass Rapid Transport is undergoing aggressive expansion to deal with the influx of tourist-actors. There are many factors for the upsurge, of course, but the data shows a strong correlation between Port Man Tou's new-found popularity and what we call the #BadChinese bump.'*

The broadcasters nod, impressed.

'In recent national surveys, respondents in their forties and over tended to select the words "shameful", "disgraceful" and "deplorable" in their reaction to #BadChinese, while younger respondents were more forgiving, and in fact tended to glamorise his Western roots. Crucially, there was strong interest across all demographics in seeing #BadChinese assume some as-yet-undefined media personality role.'

Baby Bao pauses for dramatic effect, then adds, *'And this is where NCTV comes in.'*

The NCTV producer says, *'Yes. As I mentioned to The Director over dinner last night, we are very impressed! We are principally in agreement. NCTV will begin our partnership with Daedalic with a special episode of our popular dating show to be set in Port Man Tou and featuring #BadChinese as a surprise contestant.'*

I glance at Yuan. She doesn't seem pleased.

'It is certain to be a ratings success,' says Baby Bao. *'He looks presentable until he opens his mouth and attempts to speak. Then everyone will fall over in hysterics. Watch this.'*

Baby Bao instructs Yuan to cease interpreting for a moment. Then he says to the group, deliberately maintaining eye contact with me, '现在我要假装说个笑话，等我说完了，你们就笑，他肯定也会跟着大笑的.'

I try to figure out what he's saying. Something about a joke …

Suddenly, Baby Bao bursts into laughter. So do the producers. Out of habit, I follow suit. This prompts further bouts of laughter.

'太好了!' says the lead producer. Baby Bao nods to Yuan to resume interpreting. *'Wonderful!'*

'Is he single?' asks the woman producer.

Everyone turns to me for the answer. I freeze.

After a moment of awkward silence, Baby Bao answers for me. '是的,' he says, nodding.

Yuan hesitates.

Baby Bao repeats, '是的,' adding, '他是个单身汉.'

'*Yes. He is single.*'

The lead producer says, '*We will have our writers invent humorous scenarios. Perhaps cue cards written in pinyin so we can hear his terrible accent.*'

'*And karaoke,*' offers Baby Bao.

'*Karaoke!*' They laugh and one of them writes this down.

'*And as previously discussed,*' says the lead producer, '*if the pilot episode is a ratings success, NCTV will order a full season to be produced in Port Man Tou, as well as exercise an option to take advantage of the city's filming incentives on three variety shows and two dramatic series, starring #BadChinese. Don't worry that he can't act. The worse he acts, the better the ratings, I promise you that.*'

Baby Bao's relief is palpable.

The lead producer clears his throat. '*It seems that Port Man Tou is the name on everyone's lips these days. We saw CNN's profile on the city last week. Very impressive, a few concerns notwithstanding.*'

'*Thank you,*' says Baby Bao, without missing a beat. '*As you can see, we are anticipating growth not only in the film industry, but also key sectors of construction, business services, retail and tourism. And I assure you, the report's concerns about the city's safety and, more importantly, its financial position were based completely on inaccurate fact-checking. My legal team is demanding a full retraction.*'

'*We have no reason to doubt you,*' says the lead producer. '*However, our superiors would appreciate a detailed financial statement before we sign the contract.*'

'*Of course.*' Baby Bao's smile is visibly strained.

Ministerial Office Complex – National Road, Canton of The Unwritten

The next morning, I find Yuan in her cubicle, translating an article from the *Port Man Tou Tribune*.

'Hey,' I say to her. She sips coffee from a mug with my meme printed on it.

'Baby Bao gave me some DVDs of that NCTV game show. Want to watch them with me?'

'You mean the *dating* show?' She makes a gagging expression. 'I'm busy.'

'Come on. Help me out.'

'You want me to help you score a date with one of the contestants? No thanks.'

'I want you to help me avoid looking like a fool on national television.'

'You deserve it for failing to point out to the NCTV producers that you aren't single.'

'*You* didn't point it out either.'

'I was doing my job,' she argues.

'So was I.'

'Being bad at something isn't a real job.'

I open my mouth, then close it again, and finally let out a deflated laugh.

Yuan looks confused.

'I was about to defend #BadChinese,' I explain. 'Defend my own badness. But if I had ended up doing *that*, then I'd know I'd become completely brainwashed by Baby Bao's own warped logic.'

'Shhh!' She nods to a CCTV camera in the ceiling.

I look at the DVD in my hand. The title reads: 选我吧.

I parse this into English. '*Choose Me.*'

'I'm impressed! You actually pay attention when I teach you new words. If you keep this progress up, #BadChinese might no longer apply.'

'#MediocreChinese just doesn't have the same ring to it,' I say.

Yuan examines the DVD. 'The show is syndicated overseas under a different title. *The Interrogation.*'

Metro Megamall – Baby Bao Road, Canton of Illegal Tender

A large crowd is gathered in the pavilion near the entrance of the Metro Megamall, waiting impatiently for the ribbon-cutting ceremony to finish and the doors to open. I share the stage with five boring businessmen-actors in suits. At the front of the stage, the presenter boasts about the mall's development: built in record time across a huge expanse – fifty-two hectares – and recently confirmed as the third-largest shopping mall in the world.

Finally, I'm summoned to cut the ribbon. An assistant hands me a pair of oversized scissors, the same one used for every ceremony. I suppose when it comes to giant scissors, you only ever need one pair.

I pose for the photographers, then snip the ribbon.

After the ceremony, I duck behind the stage and slip on a baseball cap to avoid being recognised by snap-happy bystanders. I look for Yuan but can't find her in the crowd. I text her. She texts back. She's already inside the mall, buying shoes.

Shoppers stream up and down the walkways while garish synth-pop blasts from the sound system. Security guards patrol the area in electric buggies.

I find the shoe store, and Yuan, who is trying on a pair of heels.

'Thanks for your moral support out there,' I say, sarcastically.

'Look at the strap on this. Slightly damaged! I'm going to get it confiscated for analysis at the Department of Verisimilitude. I bet I can get Eric Lai to release the evidence to me later.'

'Yuan, I am shocked and disgusted. That is an egregious misuse of power.'

'We can head to the electronics department later. Eric can probably get a stereo confiscated for you, too,' she says.

'Cool.'

Yuan and I take the escalator to the top floor, where a huge crowd is lined up at the cinema ticket counter.

'What's going on?' I ask.

Yuan translates the titles on the marquee.

'*Death of a Pagoda. The Funicular. Untitled. Don't Encourage Him. Maximum Overdrive: The Director's Cut. A Great Gatsby. A Great Gatsby II. The Imperial March. Selected Shorts 1992–2017.*'

'That's weird,' I say. 'A cineplex that shows only films by one director? *The* Director? Look, most of them are sold out. I find it hard to believe that this many people want to watch *Untitled*.'

Yuan shushes me, then whispers, 'It *is* out of the ordinary. Maybe this is how The Director justifies his success? By ordering his citizen-actors to frequent his films, over and over? All those salaries flowing back to him.'

'You were right. It is a scam.'

'But what can we do?'

I shrug.

A middle-aged cinemagoer-actor stares at me in passing and whispers to her husband.

I don't have the energy to take a selfie or do a signing. Oh shit. She's calling to other people around her and pointing at me.

'Quick,' I say. 'Let's go this way.'

We head down the escalators. A small group of people follow after us. Downstairs, we approach a security guard. Yuan exchanges some words with him. He peers closely at me, then breaks into a grin of recognition. He hands her the keys to his security buggy. I jump in the driver's seat of the buggy and key the ignition. Yuan sits in the passenger seat. We peel away from the swarming crowd.

'You sure you know how to drive this?' asks Yuan.

'Sure, but the steering wheel's on the wrong side.'

We weave through the human traffic.

When it looks like we're free of the citizen-actors following us, I reduce the speed to a more leisurely crawl.

'Most of the citizens in this canton are locals,' Yuan explains.

'How can you tell?'

'Their accent. They speak in the Zhongyuan dialect. These are the villagers who were forced to sell their land for the development of the city.'

'Forced?'

'Regulations on resettlement and land requisition are pretty strict in China. It's common to hear about displaced villagers numbering in the millions. If they refuse to move, they are ... *persuaded* into accepting the terms of resettlement. Usually, there are many petitions to stop the development, but you can see what happened here. If there were petitions, they failed.'

We come to a traffic blockade. I jump out and push the blockade aside.

'What are you doing?' Yuan asks. 'We can't go in there.'

'We're never going to know what's real if we don't stray off the path.'

We drive into the incomplete section of the mall. It is cavernous and dusty. I switch on the headlights and we barrel through, passing empty directories and signs pointing to different international zones – France, Greece, Italy. The mall's unrealised ambition. In the middle of the track there is an empty Venetian-style canal that runs the entire length of the wing. Its walls and ceilings are painted like frescoes.

The fixtures soon disappear; the walls become unpainted concrete blocks. There are square holes in the concrete where windows ought to be, hastily boarded over with bamboo. The afternoon sun pokes fingers of dusty light through the thatches.

I stop the buggy. We get out.

On a nearby wall, I see some graffiti in Chinese.

'Something The Director?' I attempt to translate.

'*Fuck* The Director,' Yuan says. 'I suppose not all the villagers were happy about turning over their farms to Port Man Tou and becoming citizen-actors.'

We walk to the opening in the wall and peer through the thatch.

Outside, we see humble patches of corn and wheat arranged in miniature rows. Dozens of tiny farms – illegal – abut the mall, hidden behind it.

Their invisible rebellion.

Dear citizens of Port Man Tou,

Pursuant to The Director's grand effort to standardise time throughout the city, the following items are now prohibited per the Regulations of Port Man Tou Municipality on Administration of Units and Measurements 2017 r 13.1:

- Clocks
- Watches
- Mobile phones (smartphones and otherwise)
- Calendars (digital or otherwise)
- Internet devices (intranet-only devices excepted).

These regulations have already undergone beta testing in the Canton of Time's Uncertain Arrow and, as they have proven a complete success, The Director has now ordered a city-wide rollout.

Officers from the Bureau will make randomised sweeps throughout your local cantons. Possession of any of the abovementioned contraband will result in immediate seizure and forfeiture. Violators will be prosecuted to the full extent of the law.

Per municipal law, televisions, personal laptops and work computers may continue to be used, provided their secondary timekeeping functions are disabled by a sanctioned officer.

Henceforth, the master clock atop Bao Tower will be the sole source of timekeeping for Port Man Tou.

All local print and broadcast media outlets have already adopted Port Man Tou Standard Time (PMTST). You may use these notifications to orient yourselves throughout the day.

As for the rumours that the date and time atop Bao Tower are wrong, any concerned citizens are welcome to contact us directly. Please leave your full name, phone number and citizen ID, and an officer will personally follow up with you. Rest assured, we treat such allegations very seriously, and are compiling detailed records of each complaint and complainant.

There is one final matter to discuss. That is the 'joke' that has been circulating among the Canton of TUA, wherein citizens have been known to ask, in a sardonic, defeated tone, what day it is today. Do not think the Bureau does not understand that this is some sort of subversive expression, however minor or inconsequential.

By official decree,
The People's Investigations Bureau

35

LU SHAN LIANG

Before the watchful eyes of the Imperial Court, the Emperor's guards extricated His limp body from the clutches of the Manchurian. There it was, for all to see. The Emperor had been assassinated.

The machine had bled from their swords and spears, but its gears continued to grind. Uncertain whether they had truly killed the demon within – and not daring to open the machine lest they unleash some secret trap – the Emperor's guards took the automaton to the blast furnaces, where long ago the Emperor had ordered the burning of the books.

Those few who witnessed the burning of the automaton spoke of having seen, amidst the roaring flame, the shape of the demon itself. Its skull crowned in melted bronze.

Whispers from the scholarly gardens completed the tale. The grand masters were certain that the body, charred beyond recognition, was that of Lu Dong Pu, the Imperial Traitor. He who had escaped the Six Levels of Hell. He who had liberated the citizens from the Emperor's oppressive reign. He who would henceforth be revered as a hero of the people.

Now came the power struggles. Ministers and generals arranged themselves into tentative factions. Court officials spread poisonous lies. Concubines pressed their claims to power by virtue of their swollen bellies. Schemers, one and all.

The Emperor chose the day of His resurrection with great intent, allowing these traitorous subjects time enough to breed their dreams and hopes that – upon sight of His return to the Imperial Court, triumphant, unharmed, astride the Imperial Swine – were dashed into despair.

To the Court He proclaimed in booming voice that His reign was never-ending, for He alone had discovered the secret to immortality.

It was a lie. He was as mortal as any man. Only that it was not He who had been killed by the Manchurian that day, but rather Child.

And so He came and banished each of these connivers to the Six Levels of Hell and took control, once more, of Court and Empire, certain that this bold resurgence would ensure the everlasting obeisance of His people.

Once or twice He wept, so deeply had He been moved by His own apparent triumph over death. But, looking about the Court, pacing down the palace hallways, peering into the scholarly gardens, the Emperor was more than disappointed to find that His 'loyal' subjects were not similarly inclined to shed so much as a lousy tear.

Ingrates.

It was not every day that a man, by divine grace and sheer force of will, could resurrect Himself! And yet they shuffled their feet, seemed listless and morose. Where was the joy and celebration at His return?

But then again, perhaps His subjects *were* properly awed and cowed and astonished, and simply could not comprehend the gravity of such an act. The more He thought about this, the more it seemed likely. Who could blame these simple folk?

To distract the people from their melancholy, and nudge them into adulation, the Emperor announced a grand contest. To the winner would go untold riches, lands, titles, Imperial boons, anything the winner desired. If it could be named, it would be given.

The terms of the competition were simple. Whosoever most moved the Emperor's heart – by song or craft or dance or tale or any other method – would emerge the victor.

Entrants came from far and wide. Each day brought new marvels to the Imperial Court.

The Emperor ascended the steps to His throne and began the proceedings. One by one, the contestants were ushered into a clearing in the hall where they would bow to the Emperor. A hundred ministers and courtiers sat upon wooden benches on either side of the Court in observation. Palace aides lingered at the entrances, passing word of the goings-on of the Court to citizens in the outer palace.

Tradesmen brought strange treasures and tales from foreign lands. Blacksmiths wrought fine and tempered blades in the Emperor's honour.

The chefs Dong, Nan and Xi outdid themselves with bold reimaginings of one of the Emperor's favourite dishes. Their *birdless* bird's nest soup, *nestless* bird's nest soup and *soupless* bird's nest soup won high plaudits from the Emperor Himself. Each dish was better than the last. Gourmands and connoisseurs shared significant looks. Surely the Imperial Chef Bei could advance this dish no further! And indeed, they were disappointingly right, for Chef Bei was curiously absent from the contest …

Dancers swept the Court with graceful pirouettes. A woman from the slums presented an old loaf of bread whose mould had spread in such divine patterns that it displayed the unmistakable image of the Emperor's face.

From the mouths of the palace aides, word quickly spread throughout the city. Never had the citizens been so entertained, and for a time they forgot their hatred of the Emperor.

Hoping to move the Emperor's heart through fear, a harried accountant simply read the logs of the Imperial coffers verbatim, the numbers telling the tale of an Empire in collapse. A farmer – deeply optimistic – brought in a horse. A better farmer brought in a better horse.

But the one who won the Emperor's heart was the new Imperial Architect, Lu Shan Liang.

As the young man was introduced into the hall, the Emperor noted the surname they shared. Could they be related? No, impossible. He had wiped the lineage clean long ago. No nobles bearing this illustrious name remained in the Empire. Only men of poor birth and little consequence.

Lu Shan Liang introduced himself to the Court as the man who had built the complex of pretenders. On this day, he brought no tricks or trinkets like the others but had come, instead, with a vision of a new Imperial City.

Once upon a time, in that first and incomplete recollection of his father, who had fallen as though from the sky and broken his back in two, Lu Shan Liang had glimpsed a scaly monument whose form might one day be adapted to something ever greater.

Lu Shan Liang described to the Emperor the Imperial City of his imaginings, innumerable cantons arrayed with purpose so that together they might appear as connected, like a great beast visible from the heavens, its vast expansion devouring the known landscape from State to conquered State, never still, coiling and undulating across the territories until it spanned the length and breadth of the known Empire.

The Emperor had no need to hear from the remaining contestants. He declared Lu Shan Liang the winner.

His fearful subjects made haste to open ledgers and accounts, and summon the necessary manpower to attempt to realise the Emperor's folly, not knowing that it was Dragon – greatly taken by the notion of a city in the fanciful shape of His own image – who ruled on this day.

Shortly thereafter, construction began in the outer cantons of the new Imperial City.

Day after day, the Imperial Architect was called to an audience with the Emperor. He brought drafts and plans for the Emperor to pore over and better understand the intricate network of angles and structures, but mostly he spoke, for the young man found he had a talent for oration.

There were days he spent describing only a single building or tower in such vast and endless detail that, had he wished, he might have charted too its eventual decay, its ruination, the rotted paths that rats one day might take. Other days he described entire districts in but a single sentence.

Once he spoke of a canton that was only made complete by its reflection in the water. Another time, his sketches of the city emerged as tales in which two lovers walked the vivid streets – each lull and argument; the way they had of stumbling, occasionally, into eloquence – so that the Emperor, entranced, began to feel as though He Himself had laid eyes upon each imagined cobblestone, had memorised every building in His periphery, and walked those very streets Himself.

36

Dear citizens of Port Man Tou,

Filming continues, as always, in the Canton of Sinae Verite.

Movie X is a gritty urban actioner. Kingpins and drugs and counterfeit goods. Justice meted out on the kerbside. Chaotic foot chases captured on handheld cameras.

It is common knowledge, however, that its production has been rocky. The Director has been filming for several years, we think.

In the first of what has come to be known as his seasonal fits of rage, The Director once destroyed all existing footage because the sky was the wrong colour. Indeed, it *was*. Extras who had come from other cities had never before seen such clear and unpolluted skies as those above Port Man Tou. There was no smog! The extras did not wear breathing masks. They filled their lungs extravagantly. They ruined takes by gawking up at the blue sky.

This was precisely the sort of artifice The Director had once prized in his past films. But *those* were filmed in Beijing, Shanghai, Hangzhou: *real cities*. Here, on the canvas of Port Man Tou – the artificial city – the inverse is true. The only thing that matters to him is the real. Only the real can please him now.

So, machines were brought in to simulate smog. Day and night, synthetic pollution was pumped into the air, greying the skies, and fixing the palette of the film. But still he destroyed the reels. Why? *Watch the citizens in this scene*, he said. *See their health and happiness. How they stroll the streets without a care in the world. They know it isn't real. Watch them cough. There. Did you see? How it does not linger? In Shanghai, the coughs are deeper, more urgent, weighted with disease …*

The Director is deeply attuned to such minutiae. It is his goal, in the Canton of SV, to stamp out all such traces of similitude.

No longer does he pay the extras. No longer do they live, gratis, in comfortable apartments in the city. Instead, they have been moved to the fringes of the cantons, where the rent is cheaper, the rooms smaller.

They commute. They work in the city to earn their keep. They hunch over assembly lines, cutting their fingers on all manner of plastics and electronics and textiles. They do not stare at the sky anymore. Now, dispersed and shuffling, they blend perfectly into the scenes of *Movie X*. Rarely do they ruin any takes.

And thanks to the proliferation of the mills and steelworks, the sweatshops in which the citizen-actors toil, the city has been transformed into a bona-fide titan of industry. Multinationals from the US, Japan and Korea are clamouring to establish local outposts in Port Man Tou. Week by week, new cement plants are being built. Factories flourish. Port Man Tou now sits at a respectable 9+ in the Global Air Toxicity Index.

Now, in this newest iteration of the city, the smog the people breathe is real. Watch this scene. The way they cough. There. Did you see? The air is thick and heavy in their lungs.

By official decree,
The Department of Industrial Affairs

Bao Tower – Daqiao Road, Canton of Time's Uncertain Arrow

I am summoned to The Director's office on the eighty-eighth floor of Bao Tower. As I alight from the elevator, I can't help but gawk at the panorama of lesser skyscrapers and giant bronze buddhas that appear to float above the thick brown smog.

A security guard posted outside his office mutters into the intercom.

'进.'

He eyes me warily, then opens the door. I am greeted by a cluster of security feeds running the length of the wall. I glimpse the drunk tank at a police station, a Mass Rapid Transport terminal, the Ministerial Office Complex. The heat and disequilibrium from the monitors is disorienting.

Baby Bao slouches in his plush leather chair, feet up on his desk.

'Ah, Xiang Lu! Oh, don't give me that hurt face. If I had told you about the dating-show plans earlier, you would have had to act surprised, and we all know your acting is almost as bad as your Chinese. Hahaha!!! Better we leave nothing to chance for such a potentially lucrative deal!'

'Look. I've given it some thought, and I can't do a dating show. That's where I draw the line.'

The Director looks amused. 'You don't draw lines. I draw the lines. You just follow them.'

'But I'm dating Yuan,' I persist.

'Xiang Lu is dating Yuan. But #BadChinese is single. Go back and read your contract.'

I feel a flash of annoyance, not at Baby Bao but at myself, to have signed myself into exploitation. What other bullshit have I carelessly pre-agreed to?

Something on the wall of monitors catches my attention. I recognise security feeds from the Efficiency and Relaxation Apartments, where Yuan and I reside.

On another monitor, masked men with automatic rifles scramble out of an unmarked white van and charge into a bank.

'Is that a movie?' I ask.

One of the gunmen takes aim at the monitor. The muzzle flashes and the screen goes blue.

Baby Bao jumps from his chair and sprints for the elevators, barking orders into his phone. I give chase. He mashes the button for the parking garage and hangs up.

'Did you call the police?'

'No,' he says. 'My driver.'

We find the Bentley limousine waiting beside the elevator. The tyres screech as we tear out of the Bao Tower car park and race through the streets, swerving to avoid oncoming vehicles and pedestrians. I can vaguely hear sirens in the distance.

The police have already cordoned off the area when we step out of the car.

'Come on,' says Baby Bao.

We approach a police officer at the barricade. He waves us through. Another officer shepherds us, with our heads lowered in a running crouch, towards the police vehicles that surround the bank. A tactical response unit is crowded outside the main doors. Snipers hold position on the roof. A helicopter swoops overhead.

'Is this real?' I ask.

'Raise that with the Department of Verisimilitude,' Baby Bao says.

One of the officers fits Baby Bao with a Kevlar vest.

'Is there one for me?' I ask.

The cop shakes his head.

I gulp. Baby Bao laughs.

There are shouts from inside the bank followed by a single gunshot. The tactical unit bursts into action. They rush the entrance, but are forced back by automatic gunfire. The windows perforate and shatter. Even from this distance the sound causes my ears to ring. Amidst the chaos, a fleeing hostage dives through a window and is dragged to safety. The tactical unit storms the bank.

We hear bursts of gunfire, then silence.

Radio chatter confirms the end of the siege.

I catch myself wide-eyed, breathing quickly, my body coursing with a weird mix of doubt and adrenaline. I keep expecting The Director to yell, 'Cut!' Instead, he puts his arm around me and walks us over to the bank entrance. The cops seem to have no objection.

We enter the scene. Two gunmen lie in the foyer, blood pooling convincingly around their bodies. The third has been killed inside the vault. There is a fourth body, belonging to a victim. The freed hostages are in hysterics.

Baby Bao saunters into the vault, steps over the dead gunman, and returns with a duffel bag.

'Hold this for me.'

The bag is surprisingly heavy. Identical duffel bags lie beside the two slain gunmen in the foyer. Baby Bao walks towards the bodies. I follow, peering closely at their bloody chests for squibs or other special effects. Baby Bao grabs a duffel bag in each hand.

'Okay, let's go.'

I don't move. I am suddenly overwhelmed with confusion.

'Let's go!' he shouts.

We exit the bank and I am bewildered to find that nobody bats an eyelid as we make our way back through the circle of police vehicles and past the barriers to Baby Bao's car. The driver pops the boot and we throw the duffel bags in.

We drive off in silence.

Nameless road, Canton of ???

Sometime later, still in a daze, drained and lethargic in the aftermath of the drama, I realise that we are driving through an unfamiliar part of the city.

Our surroundings become devoid of modernity. No high-rises or powerlines in sight. Smooth asphalt gives way to roughly paved cobblestones that make my teeth rattle.

In the distance, a walled palace emerges, its yellow roof tiles glinting golden in the sunlight. Parts of the palace remain unfinished, girded by steel beams and braces. A construction crane lingers nearby like an object out of time. I look to Baby Bao, thinking this must be our destination, but we hurtle past without slowing.

'Where are we going?' I ask.

Baby Bao ignores me.

The opulent landmark fades behind us. I see farmland in the distance, row upon row of swaying millet. Farmer-actors work the fields, their heads barely visible above the stalks. No one regards the passing Bentley with any interest.

Soon, even the cobblestone road disappears.

Dusty two-storey buildings flank the abruptly narrowed, unpaved streets of a tiny village. I feel like we have gone backwards in time.

The driver honks in frustration as the car slows to a crawl. Suddenly I am overcome with déjà vu. This canton is a replica of Min Qiang, my ancestral home. Through the windshield, I see a slow-moving funeral procession and, impossibly, my grandmother's smiling face, so familiar from weathered photographs and faded childhood recollections, in a moment that is unfathomably slow, yet over all too soon.

37

MOUNTAIN

It came to him like a dream, though the Grand Prolonger of Autumn had not been dreaming but rather drinking at the Phoenix Tavern, distracted by the badly rebuilt wall that separated the bar from the brothel next door. If the Grand Prolonger placed his ear to the wall in a pretence of slumped drunkenness, he could hear the moans of some couple loudly coupling.

This was the Grand Prolonger's favourite seat. On the nights he entered the tavern to find it occupied, he would sulk into his drink and wait for it to become available. Then he would resume surreptitiously peeling back the wallpaper and picking at the plaster until he finally uncovered a finger-sized peephole into one of the brothel's bedrooms.

Though he had long ago been deprived of his manhood, did he not still feel the phantoms of desire?

He often considered throwing caution to the wind and putting his eye to the hole (it would have been so easy!), but he never did for fear of giving it all away. He could only ever bear to listen, the right side of his body in that tricky embrace with the wall.

In all these years, he had come to desire the Imperial Consort. He had never felt more alive than in that hopeless labyrinth, for he had become convinced that by his works and good deeds he would one day win her affection.

Through time and rote persistence, he had attained the competence to navigate the contours of the outer labyrinth. But the inner labyrinth's constantly shifting pathways remained unknown and unknowable to him. How many times, with mind adrift, had he misjudged the route to the heart? How many times had he become lost and cried out in fear for the Imperial Consort to save him? And he called himself her protector!

When he was with her he seemed to understand the inner labyrinth completely. He watched her mend the great crack that ran along the Endless Corridor, using the mortar and slaked lime he had brought at her request. It occurred to him then that the texture of this stretch of wall – unique in its ruination – might aid him in differentiating the perilous and seemingly identical forks within the inner labyrinth. Thereafter, he came to think of it as a guidepost.

Recall that time when, drunk and staggering, he had found his way into the heart by that very method. The heady exhilaration of having finally made it through the inner labyrinth and finding her there, like a hidden treasure! What a vision of loveliness! The memory of the words he had whispered (subtle, surely, and – knowing himself – perhaps even noble) had faded, but the sting of her repudiation had not. The way she had then averted her eyes, as though he were beneath her consideration.

The Imperial Consort had gently bidden him to forget her and the labyrinth.

But he did not. He often returned but was never able to find her, or the heart, again. He was crestfallen to discover the storerooms restocked with supplies and materials. It had not occurred to him that Wuer had never been contained by the labyrinth's walls. That she had chosen to stay and might just as easily have chosen to leave. Had she ever truly needed him?

Nursing his drink in the Phoenix Tavern, he recalled her instructions, in those earliest of days, that he must never make a map of the labyrinth.

But that was then, when loyalty had been the sole and sufficient measure of his love. Between slow sips of rice wine, with eyes half closed, he realised that everything she had said to him had been a lie. His affection for her calcified into bitterness. In the vicarious ecstasy of that moment, ear to wall – entranced by the rapturous moans and hurried slapping of flesh – he was overtaken by an inscrutable conviction: that in creating a map of the labyrinth, all his problems would be solved.

The time came for the Emperor to bestow His boon upon the Imperial Architect. He asked Lu Shan Liang what prize he sought. He replied that he sought an audience with the scholars who had authored the books of the Imperial Library.

It was a simple request to grant. The Emperor gave orders for the men to be taken from the Six Levels of Hell to an audience with the Architect. But how could the Architect – a foreigner to the Imperial City – know these exiles, whose names had for years been lost to the wind?

Lu Shan Liang replied that he had read these books in his village, and each had sparked in him a great longing for the Imperial City.

The Emperor was intrigued. So the books had survived the flame by migrating south like birds in flight. The Emperor enquired about the village of the Architect's childhood.

Lu Shan Liang described Min Qiang, of the Fuzhou province. In his recent travels he had often heard it referred to as the armpit of the armpit. But it was not so to him. He spoke with deep fondness of the simple life he had left behind: the kindness and concern of neighbours and friends, the summer breeze that made his eyelids heavy in the afternoon, the road he walked to visit his father's grave, the crowds at the market where fresh fish and milk and woven silk were sold, evenings lit by stars and candlelight. And come the golden glow of dawn, the scores of silent fishermen, transfixed, upon the frozen surface of the lake. There, time seemed to flow in stranger ways, like memories returning to shore. The village was unremarkable in every way, he said, except to those who lived there.

On this day, it was Mountain who ruled.

In truth, He was most at ease in the tower, where He could gaze down at the lives of His citizens with cool detachment. The throne in the Imperial Court – elevated by a dozen marble steps – provided, too, some comforting altitude.

Mountain was not petty or cruel or filled with rage, but silent and contemplative. The courtiers were accustomed to His mood swings and called these days the calm before His storm.

He would often quiz His scholars and advisers on matters that aroused His curiosity. Why were the citizens' taxes paid in salt? Why, for that matter, were the poorest taxed at the highest rates? Their stammering digressions and non-answers drove him to put aside His social reticence and descend into the poorest canton at the outskirts of the city.

Mountain dismissed His entourage and walked the streets alone. He sought to live, for a time, among His people. To eat as they ate. To speak as they spoke. The peasants and slum dwellers welcomed Him with full hearts and open arms. If any had heard the tales of His jealousy or cruelty or perfidy, they did not betray such knowledge.

Children ran circles around Him, tugged at His fine brocade and even His beard. He allowed them to climb upon His broad shoulders, to steer Him into their homes and show Him their most treasured possessions. Outside, in the dusty streets, they invited Him to join in their invented games. In turn, He bestowed upon each urchin a grand and lofty title: Chivalrous Separator of Heaven and Earth, Chronicler of Playground Bruises, Grand Maestro of the Air-zither. And He taught the children of the slums to sing the song of Mountain.

The ministers and generals and advisers of the Imperial Court reacted with suspicion and incredulity for they could not reconcile His sudden magnanimity with the tyranny they had long suffered under His reign. Of course, over the years they had caught glimpses of the Emperor's capacity for kindness, but never without ulterior motive.

Their spies reported observing Him in an artist's studio, patiently sitting for His portrait. They must have been confused, these spies, for how else to explain the night they broke into the studio only to find on the canvas no likeness of man, but instead, of Mountain.

When Mountain tired of the company of men, He returned to nature, enjoying solitary walks through the scholarly gardens or boat rides on the lake.

Mountain was musing upon the construction of a nearby canton – the shape of its reflection in the water – when His boat collided with another and was overset. The shore was not far. There were many who could have easily aided the drowning Emperor. But they remembered the third Imperial Edict – that to touch Him was an offence punishable by death – and so they watched as He swallowed dangerous mouthfuls of water, trying to grant someone, anyone, the necessary permission to save His life.

And so the Emperor was dragged to the bottom by His own mountainous weight.

38

Ministerial Office Complex – National Road, Canton of The Unwritten

I come to pick up Yuan from her office.

'You're dressed up,' she says. 'Another promotional appearance today?'

'Yup. There's a new wing opening at the Port Man Tou Replica Art Museum. We can check out the gallery after I'm done with the promo stuff.'

We walk in silence. The streets are deserted. A new city-wide directive has prohibited citizens from engaging in 'subversive' activities, including publicly criticising The Director. The legislation has been written in troublingly broad language and no one is exempt, not even ministerial officers.

I don't need words for her to know what's on my mind.

'Hey,' I say, suddenly. 'Let's take the bus today.'

'But the Mass Rapid is just around the corner.'

'Come on, let's change it up a bit.'

'Why?' she asks.

Because on the roads you can at least watch the passing landscape, remain reasonably sure of the route. How can we be certain, careening through those strobe-lit tunnels, in those sleek and shuddering train carriages, that we are arcing in the right direction? That we are even moving at all? That it's not all an illusion made up of LED windows, carefully timed lights and sounds, and complex hydraulics?

I try to communicate all this in a look. 'Why not? We haven't taken the bus in ages.'

'Fine.'

Yet even on the bus my anxieties have not abated. I open the window, stick my hand out and feel the wind passing through my fingers. But even this proves nothing. Even the wind can be orchestrated.

Port Man Tou Replica Art Museum – Ansha Street, Canton of Sinae Verite

I stand before a long paper scroll by the seventeenth-century painter and poet Shitao. It spans the length of the wall and depicts some mythic landscape. To the left, a handful of seals comprising Chinese characters are stamped in red ink, and beside them several lines of poetry are rendered in a calligrapher's brushstrokes.

Now I realise my mistake: what I thought was the beginning is really the end – right to left and not the other way around – and I walk to the other side to begin again.

I recall something Yuan said, about being able to spend her whole life re-reading a single book. So instead of moving on to another painting, I reappraise the work. And I realise that this landscape was not painted, but written.

The same graceful flick and flourish in the lines of the poem reappear across the rest of the canvas, in blades of grass, rocky outcroppings, weeping willows and the figure of a farmer, whose bent posture might conceal a written character. Were these icons of the land not rendered with the same calligraphic brush? Is the painting the poetry or the poetry the painting?

The leaves on the trees form almost-words.

In the shadow imprints and inkblots, amidst the pressure and stroke of the brush, I think I see some hazy dreamscape – a second China – in which the art and the words are all but inextricable.

Outside, our eyes slowly readjust to the light of day.

'Where were you?' I ask. 'We sort of lost track of each other in there.'

'I was in the Ming Dynasty, mostly,' Yuan says. 'Well, actually, I was just wandering all over, and eventually I started following the old security guard. He was so funny, patrolling the room, scolding people who were taking pictures. He reminded me of a cartoon villain. I even saw him stop a teenager from completing a sketch in her notebook!'

We both laugh.

'Yes, he eyed off my camera as soon as I walked in, and hounded me for a little while,' I say. 'But there was only one of him, and many of us, and it became a kind of game for everyone. We'd all wait for him to move on, then quickly take our photos, like Cold War spies.'

'Nice work! How did your photos turn out?'

I peruse the photos on my camera. All blurry. I shake my head.

'That's too bad,' she says. 'I guess the guard is doing the gallery a favour. Prohibiting photographs so you might buy the official book from the gift shop later on.'

'I admit, I suddenly feel all the poorer for not knowing how to read Chinese.'

'Suddenly?' she teases.

'Yes. Enough people in my lifetime – relatives, friends, strangers – have given me enough grief about not knowing how to speak, much less read, Chinese. Even after finding work as a translator, and now here, doing whatever the fuck it is I'm doing, my default position on the state of my Chinese language skills has always been something like defiance. Watch me give a shit, you know? But back there, in the gallery, taking in all the art ... I've felt *other* people's shame, but it was the first time I've ever really felt my *own* shame that I don't know Chinese. The plaques in English were useful, but they rarely translated the text of the poems on the scrolls. I felt like I was missing some vital aspect of the art, something significant. Honestly, I never thought I'd be so blown away by calligraphy.'

'That's good to hear! But the proper term for it is *shufa*. You must not call it "calligraphy". My friend Xian Jing's husband, Ah Ray, who is a scholar on the matter, feels very strongly about this, and will correct anyone who'll listen. Calligraphy, you see, quite literally means "beautiful writing". The written word is beautified by the addition of the artistic flourish. But *shufa* is entirely different. *Shu* means "handwriting" and *Fa* means "way". To call *shufa* "beautiful writing" would be inaccurate, and even demeaning. Because in *shufa* the writing itself is the art.'

'And those red seals are the artists' signatures, right?' I ask.

'No. No. They are the seals of prominent art collectors who owned the work over the centuries. Before these artworks were in museums, the art belonged in their personal collections. And years from now, the works will return to the private realm, change hands, and perhaps one day another seal will be added. What's wrong? You look shocked.'

'I don't get it. Any collector can just come and print his seal on the canvas like that? It just seems like ... okay, what if every dude who owned the *Mona Lisa* over the years just went ahead and graffitied his autograph on it? The art would be ruined.'

Yuan shakes her head. 'That is the Western way, the Western understanding. In *shufa*, the addition of a seal is not a weakening of the art, it's not an act of vandalism or disrespect. It is an *elevation*. The collector does not add her seal flippantly or without much thought. In fact, she may only add her seal to perhaps a handful out of thousands that live in her collection. Her seal is the deepest sign of respect to the art.'

I think about this as we walk.

I begin to see. 'It forms part of the art.'

'En. That's what I was saying. The seal is as much the art as the landscape and the poem. And there is a real artistry to the imprint of the seal itself. To me, the seals are the most exciting part of *shufa*, the reason why *shufa* is known as the living art. The piece that we observed today has more seals than it had two hundred years ago, and it will perhaps have more two hundred years from now. By then it will be a different work of art. The art is not stagnant, but over time accumulates a greater weight. It lives.'

'But' – I cannot help being obstinate – 'the seal doesn't belong to the artist. It wasn't part of his vision. He didn't intend it. Others add to it and the work is changed, irreparably.'

'What's wrong with that? We change art just by observing it, or thinking or talking about it. After this conversation, the two of us will never know Shitao's landscape in quite the same way as we did before. Did the artist intend for us to talk about his art? If we perceive his art differently from each other – or from the artist himself – or even from ourselves over time, then are those differing perceptions any less legitimate?'

'No, not at all.'

'Ah! I was expecting you to put up more of a fight. Now I'm disappointed, I was getting ready to defend my position—'

'You don't have to, I'm agreeing with you!' I say.

'Let me finish, otherwise I'll forget!' She pokes me in the shoulder. 'Because, in the first place, the artist's rendition of the landscape is an interpretation, the poem an interpretation, each stroke of the brush an interpretation. In *shufa*, even creators are interpreters. Especially creators, I think. They are the foremost interpreters of nature and the word.'

If art is a language then it seems she is fluent in this, too.

'So which pieces did you like in there?' I ask.

'If I were a burglar, I would steal Liang Kai's *Immortal in Splashed Ink* and hang it in my room and gaze lovingly at it every day. And you?'

'I liked Shitao's works the best. I was blown away by all of his pieces, in fact. I can't get his *10,000 Ugly Inkblots* out of my head,' I say. 'There's something fucked-up and wild to me about how it starts off with a traditional landscape, then breaks into abstraction, all those inkblots suddenly blowing out across the canvas. As though he were inspired to ruin the art, to ruin beauty.'

'Actually,' says Yuan, 'I was insulted that the plaque described that piece as Pollock-esque. Shitao was a seventeenth-century painter! If anything, Jackson Pollock was Shitao-esque.'

'I actually took the tour of Jackson Pollock's studio a few years ago, in New York. That was a great experience. Great tour guide. She had this way of whispering and tiptoeing around the place that made us feel as though we should too. You could see that she revered the spot, as though the studio were somehow mythical to her, like some special place that might *itself* inspire art. It reminded me of the story of how Stephen King wrote *Misery* at Rudyard Kipling's desk. Or how musicians seem to channel The Beatles when they record at Abbey Road Studios. It's the site of significance, you know? It's Kerouac's scroll of *On The Road*. It's the object imbued with meaning.'

'In the absence of the creator, we revere her tools,' Yuan says.

'Yes! Exactly. Where is that from?'

'Me. I just made it up.'

I stop walking and look at her.

'But what was I going to say? Ah, the guide,' I continue. 'She showed us how Pollock would lay his canvases flat on the ground and then drip and flick paint on them from above. That was his method. Dozens and dozens of canvases. Over the years, the studio's floor became soaked through with colour. The aftermath of his works. I remember looking at the floor, and the thing that made my heart leap was this. *It looks just like his art.* Or, at least, it seemed *indistinguishable* from his art. All the accumulated paint that had seeped through, the spatters that had fallen beyond the canvas and stained the floor forever. Was there intent there? Surely, over time, he must have known at some point. Must have become aware of the resemblance.'

'That the floor had begun to resemble the art?' she asks.

'Yes!'

'I don't know. I don't like Jackson Pollock's art. It could mean nothing or it could mean everything. You say his floor was

250

indistinguishable from the art. I say his art was indistinguishable from the floor. Oh, don't give me that face. I don't mean to insult him. That's just how I feel. It is very like you, I think, to search for patterns in the paint. To rearrange meaningless things until they become significant. You construct theories about things, the world, and latch tightly on to examples that will prove your theories beyond doubt, ignoring any troublesome pieces that don't fit and therefore might harm your theories. Am I right?'

'You aren't.'

She is.

I want to say something to her, but I am distracted by a towering buddha cresting over the horizon – one of the many enormous statues that have been erected around Port Man Tou. Struck by its visage, I cannot expel the words that have become stuck in my throat, or in my head.

What I was on the cusp of saying to her then, on the street, halfway between the gallery and the ruins of the neighbouring canton, and what I *did* say to her eventually, much, much later, once, after emerging from the shower, brow furrowed, eyes down, because it is much easier to remember the order of words like that, a mini-speech practised in my head, was this:

If you are living a life aligned towards art – the making of it, the receiving of it – then the patterns you leave in your wake, whether you are aware of them or not, whether you intend them to be or not, will be indistinguishable from the art itself.

Dear citizens of Port Man Tou,

Finally, after months of setbacks and delays, the towering colossus that straddles the lake's harbour is now complete. Behold its magnificence, the likeness it bears to our great Director, the way its vast dimensions protect us from the sun by casting a shadow across the Canton of Our Subconscious Choreography.

Did we really need another sculpture? It is a valid question.

Indeed, the Canton of OSC is already brimming with a pantheon of great statues and bronzed titans, behemoths that pierce the skyline. One cannot traverse the canton without passing serene buddhas contemplating our roadsides and turnpikes. The gods among us.

They are a ubiquitous part of our landscape and inextricable from our reality.

See the way in which they subtly guide the movements of the city.

How the flow of traffic is forever altered by their presence. The streets and detours we much prefer to take, so as to remain only in the periphery of their sight (for we cannot stand their gaze directly).

How, in Diomira Square, a gas station within the sightlines of a ten-storey effigy reported a marked decrease in the sale of smutty magazines because patrons were suddenly embarrassed and ashamed.

How we citizens adopt a tone of reverence whenever the statues are within earshot. We whisper so as not to disturb them, and shy away from such displeasing topics as politics and scandal, or our concerns about The Director. We are silenced by the city's architecture.

It is said that the Canton of OSC is the pride of the People's Investigations Bureau. The Director boasts that the rates of criminality here are low compared with the other godless cantons. And yet, vicious crimes do still occur – muggings and rapes and murders – carried out at certain wretched hours of the day, out of sight and behind the backs of bodhisattvas.

The Director was overheard expressing some measure of regret that the colossus was built to face the lake. If only he could have turned it, re-cast its panoptic gaze towards the city, perhaps those unruly citizens in the Canton of OSC might then have better understood the nature of obeisance.

By official decree,
The Department of Circumspection

Efficiency and Relaxation Apartments – Fuxing Road, Canton of The Unwritten

Yuan is cooking up a pork stir-fry in the kitchenette.

Even here, in my apartment, we are careful with the topics we discuss. Once, moving from the bed over to the couch, I caught the squeal of something that sounded suspiciously like microphone feedback.

I set the table and pour wine. As she puts on the finishing touches, I linger by the bookshelf and pick out the pair of books we bought as mementos. Yi Shu's *Xibao* for Yuan, Milton's *Paradise Lost* for me.

I open the books. Still bearing that single line, though the ink is smudged.

Yuan sets the food on the table. It smells amazing. We sit down to eat. I set the book down alongside my plate.

'It's too bad that these books ended up being empty. There's a passage from *Paradise Lost* that I'd show you if I could. It's where the second Adam ascends the highest mountain and surveys the lands below and the mighty nations that history would create. The Russian, Persian, Indian empires. But China twice ...'

'What do you mean?'

'Milton refers once to Sinae – China, that is – and then, in a later line, he refers to Cathay. Also China. So what gives?'

'You have that annoying look on your face,' she says, 'like you're going to tell me something that is not as interesting as you think it is.'

'Well, forget it then.'

'Oh, you're too sensitive. Just say it.'

'Well, I've always thought of great literature as myth. Or that there comes a point where great literature acquires the *status* of myth. *The Iliad, Ulysses, Moby Dick, Paradise Lost*. And myth is truth, of a kind. So what if it *wasn't* a mistake? What if the second Adam *did* see two Chinas? Which Chinas might they have been? A real China and a mythical China, side by side? Even culturally, I think the Chinese are more attuned to myth than Westerners. Every animal of the zodiac is real except the dragon, which is mythical.'

'废话! The dragon existed in ancient times!'

'*Yes*, in the imagined China.'

She sighs. 'There's no arguing with you. And your food is getting cold. When you get in these philosophical moods you hardly touch your dish.'

'How about this? Every Western city has a Chinatown. Yet not one of those Chinatowns looks like China. They only resemble the China of our imagination.'

'En, I agree with that, at least. In Hangzhou, where I studied at university, there are restaurants in the tourist districts with signs that say they serve "authentic" Chinese food. And yet no restaurant in China with such a sign can be authentic! They only serve food that caters to Western tastes.'

'Boneless lemon honey chicken,' I say.

'No such thing!' She laughs.

'Only in the imagined China,' I say, thumbing the blank pages.

An empty book, waiting for my words to fill it.

39

TRICKSTER

The Emperor announced a great reward for any information that might lead to the capture of the Imperial Consort.

Over the subsequent years, ambitious or desperate men would enter the labyrinth armed with flasks of water and dubious directions. Trapped in maddening loops and suffering from exhaustion, they eventually curled into darkened corners to await death. Inexplicably, they would awaken near the safety of the labyrinth's entrance, like sailors washed upon the shore after a storm. All had seen the woman in their labyrinth-dreams. Some said she fed them; others said she had led them back by hand or they had followed her whispers to safer corridors. All were stricken by her melancholic beauty and chastened at having interrupted her solitude.

The eunuch, flanked by Imperial Guards, was thrown upon the floor and made to kneel before the Emperor.

Two degenerates identified him as the same eunuch they had overheard in the Phoenix Tavern, drunkenly boasting that he possessed a map to the labyrinth. It had not taken much convincing on their part for him to show them the contraband map. Also, they added – the smell of cheap wine still on their breath – perhaps there might be some reward for their good citizenship?

The Emperor thanked them for their service. A reward? Of course. And what better gift for two obvious connoisseurs of fine drink than a bottomless flask of rice wine, specially conjured by the Imperial Apothecary!

They could hardly believe their ears. As they were led away, they wept with joy and praised Him as a most fine and generous ruler, not knowing on this certain day that He was, in fact, Trickster.

The degenerates were never heard from again.

The map was shown to the Emperor. It was not much to look at: an ugly scrawl of ink on parchment with copious notes crowding the margins. Though the majority of the map's terrain remained uncharted – terra incognita – there was a crucial landmark called the Endless Corridor, where the Grand Prolonger had secretly marked the walls. It appeared to be sufficient information to reach the inner labyrinth.

Tell me, Trickster enquired of the Grand Prolonger, *why does the Imperial Consort remain within the labyrinth?*

The Grand Prolonger trembled in fear, but refused to speak.

Trickster reassured the Grand Prolonger that he would not be punished, but rewarded. After all, the Grand Prolonger had delivered Him a map to that which He most desired!

Still, the Grand Prolonger remained silent.

Trickster did not seek to harm her, but rather take her back into His harem. Oh, He most preferred virgins, to be sure. And He had a certain type, a certain shape, as all men did. But He was a generous Emperor, Trickster was, and sampled every sort of woman in His Empire. Tall ones, short ones, the supple-skinned and the deeply wrinkled. He did not discriminate. But try as He might, none of these women could satisfy His seemingly unquenchable appetite.

He asked the Grand Prolonger to name a boon.

Leave the Imperial Consort be, the Grand Prolonger replied. *Do not seek her out.*

Impossible! Trickster scoffed.

Then do not take her into Your harem.

A most unreasonable request!

But in the eunuch's desperate pleas, Trickster sensed an unrequited affection for the Imperial Consort. And, slyly, He made the Grand Prolonger a most generous offer: He, the Emperor, would take her back into His harem. Of that, there could be no dispute. He would have her body. But the Grand Prolonger would have her *mind*.

The Grand Prolonger's eyes flickered.

Trickster explained that, in all these years, His chemists, disappointments that they were, had been unable to craft Him a potion of everlasting life. They had by chance, however, conjured a potion of everlasting *love*, which He would deign to serve the Imperial Consort. Then she had only to rest her eyes upon the first she saw – the Grand Prolonger, of course – allow a moment for the liquid to flood her heart's meridian, and she would return the Grand Prolonger's love for her in kind.

Trickster, His guards and the Grand Prolonger of Autumn prepared for their entry into the labyrinth. Trickster spoke of the entrance in the east wing of the palace, but the Grand Prolonger preferred the route outside the palace, connected via the sewers, with which he was familiar.

The Grand Prolonger led them into the winding labyrinth. He felt sick with anticipation at the promise of finally winning the Imperial Consort's love, and sicker still that he had to enter the Emperor's bargain to get it. But did it not show the depths to which he was willing to go in order to win her heart?

Trickster ordered His guards to light their torches. In all these years, the Grand Prolonger of Autumn had learned to navigate the passageways by dimmest candlelight. Now, with each of the guards' torches brightly illuminating the labyrinth, the Grand Prolonger cast his eyes around at the pathways and the walls made of cobbled stone and felt disoriented.

He lowered his eyes and found his confidence returning. With practised step, he led them in single file. They did not speak, for the Grand Prolonger required his sharpest wits about him in order to navigate the pathways of his betrayal.

The deeper they went into the labyrinth, the more convinced he became that the Imperial Consort was observing their movements from adjacent rooms or pathways, impossibly close but always beyond reach.

At last they approached the threshold to the inner labyrinth. The Grand Prolonger placed his hand against the wall. In his fervid desire to map the labyrinth, he had secretly carved nicks and grooves along the walls, which he used to guide him. From here, the route to the heart was simple enough.

But as they crossed the threshold, the Grand Prolonger became confused. In his recollection, the inner labyrinth had been in a state of collapse and decay. But the ground beneath his feet was no longer uneven with rubble. The walls were smooth to the touch, his landmarks erased, his path undone.

He opened his eyes. By the torchlight, he bore witness to the labyrinth transformed. Wuer had abandoned the tainted parchments he had brought her to transform into books, and had begun to write upon the very walls. Calligraphic brushstrokes adorned the inner labyrinth from top to bottom. In the wavering light, the vivid sweep and flow of ink seemed to rush like river currents through the whispering passages.

The Imperial Consort had foreseen her subject's betrayal. But far from chastening the Grand Prolonger of Autumn, this caused him to desire her even more, and he pressed grimly onward. He was certain she would change her mind about him after he gave her the potion.

Trickster, regarding the wall in some mesmeric state, began to read its words aloud. And so, too, the guards behind Him, their voices overlapping cacophonously. This caused the Grand Prolonger – still feeling for telltale flaws in the edifice – to lose his concentration and lead the men astray. Having lost the way, the men turned on one another, hurling accusations and blame.

Under vague and conflicting instructions from Trickster – *Kill him!* – the guards ran their swords through each other until only the Grand Prolonger and Trickster remained. The two bickered for a time before agreeing to reverse their path and find their way back to the entrance. But they failed to retrace their steps, and instead followed the procession of words, sinking deeper into the uncharted depths until the labyrinth consumed them.

They wandered in circles for days. Their supplies dwindled.

On the fourth day, having run out of water, Trickster and the Grand Prolonger of Autumn fought one another for the final flask of sustenance: the love potion prepared by the Imperial Apothecary.

The Grand Prolonger – desperate to save the flask in order to capture Wuer's heart – resisted to the bitter end. But Trickster's thirst won out. He strangled the Grand Prolonger and imbibed the love potion. Dropping the flask, He gazed upon the body of the Grand Prolonger of Autumn and spent the next few hours in great pangs of love for the man He had just murdered, before He, too, breathed His last.

40

Port Man Tou Lake – Century Lane,
Canton of Our Subconscious Choreography

'Yuck. This is no good.' Yuan looks glumly at her corn on the cob. 'Want it?'

We are at Port Man Tou Lake, eating deep-fried treats and watching a man with a mop and bucket write calligraphy – *shufa* – on the ground. The water-words from moments ago already beginning to evaporate in the sun.

'Ugh. This tastes a little funny, too. Oh man. This drink is expired.'

I throw the stuff in the nearest bin, and return to Yuan, putting my arm around her.

We used to be paranoid about such public – and even private – displays of affection. Wondering who was watching, where the cameras were, et cetera. But no longer. Or rarely, I should say. Everything becomes normalised with the passage of time. We forget we might be on film, lose our self-consciousness. And yet, at odd times, we remember all over again, and the kiss, or the laugh, or the smile becomes performative. Although, city aside, it is much like this anyway in the early months of dating, when we constantly strive to show some better, more Hollywood version of ourselves.

We walk down the boulevard, past the southern edge of the lake where hundreds of workers swarm a construction site on an embankment.

'I was thinking,' I say, 'now that I've been practising conversational Chinese, the act of speaking is somehow easier.'

'Well, of course. You become more confident through practice.'

'I mean, yes, that's very obvious, but what I was trying to say – and not very well – is that it somehow seems *easier* than English because I know fewer words. Right now, I only know *one* way to say something in Chinese because I don't have the vocabulary, you know? Whereas in English I can sort of become paralysed searching for the right word. Like sometimes, in the middle of a conversation, I will pause because I know it – the perfect word – but maybe it's too pretentious to say it aloud and so, instead of just blurting it out, I lengthen the pause, try to recall another word, the commonly said word, the acceptable one, which just makes it all the more awkward in the end. This happens frequently. Makes me look like I have forgotten, momentarily, how to speak like a normal person.'

'En, this happens to me sometimes. Forgetting how to speak. I stumble over my words and make a fool of myself, but it seems to happen only with people I don't know how to connect with. I become flustered and my translation suffers. It's embarrassing. I once had a' – and was it a glitch of the tongue, or did she pause here, also searching for a more perfect word? – '*friend*. A professor. An Englishman. I was his interpreter. He was verbose and very precise. A difficult combination. It was sometimes a challenge to keep up with him, conversationally.'

Some twinge of jealousy. 'Uh-huh?'

She ignores me.

'In any case,' she says, 'it made me think. I suppose it is a hazard of that job – the professor – to profess. He was always trying to teach me or lecture me about this or that, which became very tiresome. But having spent enough time in your company, I realise you are the opposite. The exact opposite of a professor.'

'What does that mean? What's the exact opposite of a professor?'

The scent of her as she leans in close to me. 'A *confessor*.'

'Ah, another one of your famous invented words. The Académie Anglaise?'

She nods. 'Makes sense, right? Professor, confessor. Pros, cons. What if we were to *profess* our sins? To entrust our university education to *confessors* of history, *confessors* of literature? Beat a *profession* out of someone?'

'You've thought this over.'

'I have,' she says, proudly.

There's something in how she dismantles language, some sense to her inversions.

'But wait a second,' I say, taking the time now to be vaguely affronted. '*I* profess things all the time! I can footnote with the best of them. What makes me the opposite of a professor?'

'Because it is in your nature – and mine too, perhaps – to confess.' Her expression is at once melancholic and tender.

'Well. Let's say, hypothetically,' I tell her, my voice lowering, 'if I were to have fallen in love with you ...'

'Hypothetically?' she asks.

'Hypothetically,' I agree.

'En, go on ...'

'And if I were to tell you so. Right now.'

'That you have fallen in love with me?' She stops walking, as do I.

'Yes. Would I not have *professed* my love to you? Like John Cusack with a boom box. Would I not be a professor in this one thing, at least?'

'But Xiang. Who would you tell?'

'Only you.'

'Then don't you see? To profess is to tell the world, but you are a confessor, in this and all things.'

'Huh. I suppose I am, after all ... To confess is Catholic. And you're right. I think, deep down, that I have always wished for absolution from my deepest pains and faults. Fine. *Have* the confession. It's yours. I love you,' I say. 'Absolve me.'

'And how shall I absolve you of your love? Tell you that I love you also?'

It is hard to know, anymore, if we are still playing with words, or if we are saying real things.

262

We come to a dock where they rent out sampans to row around the lake. The more expensive ones are decked out with motors and canopies. The basic ones are little more than wooden rafts.

'Want to jump on one of these?' I casually ask, as though it were simply a spur-of-the-moment idea.

'Sure,' she replies, nonchalant, as we'd agreed.

We choose the most rickety, primitive-looking sampan. Not because we are cheapskates or have a death wish, but because to our eyes it is the plainest one, with no doohickies or engines or hiding places for pesky electronics. We give our life jackets a good once-over. No microphones, as far as we can tell.

I row us out slowly, cutting a path through the water lilies, past the moorings, past the other sampans filled with couples and families, pulling the oars until we are as far away from anyone and anything as we can possibly be.

'What do you reckon? Far enough?'

'En.'

We are occasional enough in our trips to the lake so as not to raise suspicion. And yet it always takes us minutes of silence to muster up the courage to speak truly, or freely – always a leap of faith – for it is not difficult to imagine the terrors of technology, the possibility of long-distance microphones, members of the People's Investigations Bureau armed with telephoto lenses.

'Betty Xia in apartment 32C has "moved out",' she says.

'Shit. That's half the building now. I knew they'd get her. She was *always* talking. What's the official line?'

'Her Temporary Departure form was approved.'

'Like hell it was.'

'I think I know where she and all the other citizens have been disappearing to,' says Yuan. 'At least, I think I do.'

'How? Where?'

'I had lunch with Eric Lai.'

'Isn't he the guy from the Department of Verisimilitude who keeps asking you out?'

She sighs. 'Is this *really* what you want to talk about right now?'

'Sorry. Knee-jerk reaction. Eric said something to you about what's happening to the citizens?'

'No. He left his lanyard behind, so I went to return it. When I got to his cubicle he wasn't there, but I noticed that *his* maps are different from mine. Remember the undeveloped land between the cantons of Eternal Ruin and Sinae Verite? According to his version, there's something there.'

'What sort of something?'

'A prison. Or wherever the citizens go when they are re-cast.'

'So what do we do?'

She reaches into her handbag and takes out a lanyard bearing Eric Lai's higher security credentials. 'We flash *this* when we enter.'

A young father and son paddle into our orbit. We smile and wave. I wait until they recede from earshot.

'We can't keep coming out here,' I say. 'Sooner or later, The Director's going to get suspicious.'

'Why? We work hard, we don't complain, we avoid the protests. We date. Paddling is a date thing. A normal thing. Nothing out of the ordinary. Dating at the lake is probably listed in our dossiers as a favoured activity.'

'But you hate boats,' I say.

'No one knows that but you. Oh, nice ad lib by the way, Confessor Lu. *I love you. Absolve me.*'

'I meant it.'

'I know.'

The final irony, I guess, is that we *have* each become actors, to protect ourselves. For Yuan and I have internalised the lesson that so many others in Port Man Tou have failed to grasp: that the absence of scripts is not an absence of direction. Our roles were to fall in love. We did not resist such a direction. Indeed, we might well have fallen in love regardless. So it has been easy for us, or *easier*, I should say, because nothing is easy, because everything is fraught with difficulty when you must whisper your troubles to each other in discreet corners, far from the prying ears and eyes of the city. Easier, I mean, only in comparison with others, who might take issue with their assigned roles, who openly rebel against The Director's will at their own peril.

Happiness Factory – Market Street, unnamed canton

We cross the Canton of ER by foot, and after thirty minutes come to a housing complex with ochre-coloured roofs. The place is teeming with citizen-actors who are riding their bikes to a large gated compound. It doesn't look like a prison, but a series of warehouses with large pathways between buildings to accommodate the cyclists.

I pull my baseball cap lower over my eyes. It wouldn't do to be recognised as the #BadChinese when we're trying to sneak through the prison gates.

We follow the workforce streaming through the gates. A sign reads 快乐工厂.

'Happiness Factory,' I read. 'Not a prison.'

Yuan nods.

A security guard stops us at the entrance to one of the buildings. Yuan flashes the lanyard. He tells us to wait.

Five minutes later, a portly man in a yellow polo shirt introduces himself as the factory foreman. He wasn't expecting us, but is more than happy to give the Department of Verisimilitude a tour.

I let Yuan do the talking.

She asks if this is part of a film.

He nods, but adds that it is also a working factory, which manufactures electronics and other consumer goods for export.

He shows us whiteboard lists of production schedules, and the factory floor where a hundred conveyor belts are lit by fluorescent rods. Colonies of worker-actors wearing antistatic latex gloves and hairnets robotically assemble blenders, irons, waffle makers.

We don hairnets of our own and descend to the lower level.

The worker-actors pay us no mind as we roam the floor. We

watch as they pull down soldering irons, press plastic into moulds and test products on voltmeters. On the other end of the floor, a team leader and his workers chant in praise of The Director.

We follow the conveyor belts from beginning to end and watch the pieces of an iron come together – spouts, water reservoirs, plastic frames, power supplies – the finished product rolling off the line in less than five minutes.

One of the workers hisses as we pass. '喂! 是我.'

The worker threading electrical wires into espresso machines gestures impatiently at Yuan to interpret. I recognise him as Baby Bao's producer.

'Farmstrong!' I say. 'What are *you* doing here?'

We look around. The foreman is no longer in sight. Yuan translates Farmstrong's words into English.

'*I was re-cast by The Director,*' he says bitterly.

'The Director said that you left to start your own production company in Shanghai,' I say.

'*Well, I am still producing.*' Farmstrong chuckles. '*Coffee machines, that is.*'

'What's it like here?'

'*The production schedules are onerous, there is nothing to do but work, work, work. Worker-actors have fallen asleep on the lines and injured themselves, halted the conveyors, and all the rest of us can think about is now we are behind by this many minutes, and this many units. You stop thinking like a person.*'

'That sounds awful.'

'*Do you know they take it out of our pay if we fail to meet our quota for the day? Maybe you can speak to the foreman for me, get me promoted to the fridge production line. I've heard stories of worker-actors hiding in fridges, smuggling themselves to freedom.*'

He glances at us to gauge our reaction to this statement, then continues.

'*Before I was re-cast, I had some involvement in The Director's finances and the finances of Port Man Tou. Simply put, they are a mess. In his great hurry to build the city, not only as a giant film set, but also as a titan of*' industry, he has leveraged funds he does not have. The only profitable sectors are film and tourism, and they are nothing compared with the losses derived from infrastructure, public utilities, expansion and other business ventures. This factory, for example, is operating at a huge loss.'

'How can that be?'

'The Director is trying to lure business away from competing factories elsewhere in China by subsidising the costs of production. Eventually, his undercutting tactics will yield profit. When that happens, the city will be unstoppable. We will have no chance.'

'No chance for what?' I ask, sensing a dangerous turn in the conversation.

'No chance to bring him down. To interrupt the flow of money before the city can absorb the loss. But I believe a catastrophic failure on one of his film deals would achieve this.'

Yuan and I look at each other.

On our way home, we approach a square, and are halted in our tracks by some kind of demonstration. A gathering of distraught citizens. Women hold up photos of children. They weep and prostrate themselves. A blank-faced wall of officers from the Bureau, here to keep the peace. Men exchange heated words with the officers. They curse and spit. The hostility is returned with force. Weapons are drawn. Screams are heard. Yuan and I back away, try to find an alternate route to our destination. But here they come now, spilling into the streets, so many of them. The angry crowds. The critical masses.

Dear citizens of Port Man Tou,

In the Canton of Eternal Ruin, there are times (and more and more of them these days) when in the sunset hour the city seems to sway and shimmer. We notice, as though for the first time, a far-off line or landmark (always at a distance, never not) that strikes our hearts and takes our breath away. And so we venture out into the Canton of ER to try to locate this brilliant and unfathomable structure.

But by the time we arrive, the hour is lost. The men and women who live in the vicinity report having seen no such beauty, and on other days, by other angles, we see that it is exactly as they say. These structures that seemed to signal to us, like siren song, appear so suddenly unimpressive – tremulous, even – like a misremembered poem that might collapse at any moment.

And indeed they do collapse, have collapsed. Broken bridges and apartments and schools. We suppose there are fatalities, but it is hard to say how many. The Director is silent on the matter.

There are those who say the ruins in the Canton of ER are the result of substandard building practices, that minor tremors and earthquakes that happen in our sleep are revealing these delicate structures as fallacies and that, eventually, each one of them will crumble to the ground. But we are not so sure. What does that say about us? It grieves us, after all, that we might have glimpsed beauty in the collapse.

Nowadays we regard every building very carefully, not only its composition – each scaffold and edifice – but also the air around it, the way the light regards it, the placement of it in relation to others (for it occurs to us that the buildings are each aligned, and might collapse without its neighbours, or its neighbours' neighbours), and we study each of these buildings in the hopes that such diversions might one day revive our understanding.

By official decree,
The Department of Verisimilitude

41

SIMA QING

The new Imperial City grew voraciously. More workers were required to meet demand, and every able-bodied man was sent to the ever-expanding outskirts. Eventually, even prisoners from the Six Levels of Hell were released and sent to the frontier in chain gangs. They were forced into backbreaking servitude building roads and ziggurats. Each day, the Emperor's forces conquered newer territories, lands rendered desolate and lifeless by warfare. But in the destructive wake of expansion came the hum of industry. The Imperial Architect and his labourers sought to sculpt the city from these ruins.

Of late, the Emperor had taken to touring the outermost cantons that spiralled across the landscape.

Here, the Canton of Sonorous Echoes, where sound travelled in mysterious ways. Each home built in such a manner that a whisper spoken in spring might reverberate against the angled roofs and eaves only to lose its way, become befuddled, and emerge instead in autumn, elsewhere and in perfect clarity.

There, the Canton of All Cantons. A codex of the entire city built in miniature. The impossible object that contained itself.

The Emperor had not forgotten His promise to grant the Architect an audience with the scholars who had authored the original books of the Imperial Library, and who were now labouring in the Canton of Apophenia. Here, in this canton, stood the hundred houses of worship, the cave temples of Xinjiang known as the Seven Stars, once burned to the ground by the Turks.

The Emperor had ordered the Architect to restore this monument to its once-glorious prime, but upon seeing it restored He had a change of heart. The Emperor understood now that, even before the original had been burned to the ground, it was destined to be a ruin. That the new temples – pristine and perfect in their re-creation – were, would always be, already ruined. All things were destroyed by their meaning. He saw this now. Only the meaningless might survive. Only as a ruin might it endure.

The Emperor gave orders for the entire canton to be razed to the ground, and for the author-labourers to rebuild the temple compound from its outset as a ruin. Corridors and entire wings left to rubble, facades torn and vandalised. Rows stocked with broken idols, disfigured statuettes. Illegible tomes filled with putrefactive ink.

Overseeing this folly, Lu Shan Liang would brave the canton daily to monitor its progress. He inspected altars and ceilings and frescoes, deliberated on whether their surfaces bore the right amounts of grime or discolouration. He observed the author-labourers at their work. He had pictured them as lucid and brimming with thought, but up close he saw that they were dull-eyed and sunken-cheeked. Clothes tattered, hair bedraggled. They picked at scabs. They wasted away in their chains. He spoke with each author-labourer in turn as they carted stones and laid the foundations.

They reluctantly admitted to having been authors once, but each man had forgotten his name and who had written what. Or else remembered all too well, but feared the Architect might be the Emperor's agent sent to collect evidence of seditious thought. Had they always been so unimpressive? Or did they make themselves so deliberately? They talked in circles, cleared their throats and made awkward digressions. They dismantled their own charms.

One spoke at length about future works he might write, but these lofty ambitions were mangled by his graceless tongue, and the more he spoke, the more he seemed like a babbling fool.

Another, who held a high opinion of himself – whoever he was – blamed his readers for miscomprehending his work.

A third claimed to be the true author of those *same books*, and the three commenced to argue ceaselessly about the perilous line between inspiration and theft.

They erected useless walls and over time succumbed to meaninglessness.

See the corrupted fruit of their labours. How they laid down new foundations already in such states of decay, tore down structures and replaced them with false signs and symbols.

Could these bedraggled lunatics really be the same scholars whose words had spoken the language of his soul? He had sought answers, but only received the deepest of disappointments.

But one among them was different. His speech was refined and singular in its learned eloquence. He feared no repercussion and hid not his intellect.

His name was Sima Qing, the Shadow Historian.

Each day, while toiling in the ruins, Lu Shan Liang and Sima Qing would converse for hours on end. They came to seek each other out. Amidst this sea of senseless symbols, they spoke with greater candour, coming to rely on the other's presence, becoming the holders of each other's secrets.

Now the true audience began.

Sima Qing spoke of his past. Was it not written in the shadow histories more than thirty years ago that *he* was once the Emperor overthrown? The Emperor's uncle. Blind to the treachery of the Emperor's father; stripped of status, manhood; thrown into the lowest caste. Thenceforth an Imperial Edict had marked him as untouchable, not to be harmed under any circumstance. And what reason for such apparent mercy? He did not know. Only one could know the truth. His brother, his deposer, who had long ago expired on a fateful chicken bone.

Learning that his companion was the Shadow Historian, Lu Shan Liang asked Sima Qing about the Imperial Artisan, his own father.

Indeed, Sima Qing knew much about the Artisan. He recalled his works: the Moonlit Pagoda, the self-portrait called *A Simulated Man*.

Upon hearing this, Lu Shan Liang told Sima Qing of the portrait. How, in order to maintain the illusion of time's arrow, his father had painted each portrait atop the other in reverse order, beginning with his death and ending with his birth, so that future patrons could view the work chronologically. How, by the time his father had commenced painting the layers of his youth, he had imbued upon the canvas the likeness of Lu Shan Liang instead. The father and son, now indivisible.

Sima Qing knew then that Lu Shan Liang was the child of the labyrinth, adopted by the Imperial Artisan, but born from Lu Dong Pu and the Imperial Consort, Wuer.

Seek out the labyrinth, he said, *where the author of your longing might still weave and wander to this day.*

42

Bao Television Studios – Yingen Lane, Canton of Western Facade

Filming for *The Interrogation: Port Man Tou* is about to begin. The harried stage manager barks instructions into his intercom headset as he whisks me through the busy passageways of Sound Stage 8. I stumble over an electrical cable that snakes across the floor. He impatiently snaps his fingers at me to keep pace.

We pass the female contestants' dressing room. The door is slightly ajar and I see the room is bursting with chattering beauties, a couple of whom I recognise from the DVDs. Suddenly, the reality of what I'm about to do sinks in: whatever my failures were before, at least they weren't *televised*. No amount of ribbon-cutting ceremonies and staged photo ops could have prepared me for this. My stomach gurgles.

The stage manager – already thirty paces down the corridor – berates me for lingering. I catch up and he ushers me into a small make-up suite. Suits and sequined leotards hang on a rack.

The stage manager tells me to wait for the make-up artist, then he takes off.

A few minutes later, the door opens. It's Yuan. I breathe a sigh of relief.

'Where *were* you?' I ask.

'I got lost out there. Then when I asked for you, they took me to the female contestants' dressing room instead.'

The make-up artist enters the room and sits me down in the barber-style chair. He musses my hair and appraises my reflection in the mirror.

The Director bursts through the door. 'Ah, Xiang Lu! Are you ready for your debut Chinese dating show appearance?'

'I guess so.'

'Don't look so nervous! There are a lot of single women in that room! You might even have a chance with a few of them!'

'I told you, I'm in a relationship with Yuan.'

He waves his hand dismissively.

'Once the show begins, the host will call out your name and the production assistant will give you the cue to walk onto the stage. Do it confidently, like you have the second-biggest balls in the room. After me, of course. Hahaha!!!'

'Will you be there?' I glance at his hair, which looks particularly luxuriant tonight.

'I'll be on the celebrity guest panel. When we get the full season order, I'll outsource the role to one of my doubles.'

'There must be a lot riding on this,' I say. 'You don't usually prep me in person for a media appearance. You just throw me in the deep end.'

'That's not your concern. You just go out there and be the best #BadChinese you can be. And remember to have fun! Live TV is always exhilarating!'

'This is going out *live*?'

'Of course! Live in China and on delay in Australia. I'm sure all your friends and family will be cheering you on! New memes await!'

It's all I can do to keep from throwing up.

He turns to the make-up artist and says, '给她化个妆.'

'Huh? Why do *I* need make-up?' asks Yuan.

'You are his translator,' Baby Bao explains. 'Would you rather be on camera *without* make-up?'

274

We peek out from the wings at the studio audience: a sea of Chinese faces. The lights are blinding. The walls flash colourful LED patterns to enhance the party atmosphere. The female contestants stand behind their podiums with perfect poise as the host, Ming Zhou – a short man in a dapper suit and plasticky hair – introduces them one by one. The celebrity guests sit shoulder to shoulder at a desk to the side of the stage. The crowd applauds. A camera mounted on a crane swoops restlessly overhead.

Ming Zhou calls for me.

The stage manager hands me a microphone and gestures for me to go.

A Chinese cover of Michael Jackson's 'Bad' blares over the sound system.

I stumble out onto the walkway and hit my mark.

'大家晚上好!' I say. *Good evening, everyone!*

The crowd whistles and applauds my more-or-less correct pronunciation.

I shake hands with Ming Zhou. Yuan is quietly ushered onto the stage. Ming Zhou introduces her and jokes that her translation skills will only be required in the event of a communication emergency.

He gestures at me and speaks to the contestants. '好了, 各位女士, 你们对他的第一印象是什么?' *Well, ladies, what are your first impressions?*

Contestant Number Six – with a peacock feather hairpin – curls her lip and snipes, '他看起来很正常, 可他一开口向我们打招呼, 我就觉得他的智力有问题.' *He looks normal enough, but once he opened his mouth to greet us, I began to question his intellect.*

Contestant Number One – with a cute bob and a polka-dot dress – says, '他看起来很自在.' *He looks comfortable in his skin.*

Contestant Number Seven – the token joke-contestant wearing pigtails and overalls – says, '他是演出来的. #BadChinese 只是一个营销噱头.' *He's not real. The #BadChinese is just a marketing gimmick.*

I was going to wait until the question-and-answer segment, but this is as good a point as any to make my move. I hold up the microphone and address her, '你说中了. 我被你看穿了, 7号选手.' *You're absolutely right. You've seen through me, Contestant Number Seven.*

275

I look at Yuan and nod.

She nods back.

I utter the lines in Mandarin – in perfect tone and diction – that we practised on the lake countless times: '事情是这样的, #BadChinese 病了. 我是他的替补. 希望我的模仿够成功, 并给各位带来一些笑声和乐趣.' *In fact, the #BadChinese has taken ill tonight. I am his understudy. Hopefully my mannerisms will be sufficiently reminiscent of his, and may give you some laughter and enjoyment despite the falsehood.*

Ming Zhou is visibly taken aback. The raucous crowd falls silent.

Baby Bao takes off his sunglasses and glares at me. I maintain eye contact with him until he puts his sunglasses back on and breaks into an uneasy grin.

One of the celebrity guests – a middle-aged matronly type – attempts to salvage the proceedings by setting up the scripted fake joke, but I pre-empt her and laugh before the punchline.

Someone from the crowd shouts, '他听得懂中文!' *He understands Chinese!*

Contestant Number Six shouts, '他不仅不是 #BadChinese, 更是一个烂演员!' *Not only is he not the #BadChinese, he is a bad actor!*

I look down at my palm card.

'郑盈盈, 那我们就摊开说吧,' I say. *Let's be clear, Zheng Ying Ying.*

Yuan looks at me in alarm. I am going off-script.

'我死也不会和你约会的. 再说, 我是不会和节目里任何一位女生谈恋爱的.' *I would never date you. In fact, I am not eligible to date any of you.*

I point to Yuan and profess: '我爱的是她.' *I am in love with her.*

The crowd boos. The other contestants jump in to defend Contestant Number Six and level insults at me. The crowd is getting riled up.

Someone hurls a water bottle. It's The Director.

An audience member rushes the stage. Security guards tackle him, but his friends have become emboldened, and follow suit.

Shit. This is not going at all like I imagined.

I take Yuan by the hand and we run backstage in search of an emergency exit. A small crowd gives chase on the studio lot. I'm not sure if they want to harm me or get my autograph. We duck behind a parked car as they rush down Yi Fen Lane. I try to think my way through the surge of adrenaline.

'This way!' I say.

We double back, trying the doors to each of the sound stages.

The door to Sound Stage 5 is unlocked. We run into the darkened hangar and collide with a solid object. The door shuts behind us. We hear distant shouts and approaching footsteps. We clamber through the dark. The lights come on, and suddenly we are facing countless reflections. We recognise now where we are: the maze of mirrors from *Death of a Pagoda*. We weave deeper into the set, trying to find another way out.

The Director's voice booms over the PA.

'You ungrateful idiot! You thought you could rewrite my script? Ruin me by sabotaging one single show? You are #StupidChinese!'

His laughter echoes throughout the cavernous set.

43

DRAGON

As the Imperial City grew in size and scope, the Emperor's absences from the capital became ever more frequent, and so too the Imperial Swine's stints upon the throne.

In many ways, the Imperial Swine was like the Emperor. It ignored the counsel of its advisers, cared only for sleeping and eating, and knew not the meaning of hygiene. And yet the Imperial Swine had won its subjects' undying affection simply by being less bad than the Emperor. It was not prone to His tyrannous whims. It did not cast out or execute any who displeased it. In fact, none displeased it, though, to be fair, none pleased it either. It was entirely apathetic, and for that the citizens revered it.

Even its minor cruelties against Tong Li Mo the Daoist were seen by the Imperial Court as endearing.

After touring the newest cantons, the Emperor returned to the Imperial City and resumed His rule upon the throne. But something in the air had changed. The people were humming a new tune. During His lengthy absence, minstrels had come before the Court to pay musical tribute to the Imperial Swine. A line about its upturned snout granted it a nobility that, in truth, it never had.

An embellished lyric turned its grunts into the most mellifluous speech.

Infuriated, the Emperor ordered the Swine be put to death.

The members of the Imperial Court wept, none more so than Tong Li Mo the Daoist. They knew not that the one who had ordered the swinging of the executioner's axe was, in fact, Dragon. He had no equivalent in this world and could not tolerate such a lowly beast being glorified in song.

Tong Li Mo was once more restored to the role of Chief Adviser. The Emperor ordered him to plan a great banquet to be thrown in His honour, with the Imperial Swine to be prepared and served as the main course.

Amidst the bleak festivities, Imperial Chef Bei emerged from the Imperial Kitchen with a surprise dish. He had returned from his travels through the Empire and beyond with new and exotic recipes. With a great flourish he unveiled the creation. He explained to Dragon and the members of the Imperial Court that by using only his signature tofu, and a handful of secret spices, he had managed to coax from the wok a meal that simulated the exact texture, consistency and taste of boneless lemon honey chicken. Gasps of shock were heard. Younger members of the Court had heard rumours of such a forbidden delicacy. Older members, who had tasted chicken before its prohibition, began to salivate uncontrollably.

Dragon applauded the Imperial Chef's audacity. True, chicken had been prohibited by official decree, but that which perfectly simulated chicken was, technically, permissible. Dragon nibbled first on a breast and, greatly impressed with the authentic taste and texture, proceeded to gobble down an entire wing.

But something caught in His throat. His face turned purple. The Imperial Chef had served Him no tofu simulation but a *real* chicken – with real bones – plucked from the false empire of the South.

In desperation, He cast His eyes about the Court for help. But none came forth to aid Him. Each courtier had sufficient reason and desire to see Him fall. All in the Imperial Court watched and waited for that long and breathless minute to expire.

From then on, all those born in the year of the Dragon were rendered luckless and downtrodden. But their younger brothers, born in the year of the proud Rooster, were destined for fortune and lives filled with significance.

So it was that the Emperor died one thousand deaths.

Ominous clouds formed above the Imperial City.

Citizens stalked the streets, searching for the last, true Emperor.

With no double left to act as diversion or shield, He felt Himself in mortal danger for the first time. He stripped off His fine brocade, shaved off His beard and descended into the slums, dressed in rags.

He sought to blend into the shadows and alleyways as He slowly inched His way towards exile. But the Imperial City had become interminably large. Each time He thought He had reached its edge He found, to His dismay, that He was still in the city. He continued to move south. Always and ever south.

In the canton called The Palimpsest, He blended into the crowds, kept His head low, spoke only when spoken to. He fought other beggars for stale bread.

In the canton known as The Truth Revealed in Artifice, He averted suspicion, when confronted about His uncanny resemblance, by thrice denouncing the wicked Emperor.

In the Canton of Graven Images, He aided in the construction of an effigy – in whose features He saw His own, rendered grotesque in caricature – upon completion of which He led a frenzied mob in attacking it, its image bending and warping out of shape as they burned it to the ground ...

The Emperor was never again seen in the Imperial City.

The clouds above the Imperial City grew darker. With a thunderclap, they unleashed a deluge that wouldn't stop until the structures of the new Imperial City lay in ruins.

Lu Shan Liang moved north, against the tide of evacuees, towards the klaxons of chaos that rang in the city's centre.

He crossed into the canton known as the Systems of Revelation, where he glimpsed the shattered gate to the Six Levels of Hell.

He passed the canton called The Artifice Revealed in Truth, and saw statues submerged beneath the rising waters.

He skirted the canton called Sense Lacuna, where ferocious winds swept the farms in ever-swifter roundelay, ripping whole acres of sesame from their very stalks, so that from the eye of the monsoon each individual grain seemed to disappear into a mass, a swarm, a ribbon that flowed as one, forming loops and calligraphic swirls, suspended for an instant in the air like some kind of living art.

He reached the ruined centre. There, only the labyrinth had survived. Tying some rope around him, he entered the catacomb-like structures. In truth, he could not have become lost – he was born of the labyrinth, after all – yet he did not discard his tetherings, for they were a comfort to him.

In time, the pathways became familiar. He had only to recall his father, the Imperial Artisan, to find the way once more. And even now, discovering stray and unfamiliar rooms, he did not lose his place or become confounded, but rather seemed to find in them a greater understanding, perhaps a solution to the very labyrinth itself. He recognised the passages he had inherited whole, and newer wings that had been grown to accommodate him, protect him. And he passed now through the veil of the inner labyrinth, with fingers that trailed the words upon the walls – a secret map encoded in their lyric – and into the heart now, where its spaces enveloped and embraced him.

44

Happiness Factory – Market Street, Unnamed Canton

Life at the factory is not as bad as I thought it would be, though it is not, by any stretch of the imagination, good. The food is decent, and free for all workers. Living expenses, too, are provided by The Director. The lodgings are humble, but not overly cramped. The citizen-actors no longer chase me for photographs. It makes no difference anymore. We are all the same now, with the same daily quotas to fulfil.

For twelve hours a day, I stand at a conveyor belt in Assembly Room L, testing the voltage of assembled toasters. Yuan fits together the plastic straps for virtual reality headsets in Assembly Room H. They pay us ฿6000 per week, a meaningless number, since we are required, per the city-wide directive, to commute weekly to the Metro Megamall and purchase tickets to the endless screenings of Baby Bao's films.

A ticket costs ฿5800.

Once in a while we hear rumours of the collapse of entire cantons, productions stuck in development hell, the ejection of all media outlets from Port Man Tou, but it is hard to sort fact from fiction. A few months ago, Yuan said she saw a man and a woman – a couple, she thinks – don hairnets before being taken on a tour of Warehouse H. She heard them conversing in English. A new #BadChinese and his translator, perhaps?

Dear citizens of Port Man Tou,

We thought it was a new and exciting production at first, the way the Special Operations Forces rumbled through the streets, brandishing tear gas and automatic weapons. They set up camp amid the expansive rubble of the Canton of Eternal Ruin, and placed the entire city under lockdown, sealing the borders.

They consulted maps of the city, scouring each canton meticulously, in search of The Director.

We were impressed by their verisimilitude, their commitment to the role; after all, even the best of us let our guard down at times and, every once in a while, we forget that we must act.

Rumour has it that, in the outside world, The Director is now a major fixture in the national news. A litany of charges have been laid against him: criminal negligence, fraud, corruption, money laundering ... the list goes on.

We keep expecting it to be a ruse, a fiction, just another scene in one of his countless movies. We keep expecting him to appear, benevolent and jovial, with entourage in tow, handing out exorbitant fines to each of us for having broken character, for having accidentally made eye contact. But he does not appear. So we suspect the rumours might be true.

The army men brought us in for interrogation. They asked us questions about the city. They wanted to know about the mysterious canton in the deepest heart of the city, where they believe The Director may have taken refuge. They had glimpsed it from above but did not know how to reach it – except by air, their last resort – for the streets surrounding it were a maddening labyrinth.

We told them that this was the canton known as Terminus. It cannot be reached by foot, or car, or train. We told the story of how, long ago, The Director had dismissed all construction workers whose shoddy work had led to the current state of the Canton of ER, and we told them of his melancholic vision for the heart of the city, that most unreachable of cantons.

From the factories was assembled an immense automaton that came to span the length and width and height of Terminus. Daily, its vast mechanical arms caressed the city, laying down searing materials, assembling entire homes and high-rises without any human intervention.

They asked us other questions about The Director, his habits and predilections. They seemed tense and solemn, and so, to lighten the mood, one of us told them a joke:

What day is it today?

Wednesday, they said.

(They seemed so sure, and we understood finally, with lumps in our throats, that the men were real.)

And the year?

By official decree,
The Department of Infrastructure and Regional Development

Cinema Level, Metro Megamall – Baby Bao Road, Canton of Illegal Tender

'It's only a matter of time before they find him and arrest him,' I whisper.

'Unless The Director's still in charge and this is all part of his plan,' Yuan whispers back.

Ever since Baby Bao's disappearance and the army's takeover of the city, all work at the factories has stopped. The citizen-actors have abandoned their compulsory theatre-going. Only Yuan and I come here now, for we have found our new sampan, the place where we might speak in private without fear of reprisal. It turns out that sanctuary was under our noses all along, in this deserted cinema where all filming and recording is prohibited.

Admission is free these days. We could even afford popcorn, if only the concessionaires hadn't abandoned their post.

'But I don't understand why they're keeping us around,' she says. 'If they're just after The Director, shouldn't they evacuate the city? Send us home? Instead they tell everyone to "carry on, business as usual". Does that seem right to you?'

'What, you think The Director's still in charge? Still filming?' I ask.

I prop my feet up against the row in front. Why not? It's only the two of us in the entire theatre.

Yuan tsks. I lower my feet.

'I don't know what to think anymore,' she says. 'In a city with no boundaries, everything is permitted. How is the Department of Verisimilitude supposed to function? Artifice has become the accepted mode of reality. We can either report everything, or we report nothing.'

Our eyes flit, every so often, to the big screen. Four hours of meandering footage of the swelling seas. *Don't Encourage Him* is The Director's retelling of *Moby Dick*, only from the whale's point of view.

Yuan nudges me. I turn to find a lone figure walking down the aisle. He sits beside me, eyes riveted on the screen. I feel like it's been years since I've seen him last.

'Is it really you?' I ask.

'Hahaha!!!'

'You know they're looking for you, right? The entire city is in lockdown.'

'Have a prawn cracker,' Baby Bao says, extending an open bag.

I ignore his gesture of goodwill.

Baby Bao fans himself with a cracker. 'Of course I know. But they will never find me. When I converted this city into a giant studio, I had my architects construct a network of utility tunnels for moving equipment without disrupting film continuity. It is accessible by a special service elevator inside each Mass Rapid Transport station.' He dangles a key. 'Those tunnels will spirit me out of Port Man Tou, towards the borders of Russia and Mongolia.'

285

'Can I see that?'

'Absolutely not.' He shoves the key back in his pocket. 'And besides, I am not simply hiding underground like a coward. No, I walk about the city unimpeded. People see me on the street and they do not turn me in because they believe I am not me. See how I dress in lesser fabrics. They understand that the real Baby Bao would never be caught dead in cheap threads, or with these sunglasses that are not designer frames. I remain undetected by perfectly impersonating an imperfect impersonator.'

'I hate to burst your bubble, but ...'

Baby Bao puts a salty finger to my lips. 'Shhh! This is my favourite scene.'

I turn to the screen. A seagull flies by. That's it. That's the scene.

'Now, what were you saying?'

'I was going to say that the army informed all citizens to report *any* impersonators. According to the memo, the more imperfect the impersonation, the more likely that man is to be the true Director.'

'Traitors! Nevertheless, the occupation of the city will fail. It is written in the script.'

'There are no scripts,' I say.

'Yes. There are no scripts. *So it is written in the script.* You have not laid eyes upon it, but nonetheless you have internalised its rhythms. This is my city. You think I didn't intend all outcomes? You think I didn't know your secret thoughts and movements? Think I could not hear you plotting on the lake? That I didn't realise that more and more, your "romantic wanderings" happened to be of airports and freight lines and the well-manned borders of the city, where if I was any less vigilant, you might have slipped quietly out of the city itself? Remember the time at the station, one week before I threw you into the factories for your insolence, when you two oh-so-casually strolled onto the departing platform, towards the only freighter bound for Manzhouli? How could you tell it apart from the rest, which were merely replicas? Oh, the pace of your footsteps was indelible, the tone of your voices, in which my microphones could detect no signs of outward stress. How you must have wanted to make a run for it, to stop acting, yet you gave nothing away. Just walked and talked in apparent aimlessness, as though the destination were not intended. Ah! You do not know that day how close you were to *escape*! Even as I screamed at my production staff to engineer crowds and impossible obstacles to block you from your path, I admit I was briefly rooting for you to succeed.'

'I don't know what you're talking about.'

'Terrible.' He stands to leave. 'When the city is back under my control, remind me to fine you for such bad acting.'

Yuan pulls out her phone and dials 110, the number for the police. The Director glares at her.

'您好, 我要举报我在美卓城电影院看到了导演, 但也有可能是他的替身.' *Hello. I would like to report a sighting of The Director. Or maybe an impersonator. He's at the cinema at the Metro Megamall.* She hangs up defiantly.

The Director wolfs down a prawn cracker then flees into the dark.

We wait until the credits roll. The lights come up. We stand. I automatically check my seat for anything I might have left behind.

There is something on the vacant seat next to mine. A key.

Mass Rapid Transport Station – Yueshan Road, Canton of Illegal Tender

The doors of the service elevator only half open, and we are forced to sidle through.

I insert The Director's key.

The lights turn off.

The elevator plummets.

My ears pop as we careen into the substratum. In the darkness, it occurs to me that this, too, might be a trap. But it is too late.

'Shit,' I say.

'What is it?'

'My head.'

'Again? Quickly, tell me something true.'

'That didn't work last time. How about *you* tell me something?'

'Okay.' She thinks for a moment. 'When I was fifteen to about ... seventeen, I couldn't remember anyone's face.'

'What do you mean?'

'Exactly that. I would forget everyone's face.'

'You're serious?'

'En. I had just changed schools. After the first day, I got home and realised I had forgotten everyone's face. I thought the feeling would pass, a momentary thing, a new environment. But it never did. People would act like they knew me. Well, they *did* know me. Their voices seemed familiar, so I kind of knew they were in my class, but I didn't recognise their faces. They were strangers to me every day. If someone talked to me I would try to remember but, even a minute later, it would just be a blank. How's the pain?'

'Getting worse. What about your family?' I ask. 'Could you remember their faces?'

'En, and all my favourite movie stars. Leslie Cheung. Andy Lau.'

'Ha! That's a relief!'

'It really was, actually. And aside from this one thing, my life was normal. I went to the library, I watched movies ... But can you imagine how terrifying it was, to not be able to recognise anyone's face, not even your friends' faces? Every day, for two years?'

'No, I really can't imagine ...'

'I was in such incredible, you know, um, anguish. I tried not to, but I would cry all the time. My grades dropped from the top three to somewhere near the bottom. My parents thought I was being bullied.'

'You didn't tell them what was going on?'

'I just told them I didn't want to go to school anymore. But I didn't tell them anything else. I don't know why. But there was a girl – Yan Jie – who made friends with me. She would sit by me every day, and hold my hand and talk, talk, talk, oh she could talk, for hours about I don't know what. Everyone called her "machine mouth" because she never shut up, but in the end I think it was her voice that saved me. Really. I guess I recognised her by her sound and gradually it all started coming back to me.'

'Are you afraid that it'll happen again?'

'Not really. I know, somehow, that it won't.'

'You seem sure.'

'I am.'

We fall silent. The pain finally starts to lessen. And I think, in the half-dark, that she is trying to recall my face. Commit it to memory.

And she says, 'But if it does happen again … you must hold my hand. Sit by me. Talk, talk, talk. Tell me about yourself, tell me stories forever … until I recognise your voice.'

We see him again, years later, on the news.

Footage shows him being led away in handcuffs, a thin mosaic obscuring his eyes. He looks bedraggled and unkempt. He stares directly into the camera. Solemn officers of the National Police Agency usher him into an unmarked car. He screams, in Shanghainese, that for years he has filmed nothing, nothing at all.

Occasionally, in each of the cities we have since called home, there have been times when we happened upon some aspect of that city that seemed unimaginable in its beauty – immense buddhas visible from the street; a stray cat giving birth in an alleyway; wizened old men in art galleries; some multicoloured autumn leaf, crisp like a treasure, that our children, James and Madeleine, have discovered on the walk home from school – and in these moments we are reminded of Port Man Tou.

Can it be? There are times, in fact, we feel as though we had never left the city.

We see Port Man Tou on the television. The streets are empty once more. But the heart of the city remains in motion. The canton known as Terminus is constantly building, razing, rebuilding, re-razing. Deep within its lattices, there is a database of architectural designs by which it remodels itself in vastly different forms. News reports show satellite footage in time lapse. We watch as the city reconstructs itself from its own materials – obeying its own dreamlike velocities – nothing wasted, everything melted down and recycled, re-recycled. On certain days it comes to resemble other cities, all cities. We have recognised, in its infinite patterns, the 7th arrondissement in Paris. Times Square in New York. The skyline of Nihonbashi Kabutochō.

Of late, its imposing structures have come to resemble nothing we know. Restlessly, it replaces itself with new and stranger iterations. The city has no referents now. Only itself.

45

CODA

Came there to remotest village of the south a passerby who lodged at the inn for a time, and in idle days thereafter was seen drinking in the tavern or else exploring the landscape, watching the swaying fields, pacing the path by the well where the road wound the bend. He once had heard another speak so fondly of this place, with its simple charm and kind people, and He resolved to settle here for a time. Perhaps forever. He liked this thought. A place to call His own.

The villagers thought Him aloof, but harmless. He had a patrician air about Him and they guessed – correctly – that He would not take to farming. They showed Him to a house upon a slender hillock that had remained vacant for some years. An artisan had once lived there, a fact that pleased Him greatly, for He had always known Himself to be an artist, of a kind. And taking up the brushes in the studio, He resolved to open a school, where He would pass along the secrets of His craft. Many students came from far and wide. Each of these He taught to discard such useless things as skill and talent and technique. Rather, He turned them to His ways, of style without style, and form without form. Under His guidance, they abandoned the pursuit of beauty, and instead committed to the canvas ambiguous shapes and lines that favoured furrowed brows and scholar-like interpretation.

Greatly was He revered for His wisdom.

Acknowledgements

An early version of this work was the recipient of an ASA Mentorship Award. I'm indebted to the Australian Society of Authors and the Copyright Agency for its support of the ASA Mentorship Program through its Cultural Fund.

There is no *Ghost Cities* without my agent and dear friend, Brendan Fredericks, and the support and belief of my incredible publisher, Aviva Tuffield.

To the talented folks at UQP: Ian See, Erin Sandiford, Kate Lloyd, Jean Smith, Sarah Valle and Maddie Byrne.

To Camha Pham, Stevie Zhang, David Brooks and Andrew Lampack for their editorial support.

To Yang Yongliang, who allowed the use of his sublime artwork, and to Josh Durham for his design excellence.

To Hayley Scrivenor and Kate Mildenhall, two of the most generous and talented writers I am honoured to know. They set the high bar to which we might all aspire. They have written books better than this one, and if you haven't bought and read them yet, well, I must insist that you do.

Special thanks to the ABIA-winning audio team, Chiara Priorelli, Emily Lawrence, Maryanne Plazzer and Yen Nguyen, who I've had the pleasure to work alongside once more for the audio adaptation of this title.

Finally, to my parents and my brother. To my children, James and Madeleine. And to Yuan, the love of my life, the signal to my noise.